MAISEY YATES

The Bad Boy of Redemption Ranch

A Gold Valley Novel

ISBN-13: 978-1-335-01504-4

9 781335 015044

50999

EAN

MAISEY YATES

The Bad Boy of Redemption Ranch

HQN

ISBN-13: 978-1-335-01504-4

Recycling programs for this product may not exist in your area.

The Bad Boy of Redemption Ranch

Copyright © 2020 by Maisey Yates

This edition published by arrangement with Harlequin Books S.A.

For questions and comments about the quality of this book, please contact us at CustomerService@Harlequin.com.

HQN
22 Adelaide St. West, 40th Floor
Toronto, Ontario M5H 4E3, Canada
www.Harlequin.com

Printed in U.S.A.

For the romance readers. You are brave. You choose to believe in love and hope, and those are two of the most powerful forces in this world. Keep shining.

The Bad Boy of
Redemption Ranch

CHAPTER ONE

THERE WASN'T A man alive who was *happy* to see blue and red police lights come up behind him on a long stretch of deserted highway where there were no other visible cars.

But West Caldwell imagined that as men went, he was probably distinctly *unhappier* than many. Having spent a couple of years behind bars, witnessing the grave failure of the justice system. Though, he supposed in the end the system had prevailed and he had been exonerated of the fraud he hadn't committed in the first place—but that initial failure meant that he didn't really have a keen view of law enforcement.

Not of any stripe.

Not that he didn't know full well that most police officers were just doing their jobs. But the thing was, something happened to you when you were in prison. There was a little bit of an us vs. them mentality. The inmates, and the ones who'd put them in jail. Of course then there was the fact that he couldn't trust half the bastards in prison.

So really, there were gradations of teams.

But either way you cut it the cops were not on *his* team.

Of course, he wasn't in prison anymore. Neither was he a criminal in the eyes of the law.

Still.

He didn't want to get a ticket either way.

This is what he got for moving to Small Town, USA.

Gold Valley, Oregon. He'd rolled into town to get acquainted with his old man—Hank Dalton—a legendary retired bull rider and man whore. One who had left half siblings littered around the country.

West had ended up staying. Because Dallas no longer held any allure to him. No, it was just the site of his financial and personal destruction.

He had been raised in Sweet Home, Oregon, before hightailing it out of there at eighteen and joining the rodeo, coming back and forth to check in with his half brother—his mother's son, Emmett.

He had other half siblings here, though. His father's children, not his mother's, so he'd figured Gold Valley was as good a place as any to settle in and start over.

He hoped he could get in touch with Emmett again. His mother said her much younger son had run off, doing whatever the hell he wanted, and she wasn't all that concerned.

West didn't feel the same.

But here in town he'd discovered a hell of a lot more family than he bargained for. And not only that, the family had taken him in more or less.

Though, part of that was that they seemed to be inured to having siblings popping up out of the woodwork.

He wasn't the first.

And if what his half brother Caleb thought was true did in fact prove to be, he wouldn't be the last.

Not that any of that had a hill of beans to do with what was happening now, and the ticket he was about to receive.

He pulled off on the side of the road, next to a copse of dense, dark pine trees. The place was lousy with pines. Totally different than the grassy rolling hills that he had learned to call home in Texas. There were Oregon grapes,

fritillarias and ferns instead of bluebonnets. And the flat fields were backed by jagged mountains.

And hell, in Texas, the cop that pulled you over might just be Chuck Norris. So, he supposed he should be grateful that at least this one wasn't a Texas Ranger.

He looked in his rearview mirror, and watched as the cop car stopped. He had hoped, just a little, that it would go on by. But no.

Then the door opened, and the uniformed figure inside stood. He could just barely see the top of her shoulders and head above the door.

It was a woman. Brown hair pulled back into a ponytail, dark glasses over her eyes. She was small. She slammed the door shut with the force of a much larger person, her belt and gun bulky on her tiny frame.

She hitched that belt up, like a bad cop show, and walked slowly over to the driver's side of the vehicle. He pushed the button on his truck window and rolled it down.

She appraised him for a moment, just a moment, before she spoke.

"Do you know how fast you were going?" she asked, lifting her sunglasses and sliding them back on her head.

"Can't say that I do, officer. But I bet you're going to tell me." It was clear from the way the corners of her mouth—not a bad mouth even given it was all severe—turned down that she wasn't into his brand of humor.

"Damn straight," she said. "Seventy-five. Max speed on an unmarked rural road is fifty-five."

"Well, see," he said. "I've been living out in Texas for the past sixteen years." He maximized his long-ago acquired drawl for effect. "Everything is bigger there. Including the speed limits."

"A shame you're not in Texas anymore, Dorothy," she returned, sharp and tight.

"You sure you want to mouth off like that? I pay—"

"You pay my salary?" She sighed heavily. "Try again. Please come up with something slightly more original if you're going to try to insult me or take shots at me in any way. And I'm going to warn you. People are not as original as they think they are. This is a universal truth. Now, go ahead, mister. While you dig for your license and registration, feel free to create a comeback that will dazzle me."

"You sound a bit jaded for a..." he looked her up and down "...nineteen-year-old. And also, it's a bit rich that you're dogging me about clichés. What's with the aviator sunglasses?"

"I like *Top Gun*."

His eyes fell to her name tag. There were no discernible female curves beneath that dark blue uniform shirt and her flak jacket beneath. "Officer P. Daniels."

"Officer Daniels will do."

"What does the P stand for?"

"Pissy and not paid near enough to banter with you."

She was quick. That didn't make her less annoying. He produced his license and his registration, and she walked back toward her cruiser, where he knew they liked to run information, or maybe in her case check her lipstick.

Maybe he would say that to her when she came back.

"You have a lot of speeding tickets," she said. "Mr. Caldwell."

"A fair few."

"A fraud conviction."

"An exoneration," he responded.

"That doesn't show up."

"A quick internet search will show it. I was in the news."

She huffed a laugh. "Well, let's hope this doesn't end with either of us being in the news."

"That would be ideal," he said.

He looked at her name tag again, and for the life of him, couldn't figure out why her name was pulling him up. It sounded familiar, and he didn't know why.

"Well, I can't really let you off for good behavior, since according to your record, you don't have much of it."

"And here I heard small towns were supposed to be friendly. This is how you welcome new residents?"

"Only when they insist on leading their own Parade of One down one of my highways in a big ass Ford truck, paying no mind to the speed limit."

"Well, damn. That kinda runs roughshod over my grand marshal fantasies."

"A shame. It's an expensive ticket, too."

Expensive ticket. Didn't the hell matter to him. He had money to burn, and he was investing a lot of it in his brother's school that he ran on the Dalton family ranch. But he was also working at getting his own place up and running. He had just bought his own property, and his own house that had...

"But what does the P stand for?" he asked.

"It's not really relevant."

"Penelope. No. That's not right." He squinted, trying to remember the paperwork that he'd gone over earlier in the week. A tenant agreement had been in there with all the mortgage stuff. And just then, he remembered the name. It was a stupid name, and that was why it had stuck out.

"Pansy." He snapped his fingers. "Officer Pansy Daniels."

Brown eyes widened. "What?"

"I believe I'm your new landlord. You going to write that ticket or not?"

By the time Pansy got to her brother's house that night, she was still reeling over her interaction with West Caldwell.

When she had pulled the truck over earlier today she had imagined it would be a routine stop. But then she had approached the vehicle, and he had been the kind of good-looking that had punched straight through her bulletproof vest and left her without air. Which was disturbing, because Pansy wasn't really prone to fits of breathlessness over men or anything else.

Life had beaten the ability to be surprised right out of her from an early age. She was tough, because she had to be. Because every last one of the Daniels siblings had to be. Raising themselves on Hope Springs Ranch hadn't been easy.

They'd had each other, but they'd had a whole lot of hard too.

She didn't often consider her name one of those hardships. Not anymore. She had gotten over her peers making fun of her at a pretty early age. And anyway, now she carried a gun, so people were much less inclined to mock her. But today, today she had *hated* it.

That man was not only good-looking, he had a smart mouth, and he was in fact her new landlord. And the whole power structure of their entire interaction had suddenly been flipped on its head when he'd said that.

She'd written him the ticket anyway.

If he was going to evict her…well, so be it.

Yes, she was in the middle of a year lease, so legally it would be difficult for him, and yeah, it would maybe see her right back at her brother's house, which she didn't really want to do, but she had to stick to her guns. There was no way that she could *not* write him the ticket just because he was her landlord.

No. Gregory Daniels, police chief, would never have

not written someone a ticket just because they might use that to hurt him.

Her father had been a man of integrity. A man worthy of his uniform and his badge. He was Pansy's idol, and always had been.

She wasn't going to balk over something like that.

She sighed heavily and got out of her car, her service weapon locked up in a special box inside. She'd changed out of her uniform and into a T-shirt and jeans. She always felt oddly light after a whole day at work in all of her gear.

When she'd first joined the Gold Valley Police Department, it had felt heavy.

Now, when she was out of all her gear, she felt strange. Plus, when she went home to Hope Springs, she wasn't Officer Daniels.

She was just a little sister. At least as far as Ryder and Iris were concerned. Rose was the youngest, but that didn't stop her older siblings from treating Pansy like a baby.

Even Sammy was a pretty terrible offender, and she hadn't even grown up with them. Though, close enough.

Her cousins would have been on hand to continue treating her like a child, too, if they hadn't all gone off to make their way in the rodeo. Now they were on the road so much Pansy barely saw them.

They were an eclectic group of siblings, cousins and friends, bonded together by tragedy.

They'd lost their parents on the same day. A catastrophic small plane crash during what had been intended to be a relaxing vacation in Alaska for their parents.

Ryder had been the oldest at eighteen, and had suddenly had not only unimaginable grief on his shoulders, but a heavy amount of responsibility. And the local Child Services had agreed to let them all stay together. Live together on Hope Springs Ranch. Agreeing that introducing instability after such a great tragedy would only be worse. Pansy had been ten. Rose had been six. They were the two youngest and had spent the longest stretch of their childhood without their parents.

At some point, Sammy had joined their ragtag crew, running from her own family issues—though her parents were very much alive.

It didn't matter who was related to who biologically. Hope Springs was a refuge for those who were out of hope.

And as for Pansy, her siblings, her cousins and Logan, they were linked. Tied together by a deep and terrible tragedy that few people would ever be able to understand.

They could just look at each other and know. That it was a particularly hard birthday or that the anniversary of the accident was weighing heavily on one of them.

That was why, no matter where she went, no matter what she did, this place was home.

And the people in it were the most important ones to her. Even if they did still treat her like a kid.

It was Sammy who rushed out to greet her, all wild blond hair and flowing skirts. Ryder's best friend was so feminine that sometimes she made Pansy downright uncomfortable.

Samantha had been one of most dominant female influences in Pansy's life. She had started coming around about six months after the Daniels siblings had lost their parents, and Pansy still had no idea how Sammy had managed to wiggle her way in. The friendship between the free-spirited woman and her taciturn older brother always mystified her.

She was half convinced that Sammy had targeted him, decided that they would be friends and simply hadn't gone away when Ryder had said no.

Nothing that she had witnessed had yet to disabuse her of that notion.

"I made lasagna," Sammy said. She grabbed hold of a mass of blond hair, wound it around her wrist and then effortlessly looped a scrunchie over it into a big messy bun.

Pansy was suddenly incredibly conscious of her own tight ponytail that had not a single strand out of place.

She didn't know why the contrast between herself and Sammy suddenly hit her so hard. Only that it did.

"Great," she said, ignoring that weird feeling. "I'm starving."

"Me too. But I've been sampling garlic bread liberally."

"You slapped my hand when I took some," Ryder said, coming out of the sprawling ranch house behind her.

"I'm the chef," Sammy said, pointedly. "I can do what I want."

Ryder shook his head, but didn't make further comment.

Like her, her older brother was a rule follower. Though she wasn't sure if he was one by nature or if he was one by circumstance. It was hard to say.

Not even she really knew when it came to her own self. Because she had a hard time remembering life before her parents' death in clear detail. It had made her terrified at first. Paranoid. She had been afraid every time Ryder had gotten in his car to drive to town to go to the store, much less go farther afield. And then sometimes she'd remember herself, her behavior, and sadness would overtake her entirely. All the ways she'd disappointed her dad, and how she'd never been able to make up for it.

What she found solace in was her dad's legacy. She had found purpose in it. She had focused in on it. And she had come to the conclusion that if she was in authority, she might feel a little more control over her life.

Ironic, since her dad had clearly still been vulnerable enough to die in a plane crash. But somehow it all made sense. In a strange way.

And even if it didn't make sense when it was all spooled out in front of her like that, she didn't much care.

In the end it might not make her safe. But it would make her good. Would do his memory proud. And that… Well her real fear was that she might not manage that.

She would rather be carrying a gun either way.

"Just as long as you left some for me," Pansy said. "I'm starving."

She walked across the gravel drive, and the four ranch dogs seemed to sense her presence, running in from the direction of the barn barking with glee. The little pack was much like her family. Ragtag and thick as thieves. Comprised of a malamute, an Australian shepherd, a border collie mix and an unidentifiable rescue mutt Rose had found on the side of a highway.

"Yes, yes," she said, bending down and petting the dogs. "I'm here."

It wasn't long before Logan followed up behind the dogs, his cowboy hat pushed up off of his forehead, dirt on his chiseled face, his blue eyes shining all the brighter for it. "Afternoon, Pansy," he said.

"Hi yourself," she said.

Logan wasn't blood related to them, but he was like a brother to her all the same. His mother had been killed in the plane crash with her parents. He'd been staying with them for the duration of the trip, and he'd never left.

"Arrest any bad guys today?" he asked.

"It's Gold Valley," she said.

"And?"

"No."

It wasn't like they didn't have crime, but actual arrests weren't a daily occurrence. There was a handful of regular troublemakers who got into scrapes now and then but didn't pose much of a threat to anybody in the community.

Of course drugs were a problem, no place was immune to that. Then there was domestic violence, which crossed all economic lines.

There were crimes that as far as Pansy could see came from a certain kind of desperation. Then there were crimes that were just hideous. Insidious. Urban, rural, rich, poor. No place or person was totally safe.

She was lucky, living where she did, that she didn't see a host of terrible things—the population was sparse, and there was a lack of anonymity in small towns that made it difficult to hide. But they had their issues.

"Thank you for your service," Logan said dryly.

"I'm not in the military."

He gave her a mock salute and headed toward the house. Pansy rolled her eyes. "Is Rose here?"

"Yes," Sammy said. "She shouldn't be far behind. I think she was out doing chores with Logan today."

Logan, Ryder, Iris and Rose still all lived at Hope Springs. Sammy's camper van had been parked on the property for the most part since she was sixteen years old. She would leave for a while to sell jewelry at different markets and fairs in the summer, but never for long.

Sammy wasn't involved in ranch work, but the rest of the family who lived here was. It didn't make sense for Pansy to live there, and anyway, she prized the independence. She followed Sammy and Ryder into the house, and the dogs trailed in behind them. She could hear her sister Iris shouting from the kitchen.

"They live here," Ryder said. "Nothing you can do."

Iris came out of the kitchen shaking her spatula. "It's our home. They don't need to have the run of it."

Both Ryder and Logan looked at each other and shrugged.

Iris sighed heavily, looking to Sammy as if she would take a hard-line stance on animals running roughshod through the house.

"Don't look at me," Sammy said. "Remember, I tried to make a case last year for us having a house cow."

As the oldest sister, Iris had taken on a stern matriarchal role, where Sammy had always been a feminine free spirit.

It didn't matter that Iris was stern. Pansy loved her anyway. Or maybe, even loved her for it. She knew that her older siblings had really taken the hit for the kids.

The house itself was worn. Wood floors with the finish worn off in high traffic areas, and claw marks from the dogs. Rugs that were shoved to one side, couches that bore the impressions of the people who sat on them in their very particular spots. There was a huge TV in the living room, a giant table in the dining room, with eclectic chairs all around. There were high ceilings and exposed wooden beams, large windows that looked out on the fields and mountains that surrounded the house.

And from the entry there was a prime view of a big sign that hung up over the end of the driveway that matched the one out on the highway: Hope Springs Ranch.

A cattle ranch they'd worked to run as a family, and keep family run, for generations. With her siblings having to take over much earlier than anyone had imagined they would.

For a long time, Pansy had hated the name Hope Springs. Because it had felt so ironically named when all of them had been left without much evidence that hope did a damn bit of good in the world.

But sometimes now she felt like she could see it. In the

way the sun spilled over the ridge of the mountains, gilding the edges of the pine trees. In the way the cows looked dotting the fields, healthy and contained by strong fences. Evidence that the ranch itself had sustained them.

They'd experienced the kind of loss that could have destroyed them. But from it they'd made a life richer than most people could ever hope for.

"Did anything interesting happen while you were at work?" Sammy asked as she went into the kitchen, grabbed a stack of chipped plates and started to place them on the table.

"Well," Pansy began. "I gave my landlord a speeding ticket."

That earned her a moment of silence in the chaotic house. "You didn't," Logan said.

"I did," Pansy confirmed.

"Before you found out he was your landlord?" Logan asked. "I mean, he's the new guy, right. I remember that you were a little worried because old Dave Hodgkins was selling Redemption Ranch."

"Yeah. I mean… I didn't know that when I pulled him over. But I found out pretty quick. And then I wrote him a ticket."

"Why?" Sammy asked.

"You probably could've negotiated for some money off your rent," Logan pointed out.

The very idea of fudging the system that way made Pansy's pulse quicken. "No," she said. "I'd never do that."

Pansy was absolutely adamant about following the rules. Doing the right thing. Honoring her father's legacy.

Pansy Daniels knew exactly who she was, and what she was about.

It would take more than a handsome lawbreaking landlord to shake that.

CHAPTER TWO

"I'm retiring, Pansy."

"Retiring?" Pansy looked at her boss, the police chief of Gold Valley, in absolute shock. He was in his early fifties, and his dark hair was still more brown than gray. She couldn't imagine him stepping down from the job. Sure. That kind of thing happened all the time in high stress municipalities. But not Gold Valley.

Roger Doering had been police chief ever since Pansy's father had died seventeen years ago, and in many ways he had become something of a father figure to Pansy himself. No, he would never replace her father's gruff certainty, but he was someone who had always been there for her.

He'd been the one who'd had to deliver the terrible news.

He had been supportive when she had applied to go to the police academy. He had been supportive all through the extensive hiring process. It was sometimes very difficult to get hired on in small towns. It was common in a place like Oregon for a police officer's ultimate goal to be to end up in their hometown, but often they had to start in Portland first while they waited for vacancies.

Pansy had been lucky. And she didn't take for granted the fact that her connections had probably come into play there.

"Retiring," she repeated again.

"Yes. And I wanted you to be the first one to know… Besides my wife, of course."

She frowned. "Are you all right?"

Chief Doering loved this town and it seemed to her that he loved his job, so she couldn't imagine that he would just leave. If he would, then her instincts needed some work. And she really didn't think they did.

She was as good a judge of character as anyone. Better.

"I'm okay," he said. "But I had a bad physical. And the doctor doesn't really like the look of my heart. I need less stress, basically."

Less stress than being police chief of Gold Valley? She didn't say that out loud, but she couldn't imagine there was police work anywhere else that had less stress. Maybe Mayberry. But then, Barney Fife was a stress and a half all on his own, so maybe not Mayberry.

"I'm sorry to hear that," she said, realizing then that her internal reaction to it was probably coated in a heavy dose of denial.

That Chief Doering was having health problems was… It was shocking. He didn't look like the kind of person who would. He was lean and fit, and his wife made tons of baked goods for the department all the time, but he never put on an ounce of fat.

She just didn't understand that. How a person could do what was supposed to be the right thing and still have problems. Weren't you supposed to be able to have some kind of control over your physical health? He made them all run like dogs at least once a month in some kind of team building exercise. They were all a lot more fit than they wanted to be because of Chief Doering.

"Yeah," he said. "But to be honest, my retirement is sufficient and the idea of slowing down isn't bad."

Again, she said nothing about the fact that slowing down from a job at GV PD sounded a whole lot like taking up knitting.

"I'm telling you because there's going to be a vacancy in my position. And I want you to apply."

"Me?" It was her dream. There was no denying that. Being police chief just like her father, sitting in the same office, having her picture on the wall, that was her dream.

All she had ever wanted since her father died was to find a way to feel like she was serving his memory well. And this… Well, this would be it.

She was twenty-seven. Not impossibly young for the position, maybe. Not here. Except… Impossibly young for the position maybe here. It was difficult to get people to take her seriously as it was.

She had worked for the police department since she was twenty-one. Six years of experience, on top of living here her entire life. She knew the town and the people in it better than most of their neighbors did.

Knew a lot of their secrets, and had taken up the mantle of fostering and protecting them when need be, and gently exposing them when that had to happen.

It was a particular thing, pulling people over and writing tickets in a town this size. Making arrests for disorderly conduct when the guy you were putting in handcuffs tonight turned out to be the son of the woman you needed to get an auto loan from the next day.

And then there were the people who insisted on making it weird when she pulled them over.

Ma'am, have you had anything to drink tonight?

Pansy! Little Pansy Daniels.

Just Officer Daniels, ma'am. Can I see your license and registration?

You know who I am.

Still. I need your license and registration all the same.

I used to teach you Sunday school. Before your parents died.

Ma'am, I'm going to have to ask you to step out of the car.

Yeah. There were people who would insist on seeing her as a child forever and ever. People who would think that her eight years' working for the police department, and her twenty-seven years of living in the town, combined with her pedigree didn't mean a whole lot. They wouldn't see her as old enough if she was twenty-seven, thirty-seven or forty-seven.

But the fact remained that twenty-seven was young no matter how you sliced it.

"That's going to be tricky, don't you think?"

Gold Valley worked with a panel of community members to select the police chief. The city manager was in charge of conducting the proceedings, and of the ultimate decision. But there would be multiple interviews with panels of people who would weigh in on the different candidates. Then she would have to undergo a physical and psychological evaluation with all the information going forward to the panels.

She was local. That worked in her favor.

She was local. That would work against her.

"It may be," he said. "Of course, I'm going to write a letter of recommendation. I know Johnson will feel a bit put out. But, Martinez told me that he would be willing to throw his full support behind you."

That was the other thing. Pansy was the only woman in their very small department. There had never been a female police chief in Gold Valley, not ever, and while she didn't think her gender would be a barrier—not when there were so many others for people to consider first—it was something.

"Well. Tell Alejandro that I am grateful for his support. I'll deal with Jay myself."

"He wants the job," Chief Doering continued. "But, I don't think he has the temperament for it that you do."

Officer Jay Johnson was at least fifteen years older than she was, more experienced and someone who hadn't grown up in Gold Valley, but had lived there for a very long time. He had a lot of surface qualifications that would make him better for the job. If he got it, he would also be in it for a long time and ensure that Pansy didn't actually make it to the position long enough before her retirement for her taste.

Granted, she could move.

But the idea of leaving Gold Valley, Hope Springs and her siblings behind wasn't something she could even consider. Anyway, Gold Valley was an integral thread that was woven through her vision for her life. A part of her dream she couldn't lift out. "What do you think I need to do?"

"Keep doing a good job," he said. "I mean, it wouldn't hurt if you managed to do some impressive police work between now and the time the selection process starts."

"Meaning what? Write more tickets? Because I have to tell you, that's not going to endear me to the populace."

"I don't know, Pansy. Trust yourself. Keep being who you are."

She took a breath, her hands behind her back, her eyes on the photos behind him. All the different police chiefs. Her father, who had come before him.

"I will. Can I go, sir?"

"You can go."

She turned and walked out of the office and through the

small department, past the two cluttered desks that the officers shared, and the front desk, where the receptionist sat.

Their very bored receptionist.

She gave Donnie a wave on her way out and paused when she got outside. She decided not to get in her police car, and instead to walk across the narrow road that ran between the police station and Sugar Cup, her favorite coffee shop in town.

The police station was a block away from Main Street, directly across from a large historic home that had been converted into a vacation rental, and several cottages that had also been converted into lodging. A narrow road with no lines cut between the cottages and the coffeehouse, and Pansy walked along the edge, on a rocky, narrow sidewalk before crossing the street and heading up the much more civilized sidewalk right in front of the coffeehouse.

She pushed on the black door and let it close firmly behind her. She smiled at the extremely unfriendly girl working at the register—it wasn't personal, she was unfriendly to everyone—and placed an order for a Big Hunk mocha before going to stand at the other end of the counter where the drinks were served up.

It didn't take long before she had her beverage in hand and was walking back out onto the street. Which was when she saw the same beat-up blue truck that she had pulled over yesterday parked in a loading zone.

She shook her head. West Caldwell was going to drive her insane.

She thought about what Chief Doering had said earlier. About her police work. And how she was going to have to work hard in order to earn the position that she wanted. West Caldwell wasn't a local. No. He wasn't. He was new in town. Which would imbue him with a certain amount of skepticism when it came to the local populace. He was exactly the kind of person she should be writing tickets to.

He is also your landlord.

Yes. He was. But in the grand scheme of things, as much as she loved the little house that she lived in, and loved being able to have her horse there for her to ride whenever she wanted, it wasn't like she couldn't find another place. She could. Not only that, she could easily find another place for her horse. After all, her entire family lived on a giant ranch. No, it wouldn't be as convenient, but she could make it work. Her having the job that she wanted, that she dreamed of, was far more important than her living in the rental that she preferred.

Anyway, her job was quite beside the point. It was the principle.

She took a sip of her mocha and charged across the street, using the crosswalk, and approached the truck. She shook her head, gathering her things so that she could write a ticket, when suddenly, he appeared.

"Is there a problem, officer?"

She had déjà vu. The lazy way he said *officer* was just as irritating today as it had been yesterday.

When she'd gone home to the little cabin she lived in at Redemption Ranch, the property he'd just bought, she'd half expected him to be waiting there on the porch with an eviction notice. He hadn't been.

Somehow this felt worse.

This man looked new and broad and big. Out of place in her familiar streets with his sharp blue eyes and the black cowboy hat he wore.

"You're parked in a loading zone, Mr. Caldwell," she said, doubling down on her officiousness because it was safety.

"I'm *loading*," he said.

She narrowed her eyes, looking up and down the street. "What?"

"Just a second."

He walked to the side entrance of the Gold Valley Saloon and propped the door open. Then he disappeared inside. A moment later, he reappeared with a giant, heavy piece of furniture, and Laz, the owner of the saloon, holding on to the other end.

Both men were incredibly fit, with large arms, and both had straining muscles, which indicated that the piece of furniture was heavy indeed.

She had no real understanding of why she was contemplating arms.

They hefted the furniture into the back of West's truck, and Laz ran a large hand over his close-cropped black hair. "Is there a problem, Pansy?" he asked.

"I guess not," she said. "I thought he was parked in the loading zone. You know, and not loading."

"I'm giving him my old whiskey cabinet," Laz said, gesturing to the mammoth piece of furniture that was now deposited into the bed of the pickup.

"He was just going to get rid of it. It's historic," West said.

"And you care?" Pansy couldn't help but ask.

"It's not historic to Gold Valley," Laz said. "I actually bought it off a guy in Texas who owned a saloon there. It's a little piece of Lone Star State history."

Pansy wrinkled her nose. "I hope you're replacing it with something local."

Laz smiled and pointed at his forearm tattoo, a giant fir tree that ran from his elbow down to the end of his wrist, bold and black against his dark brown skin. "As a matter of fact, I did. Showing my state pride." He placed his hand on the back of the truck. "The historical society gave me permission to go hunt around the basement of the old museum and I found a new cabinet. Gold rush era, and maybe from the original saloon back in the late eighteen hundreds. I've been having it restored. So, I'm trading it out."

"And we were *loading* it," West said.

He shook hands with Laz, and clapped the other man on the back. Laz smiled and waved him and Pansy off, heading back into the saloon.

Pansy turned back to West.

"I didn't know you were a history buff," she said.

"You didn't ask," he replied.

"How do you know Laz?" she asked, feeling suspicious.

He shrugged. "I drink and I've been here for a few months. Anyway, who *doesn't* know him?"

"And last night over beer he struck up a conversation about cabinetry?"

"As it happens, it came up that I moved here from Texas, you know, when I opened my mouth. And Laz mentioned he had some stuff that he had originally furnished the place with that came from the Lone Star State. I told him I was happy to buy it off him, and here I am. Are you going to write me that ticket?"

"No," she said. "You were loading."

His smart mouth twisted into a half smile and as the corner of his mouth tugged upward she felt an answering tug in her stomach. She didn't like it. "And you were ready to assume the worst of me."

"It's important," she said. "That's where the delivery trucks park to bring the beer. What if they couldn't bring the beer?"

"Surely the whole town would come to a complete stop.

Just so you know, I'm going to be taking this back up to the house, and then I'm going to go get some fencing. Which I will also be loading. Though, I will be doing it in the actual parking lot of Big R. So perhaps you won't see the need to write me a ticket. But hell, I don't know. You seem to like me an awful lot, Officer Daniels."

"I like law and order," she said, her voice sounding ridiculous and clipped deep into her own ears. "And I like coffee, which I'm going to go back to drinking now."

"Good for you, sunshine," he said. "I guess I'll see you back at the homestead."

"I guess you will," she said, turning away from him and walking back toward the police station, toward her car. Her face was burning. That had not gone well. No, it hadn't gone well at all. She couldn't remember the last time she had felt stupid. Hot faced and uncertain. But, boy had he managed to make her feel that way. She wanted to punch him in the face. But she wasn't going to let herself be defeated. Not by him, not by anything. She was too determined to let one smart-ass cowboy get the better of her. That was just a fact.

CHAPTER THREE

BY THE TIME West was unloading fencing, he was in a bad mood. It had been a long ass day, and something about Pansy Daniels was starting to get under his skin. Perhaps it was the fact that she seemed to have a hard-on for him. And not the kind he would've preferred a woman to have.

Not that he wanted that particular woman to.

She was a tiny menace.

He couldn't believe that she was putting a ticket on his truck when he'd come out of the Saloon.

He snorted, hefting fencing out of the back of the truck and laying it in front of the spot where he was going to do the deed.

He would get a little bit of a start this afternoon, but there wasn't a whole lot to be done with the daylight that was left. Thankfully, it was getting into summer, and that meant that the sun was sinking behind the mountains later and later.

He pushed his sleeves up and went for the posthole digger.

It was then that he heard the sound of a motor, and saw a truck driving up behind him. It was his half brother Caleb's truck coming up the drive. He sighed heavily.

When his brother parked and got out, he folded his arms over his chest. "What are you doing here?"

"I came to help you with the fence."

West snorted. "I didn't say I needed help with the fence."

"Yeah, only Jamie mentioned that she saw you down at Big R buying fencing, and she told Ellie, who mentioned it to me. I thought maybe you needed some help, but you were too hardheaded to ask for it."

There he was, back on the gossip chain. And he'd like to be mad about it, but he couldn't be. Not now. Not when the telephone game was proving for the first time in years that he was connected to a line.

His half brother Caleb liked him for some reason that West couldn't quite discern. He knew it had something to do with the fact that he had given the other man advice when he had been in a difficult place with the woman who was now his fiancée.

If West had known it would forge this kind of a bond between them he might not have given the advice.

People popping over unannounced wasn't quite the level of family he was after.

But then, given that Ellie and Caleb were decent people who'd found happiness with each other, West supposed he couldn't be too put out about the whole thing.

West thought love was like a forest. You came to the edge of it and went right in, but until you were a ways down the path it was impossible to tell if you were going on a pleasant walk through beautiful scenery, or signing up for an uphill battle with brambles, rocks, mudslides and in his case a bear that wanted to eat his head.

Metaphorically.

"Well. I was just going to do the fence myself," West said. "And I have no problems with that. Not in any particular hurry to get it finished. So, me not asking for help was hardly being hardheaded."

"Disagree. If I needed help with something I would ask."

"You would have a whole crew ready to show up. And I said I didn't *need* help."

Caleb ignored what he'd said about needing help. "You could have a whole crew too. If you asked."

His situation with the Dalton family was…complicated. He still wasn't entirely sure what he wanted from them. Or what he expected.

All he knew was that he had reached the point where in Texas there was nothing for him.

His relationship with his mother was nonexistent, she didn't even know where his younger half brother was at, and thanks to his stint behind bars, he knew just about every law enforcement official in the area was bound to treat him the way Pansy had when she'd first pulled him over. With a hell of a lot of suspicion. That he'd been cleared just never seemed to matter all that much.

Back in Dallas, he'd had a difficult time being accepted back into the circle that he had once been in. The fact that after he'd been imprisoned for three years, new evidence had been unearthed by his lawyer and then his ex-wife had been tried and convicted for fraud might have exonerated him legally, but it hadn't done it personally.

No. Instead, everyone who sided with her old money family had turned their backs on him completely. They had thought that whatever she had done, it was obviously to escape from a situation with him that had been untenable.

No one would believe that he—a roughneck from the wrong side of the tracks—had in fact been victimized by her—a pampered petite blonde who drank blood in her spare time.

At least, she drank his.

Again, metaphorically.

But, he felt drained all the same.

"Yeah, well. I don't know y'all well enough yet."

"You could. If you wanted to."

"Maybe."

"Just shut up. I'm going to help you with the fence."

"I don't have an extra post hole digger," he said.

"You're in luck," Caleb said, grinning. "I brought my own."

"Of course you have your own," West muttered.

Caleb chuckled. "Yeah. Well, I have a whole Christmas tree farm. I need to dig holes sometimes."

"You are the most random bastard I have ever met."

"It's funny, don't you think?" Caleb asked when the two of them were in position.

"What? The look on your face?"

"No. The fact that we were both in the rodeo for a time. I mean, I was directly following in my old man's footsteps. You were… I guess you just had it in your blood."

Discovering that he was the illegitimate son of rodeo royalty had been something of a trip. West didn't really know how he felt about it. He'd discovered that Hank Dalton was his father some time before he had gone to prison. It was information that would have changed his life when he was younger. But, at that point he had already changed his own life. Made his fortune and all of that.

He didn't care.

Not especially. Because he had grown into a man who didn't really need anyone. His half brother was eighteen years younger than him, and they were separated by a whole lot of distance but he'd done his best to try and make what relationship he could with the kid. Have him out to Texas sometimes. Before he'd gone to jail, anyway. Otherwise, he didn't have much use for family. And he couldn't say that he had much use for *Emmett*, it was just that he felt sorry for the kid. Because he knew what it was like to grow up in the fluttering shadow of Jessa Caldwell.

But by the time he'd gotten out of prison, his mom hadn't even known where the kid was.

It ate at him.

That was something he could talk to Officer Pansy Daniels about. But then, she'd probably write him another ticket.

"What do you know about that little lady police officer?"

He hadn't meant to ask about Pansy, it had just sort of come up.

"Pansy? That's her name, I think," Caleb said. "Not much. I vaguely remember she's part of a family... All the parents died. I mean, her parents and her aunt and uncle. So they all grew up on a ranch on the outskirts of town. That's one of those things you don't forget."

West was surprised to hear that. He hadn't imagined that she... Well, fundamentally he had imagined that somebody like her probably hadn't been through many hard times. A cop in a small town where there was probably barely any crime. He would have guessed that she didn't know much of anything about difficulty.

"She lives here," West volunteered. "On the property. She also gave me a speeding ticket the other day. And tried to give me another ticket today."

"Were you breaking the law?"

"No. I was getting ready to load in a loading zone. Why does everybody think that I'm a second away from breaking the law? I was exonerated."

"And you never broke the law otherwise?"

"I never got caught. I'm not that sloppy."

Sure, he'd been involved in some petty break-ins and things when he was a kid. But for a while he'd really hung out with the wrong crowd. Then he'd gotten his first job

on a ranch in town and had found that he enjoyed building things a hell of a lot more than destroying them. That
fixing a fence and earning a wage meant more than stolen cigarettes ever could. He had made a success of himself, and then his ex-wife had ruined everything. Sure, he
was getting back on his feet now, but he had already gotten on his feet.

And Monica had been born on her damn feet. Complete
with a silver spoon in her mouth and a high horse to sit on
so she had a view of the peasants down below. She had no
idea what it was like to struggle, not a day in her life.

Of course, she was probably struggling a bit now in
prison. So there was that. She had taken so much from
him, and fundamentally had no idea the amount of work
it had taken him to get it, and what it had entailed for him
to lose it.

He was still angry about it. He always would be. He
wasn't the kind of guy who let things go. He didn't get to
where he was by letting things go.

"Like I said," Caleb continued. "I don't know that much
about her. But then, I've never had a speeding ticket."

"You're an ex-firefighter turned cowboy. How the hell
can you be this boring?"

"Ellie doesn't think I'm boring," Caleb said.

"Well, that's why the two of you are suited to each other,
I guess."

"Do you want to come out to the house for dinner tonight?"

West found that he…almost did. But it was still weird.
Going over to the Daltons' for things. He preferred to be
there when school activities were happening. Big outdoor
barbecues, where it wasn't people sitting around a table.
He had participated in the family Christmas a few months

earlier, and he had felt…patently uncomfortable. He didn't have any experience of Christmases outside of the years he had been married to Monica. Then, he had done the whole holiday thing. They had decorated their ridiculously showy home on the outskirts of Dallas in a way that would make the Joneses get stressed out about keeping up with them.

But growing up… His mom hadn't done anything like that. No, she had usually hauled herself off to the casino and left him to fend for himself.

"Not tonight," he said.

"Suit yourself. But you know you're always welcome."

"Yeah," he said.

They continued working in silence for a while after that.

"I know the whole situation is weird," Caleb said. "But nobody has any issue with you or McKenna."

"I know," West said.

Actually, the way that the Dalton family had accepted him was endlessly weird to him. He had a standing invitation to weekend barbecues from Tammy, and even though he didn't really want to pursue a ton of quality time with Hank, the old man had been…well, friendly and charming in every situation West had seen him in. If it had all been reversed, and his mother had been the one that had to accept random illegitimate children it never would have happened. She barely accepted the children she had.

"When are you going to finish this fence?" Caleb asked.

"I'm going to be working on it off and on over the next few weeks."

"And when are your cattle getting here?"

"I'll tell you what," West said. "I promise that once I have a timetable I'll give it to you."

He wasn't sure if he was telling the truth or not. He hadn't really decided yet.

"Okay," Caleb said, nodding once. "I better head home. Gotta wash up before I eat."

West, for his part, was going to wash up and reheat a burger he bought at Mustard Seed earlier in the day, in preparation for dinner.

But after Caleb bid him farewell and he made his way up to the house, West saw a lone figure standing on his front porch that he recognized from the stance alone. Hip cocked out to the side, arms crossed over her chest. She didn't need a uniform for him to know with absolute certainty that Officer Pansy Daniels had come to harass him again.

THIS HAD SEEMED like a better idea prior to actually seeing the man himself.

She was still feeling high-strung from her interaction with him earlier in the day, and she didn't like it. Pansy was great with people. It was a huge component of her job. She often worked with people who didn't like her very much. People who hated her, as a matter of fact, because she was either fining them for something or arresting them. Breathalyzing them. You name it.

And she was usually able to do it without feeling affected. But there was something about West that made her feel like there was an itchy, prickling fire beneath her skin, and she didn't like it at all. So when she had gone home she had gone to the refrigerator and pulled off a list that she had been working on for the past few weeks. She had started prior to Dave Hodgkins putting the ranch up for sale, and when she had presented it to him he had said that she was going to have to wait until the new owner took over.

Home improvements.

The little cabin that she lived in was great, but there were a lot of things that had fallen into disrepair, and they needed handling. From the nonfunctional garbage disposal to the slow drain in the bathroom sink, drafts in the walls that let in both cold air and spiders, a leaky roof, and several other complaints, she had quite the list of demands.

And it had seemed right that she go to West and make sure that he did what she needed him to.

But then he got out of his truck, unfolding that long, lean body and mirroring her posture back at her. But when *he* folded his arms over his chest they looked vaguely like the size of old-growth tree trunks.

His forearms were massive. And she told herself that that only bothered her because while she had weapons, her instinct when confronted with large men was to be slightly nervous. Her goal was never to use her weapon on someone, but she was a woman, and that meant she was at a physical disadvantage. Not that she thought West was going to hurt her. But… It was something to bear in mind in her line of work when it came to dealing with large men.

And that was why her stomach felt strange and twisted. Fluttery.

She would not show him that she felt intimidated, though. Or whatever this feeling was.

She wouldn't show him, because she wasn't in the wrong here. She was absolutely in her rights. Because she was a tenant, and he the landlord. And per her agreement these sorts of repairs fell under his purview. When he had bought the property, he had gotten the lease right along with it.

"I've been meaning to talk to you about the list of repairs that need to be made on my house."

"Why don't you come inside," he said, walking up the stairs past her and pushing the front door of his house open. She had never been in the big house on the property before.

"Why?"

"Because I'm hungry as hell and I'm not going to stand out here and talk to you feeling irritated. Because I've already done that today and I have to tell you while your patience for repetition seems to be at an all-time high, mine is pretty low."

She followed after him into the massive entry. She had no idea that the place was so fancy inside. A big, open living room with a mezzanine floor that overlooked it. Large floor-to-ceiling windows that made the most of the view. What she did notice, though, was that there wasn't very much furniture. And there was absolutely nothing personalizing the place. No pictures. No decor.

A couch. A couple of recliners. There was a TV tray sitting in front of the couch, and it had a plate sitting on it. The plate was dirty.

There was also a bottle of beer sitting on the floor by the couch that she assumed was empty.

She followed him into the kitchen, and he pulled a Styrofoam carton out of the fridge and popped it in the microwave.

"I don't think you're supposed to microwave Styrofoam," she pointed out.

"Says who?"

"The surgeon general, I think. It's bad for you."

"Everything fun is bad for you."

"You think that microwaving Styrofoam is fun? I thought my bar for fun was low."

"You know what I mean," he said, casting her a baleful look before pulling the Styrofoam container back out of the microwave and opening it up. Steam came off of the hamburger and the french fries that were inside.

"French fries in the microwave." She pulled a face.

"I didn't invite you in for you to pass judgment on

my dinner. Why don't you just tell me about your home-improvement issues?"

"Oh," she said. "Well."

He took a beer out of the fridge, and held it out toward her. "Want one?"

"No, thank you," she said crisply.

"Sorry. I'm fresh out of apple juice." He took the beer for himself and closed the fridge. Then he wandered into the living room as if she wasn't there, put the Styrofoam container over the top of the dirty plate and sat down on the couch.

"You're taking this bachelor thing very seriously," she said.

"I am," he said. "That's the beauty of divorce."

For some reason, her eyes went straight to his left hand. As if she was looking for a tan line or some evidence that his marriage had existed. She had a hard time imagining him married.

You don't know him.

"I've been divorced for four years," he said. "It's just that I was in jail for most of that. I told you. I was exonerated."

There was clearly a story there, but while she waffled over if she was supposed to ask about it, or if she was supposed to pretend there was nothing to the statement, he moved on.

"Tell me about your list."

She was a little bit relieved that he had moved past the point where she could ask him about his wife. Because for a moment curiosity had almost overrode her typical caution when it came to asking people about their pasts. Because if she asked, then they did. And her story was nothing if not one giant bummer.

It wasn't that she was resistant to talking about it necessarily.

It had been seventeen years since her parents had died. In many ways it was part of her past in the same way the broken arm she had gotten falling out of a tree when she was six years old was part of her past. Part of what had made her who she was today, some of which had left scars.

But, it did tend to make people uncomfortable.

"I need a new garbage disposal," she said, launching into the list as he had asked, and by the time she was finished, he was staring at her.

"Okay," he said.

"That's it?"

"If you need those things, you need them. They call these kinds of things investment properties for a reason, I guess. I have to invest."

"Well," she said. "Thank you. Dave was pretty resistant to the whole thing, in part because he was selling."

"Yeah, and he didn't mention anything to me about those improvements that were needed. But, I did get a pretty good deal on the place, all up. The huge excess of money I used to have is gone. Honest truth. But I got a decent chunk selling my McMansion. So, I was able to buy this place, and get set up to invest in cattle. Plus live." He gestured at the burger, as if that was an indication of the living that he was doing. "I mean so I'm doing fine. But you know I used to be… Well all that was extra anyway."

"Oh," she said, not really sure what to say to any of that. He was looking at her. Those eyes like lasers. Cold and blue and bright. But they made her insides feel anything but cold.

She suddenly wished that she still had her flak jacket on, because she felt very exposed standing in front of him wearing only a T-shirt, and for some reason her breasts felt heavy. She would have liked a little bit of extra support. That jacket squishing them flat.

"My family owns a cattle ranch," she said.

"Are you afraid that I'm going to be competition for you?"

"No," she said. "Hope Springs is as big as it's going to get. It's profitable, and it's functional. There's no way for us to buy more land, not with the way things are spread out. I mean, we could, but not on the original homestead. All that to say, we can only produce what we can produce. The land only supports so many head of cattle, as I'm sure you know if you've done your due diligence."

His mouth worked up into that same smile she had seen earlier today. The one that made her feel like he was making fun of her a little bit. "I always do my due diligence, Officer Daniels."

The way his tongue lingered over the syllables of her name made her antsy.

"If you need any help… I can give you my brother's phone number," she said.

"Are you setting me up on a blind date? Because I'm going to go ahead and hazard a guess your brother's not my type."

"Maybe a blind *business* date," she said.

"Nice. We can talk about cows over a bottle of wine."

"Ryder would rather die than talk to you over a bottle of wine, about cows or anything else, that I can guarantee you."

"Give me your list," he said.

She started to comply, and he leaned forward, taking it out of her hand.

His fingertips brushed hers. They were shockingly rough. Hot.

She shrank back quickly. "Thank you," she said too quickly. "Again. I…"

"You could apologize for the whole ticket situation," he said.

The heat from her fingertips spread like a bolt of lightning to her chest, and transformed into annoyance along the way. "I don't need to apologize to you. There was a small misunderstanding, but it was clear that I was just doing my job."

"You seem to do it very thoroughly around me."

"You seem to make marginal choices around me. It's not my fault. Protecting the community of Gold Valley is my responsibility."

"Yeah. Protecting the community from people parking in loading zones. What a life, Officer Daniels. What a life indeed." He lifted up the list. "But I'll fix your garbage disposal nonetheless. Still…you're lucky I'm not docking the cost of my ticket from the repairs."

"You can't do that," she said. "I have a rental agreement."

"I don't know. I think we've proven I can do anything. From speeding on rural roads to…loading in a loading zone."

She really was feeling antsy to get out of there. She'd had three conversations with the man, and things had escalated to where she felt like they'd had at least thirty more conversations than that, and she didn't know how that worked. But suddenly, she couldn't remember what it was like before she had seen his face for the first time, and that bothered her on a cellular level.

She didn't have time for this. She had to prepare for her first panel interview for the police chief position, and that meant making sure that she was completely on top of the municipal code.

"And stay out of trouble," she said.

She turned away from him, and somehow she could feel

the smile that spread over his lips even though she wasn't looking at him.

"You too."

By the time she was back home, she felt like she wasn't entirely sure which way was up. And for a woman who prided herself on control, that was the most disturbing realization she could've possibly had.

CHAPTER FOUR

BY THE TIME West got down into town the next day he had been possessed by some kind of devil. He wasn't sure which one.

It didn't particularly matter which.

But he pulled his big blue pickup truck right into the vacant spot on the curb beneath the sign that said Loading and Unloading. Even though he knew full well that it was going to be a pain in the ass to walk from there all the way to Big R and back with the different things he needed—nothing too heavy.

A pair of wire cutters, a new pair of work gloves, just some basic things. But, even so, he figured that carrying the bag of items back would be worth it.

He wasn't sure why in hell he felt so driven to poke at Ms. Pansy Daniels.

Well. *Officer*, he supposed.

Maybe that was it. Maybe that was what stuck in his craw. He wasn't in prison anymore. He was out, and he was free, and he had a hell of a lot more wiggle room on this side of the bars.

He snorted as he walked down the sidewalk, crossing the street and heading down in the direction of Big R. He paused for a moment inside the building after acquiring his things to speak to the woman who worked there. She had two small dogs behind the counter with her.

West liked dogs. He'd never owned one.

When he was a kid his mother had told him that he couldn't have one because she didn't trust him to take care of it.

He'd found a dog once. He'd fed it scraps from his lunch every day after school. Not that he'd been able to afford to spare that food, but he'd been captivated by the dog, and had wanted to make friends with it.

He'd tried to bring it home. His mother had refused. The dog kept following him. Day after day. It hadn't understood why West had brought it home one day, and then not the next. And then the dog had disappeared. He had felt guilty about that for a long time after.

Like he'd failed the dog in some way.

His mother had only assumed he couldn't take care of the dog because she couldn't take care of her own kid. But that, West felt, was hardly his sin. Still, he'd had his share, he supposed.

That he'd never gotten a dog after that suddenly stuck out as odd to him.

His ex-wife hadn't wanted a dog in the house, and West didn't really see the point of a dog if he couldn't have it come indoors with him. Not a judgment on anyone who did it differently. But he just felt like if he were getting a companion, it would be his companion wherever he was.

But he didn't have a dog.

Never had.

So he supposed it didn't matter.

West walked out of the store, bidding the woman a good day before heading back toward his truck. He deliberately didn't use the crosswalk when he crossed back over to the other side of the street. If Pansy didn't get his truck where it was parked now then she could always give him a ticket for jaywalking.

He didn't know why he was looking forward to sparring with her again. Just that he was. And when his truck came into view, he wasn't disappointed. Because there she was, standing next to it, her arms crossed, her expression blank.

"Pansy," he said. "Fancy meeting you here."

"Why are you doing this?" She asked the question as if none of this gave her any joy. And he didn't think that was true. He thought that she got a certain amount of joy out of it, actually.

"What's the problem?" he asked, echoing a question he'd asked her at least twice now.

"You are parked in the loading zone." She stared at him blandly, and he didn't respond. "Again."

"Look," he said, moving to the truck and jerking the door open. "I'm loading. And when I got out of the truck I was unloading."

"That's not what that means," she sputtered.

"Well, the sign does not clearly define *loading* and *unloading*. There is no time frame indicated there in which the loading and unloading needs to occur."

"There is an accepted definition." She was fighting to keep cool but her pitch had risen a half step.

"Is there? I don't feel like I ever accepted it."

"You don't have to," she said fiercely. "Because that's not the point. It's a rule. And people understand what it means."

He kept his expression neutral. "Clearly I didn't."

"That's it. I'm giving you a ticket. I'm giving you the ticket I didn't give you the other day. And I think you expected it."

He couldn't tell if she was angry about writing him a

ticket or if she was angry about having to give him what he had clearly been after.

He didn't really know why getting a ticket from her had been his goal. But she was mad, and he liked that.

You are being an immature dick.

Maybe. But he had the freedom to do so, and he kind of enjoyed that. She huffed, shifting position and reaching into her pocket. And as she did so, he caught himself giving her body a leisurely tour. Her curves weren't visible in the uniform she was wearing, unlike when he had seen her last night, and he'd been able to get a good look at the shape of her toned, athletic body in the T-shirt and jeans.

No, he couldn't see anything particularly feminine or curvy in the getup she was wearing now, and he found himself drawn to her anyway.

Was that what was happening? Was this the adult equivalent of pulling a girl's pigtails?

Yeah. Actually, as he stood there and looked at her, he thought she made a pretty neat little package. And he couldn't deny that part of him thought it would be pretty hot to strip that uniform off her body and put her up against the side of his illegally parked truck.

That was something deeply psychological. The fact that he wanted to quite literally fuck the police.

Was he that basic?

Hell. That wasn't a huge surprise. He'd tried to domesticate himself, he really had. He'd thought that was the key to life. The answer to everything. And his ass had landed in prison.

He didn't much care anymore if there was only a thin line between him and a beast.

But the thing that set him apart from the animals was that he wasn't going to act on his impulse. He could have sex with any number of women, and he didn't need it to be this one surly pain in his rear. And gazing at her particularly angry face told him that she wouldn't want to get involved with him either way.

She wrote her ticket and shoved it in his direction. He took it, then touched his fingers to the brim of his hat, the ticket held between his fingers. "Thank you kindly," he said.

"You know how you could avoid this?" she asked.

"Move to another town?"

"Park literally anywhere else on the street and observe the time allowed for parking on the sign."

"Aw, well, thank you for that, officer. I will bear that in mind."

And somehow he knew he wouldn't. There he was, a grown man going toe-to-toe with a woman who came midway up his chest, essentially acting like she was being an asshole while he'd made the choice to park in the wrong place.

Her radio went off and she jolted, turning her head and answering the call.

There were codes that came out over the speaker that he didn't understand, and her dark eyebrows shot upward. "Really? Okay. I'm on my way."

"Got a code nine from dispatch?" he asked. "What is that? A cat in a tree?"

"You call the fire department for that," she said, dryly. "Someone broke in to a car. I'm as surprised as you are. But sadly, that means I have to cut this short. I'm sure I'll be seeing you around."

"Sure you will." He waved her off with the ticket in his hand still.

Then he got in his truck and shoved it in the glove box

along with the other ticket she had written him. And he headed off toward home. Then, he pulled over to the side of the road and did a U-turn, taking his way back into town. She wanted all the things in her house fixed. And he had been intent on calling someone to handle it. But he had time. More than enough time. So there was just no reason he couldn't handle Officer Pansy Daniels's list himself. All he had to do was go and buy some supplies.

"Technically it wasn't a break-in," Pansy said, making a note on her pad.

"It was," Barbara Niedermayer said, her expression fierce. "Someone got into my car, unauthorized, and stole my wallet out of it."

"Yes, but your car wasn't locked."

"Does that matter?"

"Yes," Pansy said. "I mean, it's still theft. Make no mistake. They'll be charged. It's just…semantics." The *truth*. Which mattered to Pansy.

"Semantics that will matter to the insurance company," Barbara said.

"No doubt," said Pansy.

Which was the real issue, she imagined.

The woman looked at her expectantly. Barbara Niedermayer was on the City Council, and the fact that it was her car that had been not broken in to was extremely inconvenient as far as Pansy was concerned. It could also be convenient, granted. Provided she could find the person who had stolen Barbara's wallet. And if anybody tried to use a card around here with her name on it, it definitely would be. But…the pressure that would be put on her until then, and the problems that would result if she didn't manage to find the culprit, wouldn't even be worth mentioning.

"Did you have any credit cards in the wallet?"

"Yes," Barbara said.

"And your ID."

"Yes, yes."

"Cash?" Pansy asked.

"About $500," the other woman said, clipped. "I do that envelope method."

Pansy gritted her teeth. "Great. Unfortunately, that is going to be more difficult to...recover."

And if she were the thief, she would ditch the whole rest of the wallet and just take the cash. Though, she imagined it depended on the manner of thief. Some duplicated cards and sold them for use online. Much better than trying to spend it at the grocery store a couple miles away, which also happened sometimes too.

"I know that Officer Doering is retiring," she said in a huffy tone. "And I saw that you're being put forward as police chief."

"Yes, ma'am," Pansy said.

"I would like my case to be taken seriously."

Pansy bit back the fact that she would not be responding to any threats, implied or otherwise.

Also that she wouldn't be taking bribes. Also that the other woman was extremely unpleasant.

Small towns and their hierarchies. She was often tempted to tell people trying to climb the social ladder in Gold Valley that it was a stepladder at best, and not one worth the hassle of getting up on.

Aren't you doing it now?

No. It wasn't the same. This wasn't about status. This was about dreams and tributes and the world getting something right.

It was different.

This wasn't exactly the dream she'd had when she'd wanted to follow in her father's footsteps. She'd wanted to make a difference.

Unfortunately for her it had taken loss for her to understand things like responsibility, and why rules mattered. To understand why her father had always been so disappointed in her when she'd gone off to a church day camp and wandered away from the group, in spite of being told not to.

When she'd talked in class, and run down the halls.

As a kid she'd thought it hadn't mattered. That what adults were telling her to do was white noise, and she could handle herself. They just didn't understand.

Her father had tried to explain it once.

It's how the world runs, Pansy. Rules hold hands with laws. And enforcing laws is what I do. We need people to follow rules, we need them to follow laws or everything falls apart. It's why we have police.

But, Daddy, nothing bad happened.

We have to work together, especially in a town this size. Not just worry about what makes you happy, but what helps those around you.

She hadn't understood. She hadn't wanted to.

She'd been too selfish. Too full of energy.

Read all the instructions first.

Why, when you could just start right away?

Don't eat cookies until after dinner.

Why, when she wanted them now?

Clean your room or you can't have dessert.

But she didn't want to clean, and she wanted cake.

It wasn't all those little things that had made her dad angry. He'd been worried for her future, she understood that now. Worried that a little girl who thought rules were for everyone else would grow up believing laws were for other people too.

She gritted her teeth and turned her focus back to Barbara.

"Rest assured this case will be given priority," Pansy said.

In part because it was the only case running at the moment. Other than the case of the mysterious broad shouldered pain in her butt that had baited her into giving him another ticket today. She had done her job, and somehow he had made her feel like she'd failed.

She didn't like that. Not at all.

She finished taking Barbara's statement, and then went back down to the station for a while. Unfortunately she had a feeling that there wasn't going to be much that could be done.

There weren't any cameras on the street, and while she had been able to get prints off the car, they weren't in the system. She had managed to ignore Barbara's request that she look for skin cells that might have DNA. Though, she did point out that if the person's fingerprints were not on file, it was likely their skin cells weren't either.

She stayed until her eyes were gritty, and then changed into her jeans and T-shirt before she got in her own car to head home.

She was bleary and desperate for dinner by the time she pulled into her driveway. But when she opened her door, she immediately heard the sound of metal against metal and a man cursing.

"Hello?"

She wasn't scared. She didn't know why. Perhaps because it just didn't occur to her that it could be anything dangerous. Or at least not anything dangerous she couldn't handle. She proceeded with an appropriate amount of caution, but when she saw the cowboy boots sticking out from under her kitchen sink, denim clad muscular thighs, a flat stomach… Very muscular forearms…

"What are you doing in my house?"

"Fixing your garbage disposal." He appeared out from under the sink. "It's a damned awkward angle. Let me tell you."

"I wouldn't know."

"Garbage disposals are a pain in the ass on a good day."

"I didn't know you knew about garbage disposals."

"I've lived in a hell of a lot of crappy places and had to figure out how to fix my own stuff. I wasn't going to be paying a repairman."

He pushed himself into a sitting position, then stood, his large frame filling up the small space. Her house was more than adequate spacewise for her on a given day. But somehow right now the white walls were closing in on her and the wood ceilings seemed to be compressing, the oak floors rising up.

"Right," she said.

"Growing up I fixed everything for my mom, too." He grabbed a rag off the counter and wiped his hands. Large hands.

She wasn't sure why she'd noticed that detail.

"Oh." She blinked.

"You know I'm a Dalton, right?"

She *hadn't* actually known that. And the revelation was enough to distract her from his height, breadth and hands.

"I… No."

He shrugged his broad shoulders. "Just another one of Hank's illegitimate kids."

"But I'm really surprised I *didn't* know that. Because the town does love a rumor mill."

"I don't know if I'm disappointed or not. I would've thought that I would be the subject of some gossip."

"Well, it could just be possible that Hank is so scandalous people don't pay attention to it anymore."

"Well, how about that," he said, sounding rueful. "Not even a good scandal."

"Actually, it's kind of amazing that you haven't been more of a focus. What with you being an ex-con and all."

"I haven't done much in town to be honest. As you know, I just closed on this house, and before that I was renting. Mostly I've been spending time helping out at the Dalton ranch. But, now I'm getting my own place set up."

"And fixing my garbage disposal."

"True." He took a step closer to her and she felt eclipsed. It was weird that she noticed his height like she did.

She was the shortest one in the family. By far. Her sister Rose was about three inches taller while Iris was an inch or so taller than Rose. The boys were all over six foot. She was used to being…well, a pansy among redwoods. But there was something about him that felt impossibly large. Big and broad, the way that he filled the space with a flagrant lack of permission.

"I think technically you're supposed to give me twenty-four hours' notice before you enter my residence," she said, the words like the wind chimes that hung on her porch. Rigid and clanking, and not in her control at all.

He lifted a brow. "Are you going to write me another ticket?"

"No," she said. Mostly because she really did want her garbage disposal fixed.

"Then quit complaining and let me fix it."

"I'm not complaining," she said. "I'm simply pointing out the law. Because I know you have difficulty with those."

He huffed a laugh. "Right."

"So… Hank Dalton is your dad?" She only vaguely knew the Daltons. But she knew them in the sense that everybody knew who the Daltons were. Hank was a local celebrity, an ex-rodeo star who had become nationally famous during his time at the top, a run of ad campaigns he'd gotten back in the eighties.

She really shouldn't start asking personal questions. There was no reason to. And anyway, it invited conversation she didn't want to have. Which she already knew. But she was curious about him. And that made her almost as angry as the fact that he had won earlier today. By *losing*. He'd gotten the ticket, and still she didn't feel like it had been a score for *her*.

She was harried and wrung out and irritated by the direction of her day, and he was part of it.

To top it all off, she didn't actually know as much about him as she should. And that irritated her even more.

"He is that," West said.

"And that's what brought you out here?"

"I stumbled out of jail with nothing. Wearing the same clothes I had on when I went in. Most of what I had was gone. If any of it is recovered, it's going to take a long time for that to come together. Like I mentioned, the sale of my house has me solvent."

"So you came here for…"

"I didn't have another place to go. I know my mom. I grew up with her. I figured I would see what this part of my family is all about."

It was such a strange and interesting fantasy. To find out that you had family you didn't know about.

Pansy had a big family. But there was no secret dad waiting for her to discover. Her mom and dad were just gone. There was no one else. There wouldn't be.

"Were you… How did you feel to find your dad?"

"Are you a police officer or a psychiatrist?"

She looked down. "I'm just curious."

"I heard about your parents," he said. She popped her head back up. "I'm sorry," he said.

It was such a simple statement. Not a whole lot of awkwardness or attempts at eloquence. Just a simple *I'm sorry.*

"It was a long time ago," she said.

"Yeah. So was my childhood. Doesn't mean it didn't suck."

"Did it?"

"It wasn't great. I guess I was curious," he continued. "I have these half siblings. And they had a different experience than I did. I spent the last few months kind of observing it. Like I said. I don't really have anything else. So… Why not. Before I went to jail… I wouldn't have cared. But the thing is, when everything went down, and my wife accused me of all that stuff, then framed me for stealing money… I realized that half my problem was I didn't have anyone on my side. That's what family is. It's what they do. They side with you, right? My mom didn't care. Not really. So yeah, I'd found out about Hank right before prison. Then as soon as I was out I came here. Because I thought…it wouldn't be the worst thing in the world to get myself a team. If I could. I got more than I bargained for. I figured I would find some way to meet up with Hank. I knew that he had other illegitimate kids. I didn't expect to be accepted by his other kids. The ones that were raised in his house. Or his wife."

"That's pretty amazing."

"I haven't decided how I feel about it yet. It all makes me a little uncomfortable, to be honest. I don't really know how to do holidays without TV trays and someone shouting at the football game."

It was too easy to picture. And the echo in that image, even if it was so different to her own life, was something she knew well.

Lonely.

She had been surrounded by family growing up. She'd had so many people who loved her.

But she hadn't had her parents.

Her siblings, her cousins, Logan, they'd known. And in their house there was a shorthand for their feelings because they all shared them. Their grief might take different shapes when it bubbled up and escaped their bodies like a breath. Their actions might look different, but it was a common wound.

But outside the house? At school, in town, at slumber parties?

No one else knew. They might know she hurt, but now *how* she hurt.

That the ache to be held by a certain set of arms could be a physical pain. Arms that were gone from the world and would never hold you again on this side of heaven.

She knew.

And somehow she had the sense that even though he hadn't lost a parent to death, West might know it too.

"Our holidays were always big," she said slowly. "Basically held together by duct tape. But I think my brother Ryder felt like he had to do something for us. Because he was…he was the only one who could." She didn't know why she was sharing this with him, but there was something so vivid about the picture he painted. TV dinners in a lonely childhood. A mom who hadn't even cared that he'd gone to prison for something he didn't do. A bunch of strangers that were related to him genetically being his only hope of ever fitting into a family.

A wife who had framed him.

It made her ramshackle Christmas seem like it might be something more magical than she had imagined it to be. She shouldn't have changed into her T-shirt. It made her feel soft. Human. She preferred the feeling of being... well, bulletproof. She was never going to feel ten feet tall, that was certain, but the other she was able to accomplish with the right equipment.

Right now, she didn't feel anything of the kind. She felt sorry for the stunningly handsome, exceedingly fit man standing in front of her.

"I'm hungry," she said. "Do you want some food?"

"Sure," he said, looking surprised.

"You're fixing my garbage disposal so let's have a truce. Just for now."

"You're not going to poison the food?"

"Pretty sure poisoning you would be a violation of the truce. And the law. And I did tell you how much I like the law."

"Yeah."

"Nothing fancy," she said. "Grilled cheese."

Her sister Iris was an accomplished cook, but Pansy had not followed in those particular footsteps.

"Why do you love law and order so much?"

He got back down on the ground, tools in hand, getting ready to attack the disposal again.

"My dad," she said, finding it easier to tell the story while she busied herself getting cheese and bread out of the cabinet and fridge. She grabbed the block of butter off the counter—something Iris said made her a heathen, keeping her butter out of the fridge, but she found it convenient, since it meant that it was always soft.

And she was always running late in the morning and she wanted immediate butter on her toast, not to struggle and tear the bread. Same went for grilled cheese.

"I see," he said.

"Yeah." She had a feeling he did see all too easily. "He was the police chief."

"Right."

He was the police chief. And she knew that of all his children he'd have thought her the least likely to follow in his footsteps.

That she'd be the last one to take on his values, to put on the uniform he'd once worn and dedicate herself to the service of others.

So she'd become the one to do it.

"I just…" She spread some butter over the bread, and put cheese slices on it. And strangely, she felt her throat get tight. She didn't usually…she didn't usually get emotional about this. Not anymore. "I like feeling close to him. And I was young when he died. I didn't feel like we had as much in common as I would've liked. This makes me feel like we do. And can."

It was an abbreviated version of the truth. Close enough to it, anyway. Something that everyone understood.

The rest of it… That was a lot harder.

She put the first grilled cheese in the pan, and let it start to brown. Then she flipped it, waited for the cheese to melt and stuck it on a paper plate. "There you go," she said. "There's a beer in the fridge."

He got up off the ground again, wiped his hands on the

rag. Then he took the plate, and followed her instructions to acquire a beer.

She finished grilling her own sandwich, and then got herself a beer.

She wasn't a big drinker. But her dad had always gotten himself a beer after work. It was one of her enduring memories of him. He would come home, start talking to their mom. His voice and laughter ringing out of the house. And he would pop the top on his beer, and go sit down in the living room. It was a strange, homey thing.

A sound that made her happy.

"I thought you didn't drink," he said.

"No, I said I didn't want a beer at your place last night. I did have one. When I went home. I only drink one a night."

"Why is that?"

She shrugged. "I don't drink to be affected by it."

He looked at her as if she had grown a second head. "That's the point of it."

"Not for me. I don't like feeling out of control."

She took a sip of her beer. He was looking at her still, his eyes seemingly glued to her lips. She didn't like it.

It made her feel jittery.

He shrugged, and lifted his own beer to his lips, and she couldn't help but look at his mouth when he took a drink. Strange, because she would have said that she had no interest in looking at a man's mouth.

But he really was incredibly handsome, and his mouth was very interesting indeed.

She tried to breathe past the tightness in her chest, but found it difficult. Suddenly, he stuffed the last half of his sandwich into his mouth. Then took a swig of his beer. "Okay. I'm going to get finished up. Just a couple more adjustments and you should be good to go."

He got down under the sink and finished. Then he flicked the light switch just there and the great beast roared to life.

"Good as new," he said. He picked the beer up off the counter. "I'll get out of your hair."

She blinked, not sure why he had suddenly decided to finish and get out of here now, when he had clearly been a minute away from finishing the whole time, and could have just done so and gone home earlier.

"I… Yeah."

"See you around," he said.

"Yeah," she said, which she knew with some certainty, given that she had seen him around much more frequently than she might have anticipated since the first time she had pulled him over.

"Tomorrow I'll get to work on that roof."

"Are you going to do all of the repairs?"

He winked. It felt like a punch. Square in the stomach. "I told you, Officer Daniels. I always do my due diligence."

He nodded once, and then walked out of the house, leaving her standing there. And it wasn't until he was gone and silence had settled over her that she realized her heart was beating so loudly that it was echoing in her temples. It was a little while longer before she realized that the sensation was not entirely unpleasant.

CHAPTER FIVE

PANSY HAD THE day off, and she decided to join Rose and Iris for a trip to the brand-new bakery, Sugarplum Fairy, which was situated across from Sugar Cup.

"I feel a little bit guilty," Iris said as they walked into the small shop.

"I don't," Rose said, immediately going to the case that held cupcakes, cake pops and macarons.

"They have cake at Sugar Cup," Iris pointed out.

"Not consistently," Rose replied. "And anyway, that's *one* cake. This is many cakes. Many, many cakes."

Pansy and Iris exchanged a glance. Their younger sister liked sugar more than any one person should. And no matter how many woeful warnings Iris had dished out about what her body would do when she turned thirty, Rose didn't care to listen.

Rose got a blended coffee drink and some sort of filled cupcake. Iris chose a morning bun and a hot coffee, while Pansy got a cinnamon roll and the same coffee as Iris. The three of them sat at a small bistro table by the window, looking out onto the street. From this angle they could just see onto Main Street, and the shops weren't very busy yet. It was a weekday morning, but given that it was just on the edge of summer, and the sky was blue, the weather beginning to turn after the long gray winter, sometimes there were a lot more people out and about than you would expect.

"Heaven," Rose said, taking a bite of the cupcake. "It's perfect. My teeth are vibrating."

"Sounds great," Iris said. Then she took a bite of her pastry, and her eyes went wide. "That *is* good."

Pansy took a bite of her cinnamon roll and chewed, giving thanks that she was eating sugar this morning and not going on one of Chief Doering's runs. She hadn't realized how much she needed the day off.

"We missed you at dinner on Sunday," Iris mentioned.

"I was tired," Pansy said. "I went home. And then… I sat on the couch and I couldn't get back up."

"Why?" Rose asked.

Leave it to her sister—who had never worked anywhere but the family ranch—to ask why in a mystified tone as if all Pansy did all day was wander around the streets of town at her leisure. And yeah, maybe that was true sometimes, but still.

"Work. You know. I want to get the new position as police chief."

"That's great," Iris said. "That's what you've always wanted."

"I know," Pansy said, feeling cagey and a little bit irritated at the idea that she might have to talk about this with her sisters.

It meant a lot to her, and she didn't even like saying it, in case she jinxed it or something.

"Is that stressing you out?" Iris asked.

"I just don't know how it's going to go. And yesterday there was a break-in… Well, somebody stole Barbara Niedermayer's wallet."

"Out of her purse?"

"Yeah, out of her car," Pansy said.

"From her *house*?" Rose asked.

"Yes," Pansy said.

"Well, that's unusual."

"I know," she said."

"Oh," Iris said. "And she's on the City Council."

"Yes. And you can bet that she'll be involved in the panel ultimately making the selection for the job."

"Well great," Rose said, rolling her eyes.

"Barbara is sad," Iris said. "She lives alone since her husband left her and her son is struggling with addiction issues…"

"She's mean," Rose said, as if that settled it.

"Someone was in the barn the other night," Iris said, as if it had just popped into her head.

"What?"

"Ryder didn't tell you?"

Pansy shook her head. "No." Her brother was not the best communicator.

"He saw a flashlight beam when he was driving in the other night, and he went to check it out. It was one of the old barns we don't use, out on the edge of the property near the woods."

"What happened?" Pansy asked.

"Oh, by the time he got to the barn, no one was there. But he's sure someone had been there. It's just weird, that's all."

"Yeah," Pansy said. "Weird."

She wasn't sure if this was the last thing she needed, or if it was a good thing. But she had some actual police work to do that might raise her profile in the community. Not that she wanted there to be crime, it was just that this was a fairly innocuous crime. Well, unless you were Barbara Niedermayer.

"Tell Ryder to give me a call," she said. "I should hear his account of it."

"I don't think he was inclined to make an official police report," Rose said. She licked icing off of her fingers, and then attacked her sugary drink.

Pansy somehow prevented herself from rolling her eyes. "Well, it would help me if he did."

"Nothing happened," Rose said.

"Someone was trespassing."

"Yeah," Rose said. "They didn't take anything."

"But I did have a theft," Pansy said. "And if there's somebody shady milling around, I should know."

"It's probably that West Caldwell," Iris said. "He's new. And shady."

Immediately, those brilliant blue eyes popped into her head, and her stomach went tight. "I don't think he's going around stealing wallets," she said. "Considering he just bought the ranch that I live on. That I rent from. He's fine." She cleared her throat. "I mean, moneywise."

"I don't know," Rose said, matter-of-factly. "Plenty of people get into tons of debt and aren't able to pay it back. Just because he bought a ranch doesn't mean he doesn't need to steal a wallet."

"True," Iris said.

"Anyway, he could be a kleptomaniac," Rose pointed out. "Someone who steals just for the thrill."

"Yeah. I doubt that." Though, he did tend to park in places that were illegal. For the…joy of fighting with her? She couldn't figure him out.

"I've seen him," Rose said. "Milling about town. I think I know the real reason you don't suspect him."

"What's that?" Pansy asked.

"Well, a few reasons," Rose said. "His blue eyes, his broad shoulders, his big hands…"

An image of all those things swam into her mind's eye

and she clamped her teeth down, willing the heat in her cheeks to go away.

"You sound like Sammy," Pansy said, making a face. "You're usually much more pragmatic than that."

"His shoulders *are* very broad," Iris agreed.

Rose nodded. "Iris even noticed. The fact is indisputable."

"I wrote him a ticket," Pansy said. "In fact, I've written him two tickets. I'm perfectly willing to investigate him."

Rose lifted a brow and smirked.

Iris's cheeks turned pink.

"You're both *awful*," Pansy groused.

"Just pointing out the obvious," Rose said.

"Get a date," Pansy shot back.

"You first," Rose said.

"I would rather go shopping," Iris said.

Rose looked chagrined by the prospect. Her sisters were such a funny mix of practical and dreamy, young and much too old.

Their background didn't allow for much else.

Rose was very much a product of being raised around a bunch of men. She was the first to crack a dirty joke, join in an arm wrestling contest—even if she would lose—and to join the men on a hiking trip if the opportunity came up, but Pansy suspected her sister didn't have any *actual practical* experience of men.

Iris was much more self-contained. But then, she was the oldest sister and she'd been the one setting an example for Pansy and Rose. Iris was always on good behavior, and Pansy actually had very little idea of what went on in her sister's personal life when she wasn't in the kitchen at Hope Springs or hanging out with Pansy.

"Wasn't there a bag with a cow skull on it that you wanted?" Iris asked Rose.

"Yes," Rose said slowly.

"I promise I won't torture you all day."

"Why don't I believe that?"

"I'll go with you," Pansy said. "Then we can both torture you all day."

Rose looked resigned to her fate and as they left the bakery, Pansy felt immeasurably cheered. Because this was exactly what she needed. An afternoon with her sisters. They put everything in perspective. And it reminded her why she loved this town so much. Because her family was part of it. Her mother and father had been part of it. Everything that she was and would be was wrapped up in this town. And she wasn't going to let West Caldwell distract her. She had a job to do.

And that was the most important thing she could think of.

After shopping with her sisters.

"SO YOU'RE TELLING me that you didn't file a missing persons report?"

West knew that at this point he shouldn't be surprised.

"He's fifteen," his mom said. "I can't control a fifteen-year-old. When you were that age I didn't always know where you were."

"Not for weeks at a time, Mom," he said. "That's not normal."

"If he needed something he would come home."

Why would he? He wouldn't get what he needed from you.

West bit that part back, found it best not to say anything. But he ended the call quickly after that, and then he called the police department in the county his mom lived in and filed a report himself. Difficult to do since he didn't have an accurate description of the kid, wasn't sure of his exact birth date, and had no idea exactly where he was last seen or what he was wearing, because that would require his mother to have told him these things. And it would require her to know them.

It frustrated the hell out of him.

When he was finished he felt pissed off and figured it was as good a time as any to go and fix Pansy's roof. He gathered his tools and walked toward her house.

The roof hung low on one side and he put his tools on the edge and then gripped the edge, hauling himself up.

He walked up to the ridgeline and looked out over the top of the trees, off toward the horizon. The sun poured down over the mountains. Mountains that went on forever in great, jagged layers. First green, then fading to blue until they nearly disappeared into the sky.

He still felt like he was a stranger in this land. An outsider asking permission to be here every time his boots hit the dirt.

Texas had gotten into his bones.

It was the first place he'd owned his own land. The place where he'd started to feel like he was his own man, and not tied to the drama his mama created around town. To the fact that he was a bastard with no daddy. A poor urchin with one pair of shoes and no winter coat.

He'd become a winner. He'd become rich.

He'd become a husband.

He'd become a convict. And when he'd come out of that prison Texas hadn't been in his bones anymore.

He wasn't sure there was anything but anger there. Nothing but an alien feeling of helplessness that he'd never experienced before, even when he was a kid. For the first time in his life he hadn't known the path. Hadn't known the answer.

And he'd realized that the only reason he'd ever *thought* he'd known was youth and arrogance. Not because he'd actually known. But because in spite of how little he'd had nothing had truly knocked him down. Nothing had shown him his efforts might not pan out after all.

He'd always had just enough glimmers of sunlight to hope.

The discovery that the world could be turned upside down into darkness, that he could be betrayed by the woman who shared his life, his bed, had shaken what he was.

Made him a stranger in the place that had become home.

Had made him aware that his own blood was a stranger to him. Had sent him across the country to Gold Valley, Oregon, to try and find something out about that blood.

So there he was. Fixing a roof. Starting a ranch.

Waiting to feel home.

He shook his head and stopped staring into the distance, and got to the task at hand.

Pretty soon the midday sun was destroying him. It wasn't that hot, but being up there on the roof, in the direct sunlight was. He stripped his black T-shirt off and wiped his face with it, throwing it down onto the roof next to him as he continued to pound shingles.

And that was when Pansy's little car started coming up the driveway.

It surprised him.

He hadn't expected to have her home today. She got out of the car, and he looked down at her, watching as she pulled out a couple of bags and then started to head toward the front door of her cabin.

"Hey," he called down. She jumped and he noticed her reflexively reaching to her side as she stumbled back. "Were you looking for your gun?" he asked.

"Don't scare me like that," she said. "What the hell are you doing?"

"Fixing your roof. How's that for gratitude."

She looked up, squinting into the light. "Why are you doing stealth repairs? Can't you…give notice like a normal person?"

"I decided on a whim to fix your roof today. Because the weather is nice." He put his hands on his hips and straightened, staring down at her.

She held her hand up at her forehead like a visor. "Still."

"Still what? You wanted the roof fixed."

"You are…you are unorthodox and I don't like it."

He chuckled. "I don't know that I've ever been called unorthodox before."

"That surprises me."

"Not because I'm *not*," he said. "Just because I often associate with people who don't have as expansive of a vocabulary. I've been called other things. Along the same theme."

"I'm sure," she bit out.

"You know," he said. "Since you mentioned it. I could really use a beer."

"I did not…mention that."

"Oh, didn't you?"

She narrowed her eyes, then stepped into the house, and he heard the front door slam. For some reason, he was sure that she would reappear with a beer, and be mad about it.

She was the strangest woman he had ever met. Constantly irritated at him for one slight or another and yet… She wasn't avoiding him. Not really. And she wasn't mean to him. And in fact, just as he had expected, she returned not long later with a beer in her hand. She stood down below, holding it aloft. "I'm not climbing up there with a beer in my hand. And, if you get drunk and fall off my roof I will not be held responsible."

"A beer is not going to get me drunk," he called down.

"I don't know how many you had prior to this one."

He chuckled, then put his hammer down and made his way down the ladder. He walked over to where she was standing, her dark eyes gone round and somewhat glazed.

"Is there a problem?" he asked.

"Why do you keep asking me that?"

"Maybe because you always look at me like I'm a problem."

Her breath hitched, like whatever she'd been about to say had gotten caught in her throat. She opened her mouth. Closed it. Then opened it again. "Then quit being one."

He snatched the beer—which she had already opened—out of her hand.

He took a swig of the beer, then considered Pansy for a moment. "How serious is a police department liable to take a missing persons report for a fifteen-year-old boy?"

She blinked. "What?"

"Just curious."

She cleared her throat. "I guess it depends on the circumstances."

"Great. So, probably not at all."

"What's going on?"

"My half brother is missing. My mom's kid. I mean, she doesn't think he's missing, that's the thing. He's fifteen, and he hasn't been home for weeks, and I found out today that she never reported it."

"Oh," Pansy said.

"I reported it," he said. "I called the department out in

Linn County. But I have no idea if they're going to take me seriously, or if they're just going to assume that he's a troubled kid who went walkabout."

"I can't say," she said. "I would take it seriously. I take it very seriously when someone from the community goes missing. Whether they have a pattern of being a runaway or not. But…not every police officer is like that. We're just people. Some are better than others. Some are better at evaluating situations without prejudice. And some… some just care more."

"So what you're telling me is there's no way of knowing what they'll do."

"Well, if he's not presumed endangered…"

"No. I don't suppose he is."

"Does he not have a good relationship with your mom?"

"I don't really know. He's got…the relationship that you can have with her. She's not…maternal. Not really. And that's fine. I mean, I turned out all right. I figured it out. Life's tough, but I stumbled my way through it. Made some mistakes. But if I could keep Emmett from having some of the same issues I did, I would. As soon as I divorced Monica I would have taken him in, but you know, then I was in prison. And when I got out… Mom was real cagey about his whereabouts. And then she finally admitted to me she didn't know where he was. She said he came home occasionally for food. Lately he hasn't been home at all."

"And Child Services never intervened?"

"They never did for me either. Like you said. The problem with everything is that it's run by people. And that means if you get the wrong person you fall through the cracks real easy. Emmett and I…we fell through cracks. That's just the way of it."

"Well, give me all the information about your brother.

I know… Look, there's not a lot I can do here. Linn County's a few hours away. But if I hear any chatter, if anyone shows up matching his description and I see it I swear I'll let you know."

"Why do you want to help me?" Standing there with the cold beer in his hand, and Pansy looking up at him with concern, he genuinely did want to know. She didn't like him much, and yet, she was pledging to offer extra help on something that wasn't her responsibility.

But then, he had told her about it because something in him had known that she would, and he didn't know why he had known that, only that he did.

"Family is everything," she said. "Family is what keeps you standing. Believe me."

"That's not my experience of family."

"You're doing that for your brother. You're not forgetting about him, you're not letting him go. I guess… Even if there isn't anyone to do that for you it's a good thing when you can do it for someone else. Family gets made all kinds of ways. Not just being raised together. Not just being blood. When my parents… When my parents died, you know my aunt and uncle died along with them. And so did my mom's best friend. She was a single mom, one child. Logan. We grew up with him. He's like a brother to me. Just as much as Ryder. And Jake and Colt are my cousins but they might as well be brothers too. We had to come together. We had to depend on each other. And we did. Family is what you make it. And what you do when times are tough."

He nodded slowly. "Well, I'm doing my best to find out what family can mean."

"Right. Connecting with the Daltons."

"And McKenna. She's a Dodge now."

"I know," Pansy said. "McKenna and Grant were a pretty hot topic of town gossip."

"Is that so?"

"Oh yes. Grant's wife died nearly ten years ago and everyone in town was pretty invested in him. Then McKenna showed up and... She changed him. She saved his life. I'm convinced of that. I mean, he was always going to live, but I think that was just surviving. Breathing. She made him alive."

"That's nice," he said.

His half sister definitely seemed to have a great relationship with her husband even if it was one that kind of mystified him. Grant seemed like a pretty sincere guy, while McKenna was sharp, witty and a little bit spiky, which was why he liked her so much.

McKenna was like him. She had grown up on the outside of any real family. Though, she had made it into foster care when he hadn't. He needed to make sure he spent more time with her. He had a feeling the two of them could relate.

"Thank you," she said. "For fixing my roof."

"Not a problem," he said, taking another long sip of beer.

She was staring and it took him a moment to realize that she was watching him drink the beer. That she was staring at his mouth. And as he lowered the bottle, her eyes went down too, until they landed in the center of his chest.

They settled there for a moment, then bounced back up, a look of extreme embarrassment behind them.

Interesting.

In spite of himself, he felt the look of interest burn through his body, igniting his blood.

He didn't want to be interested in her. He didn't want an entanglement, and Pansy Daniels had *entanglement* written all over her. She was complicated. And if ever there was something he didn't want, it was complicated.

Sex could be simple. Relationships he discovered could come with claws and snarls and brambles he had never even considered. He was not doing a relationship again.

Sometimes he wondered what the hell he had been thinking.

Marriage had been a foreign concept to him. His mother had never been married. He had never seen that kind of household. That kind of life.

And when he had met Monica—all pretty and blonde and soft—he had thought she was the kind of woman who would make the sort of household that he'd never gotten to be a part of before.

He'd had a whole fantasy of suburban life—upper-class suburban life, but suburban life nonetheless—and it had all been wrapped up in her.

He hadn't been in love with her so much as he had been taken with the idea of claiming a life that had seemed beyond him.

And it had turned out that it was.

No. When he wanted sex, he would get himself a one-night stand. Go to the next town over. He was not going to get himself involved with a local. And he was sure as hell not going to get himself involved with a local who also lived on his property and happened to be a police officer.

Who had a great many brothers and surrogate brothers who would probably take him to task in painful and unpleasant ways.

No thank you.

A lot of women were pretty. And a whole lot of women would look at his chest if they were standing there right now.

She wasn't special.

He took another swig of beer.

"Can I help you with something?" he asked.

Her cheeks went pink. "No. Just… The roof. Thank you."

"No problem." He handed her the empty beer bottle, and their fingertips brushed together, like they had done last night when they had exchanged food and drink. Damn. Her skin burned.

"Great," she said. "Thanks again."

She walked almost self-consciously steadily into the house, leaving him standing outside. The breath rushed out of his lungs in a gust.

Until that moment he hadn't been aware that he'd been holding it in.

She was still annoying. It didn't matter that she had said that she would help with his brother. It didn't change the fact that she was an irritation and a complication.

And he was only here to fix her roof. Nothing more.

CHAPTER SIX

PANSY CHECKED HER reflection in the bathroom mirror again. She was waiting for her interview at City Hall to start. The first of multiple panel interviews she was going to have with the selection committee. Her hair was neat, her uniform was perfect.

And she felt off balance.

She had felt off balance since she had come home to find West Caldwell shirtless on her roof.

And then, he had come down from the roof shirtless. And she... Suddenly all of her jittery feelings when he was around made a lot of really irritating sense.

Her sisters had been right.

She thought he was attractive.

Somehow, her mind had been able to ignore the fact that he had broad shoulders and big muscles while he had been wearing a T-shirt. Her body had internalized it for sure, but her brain had blocked it out.

But when he had come down that ladder in all his half naked glory, the muscles on his back moving and shifting with each motion, it had all sort of fit together.

She had been prepared to be frosty to him, something, *anything* to combat the foreign, riotous attraction that was moving through her body, and then he had told her about his brother.

Everything in her had gone soft. Like it had been melted

by the scorching heat of his body, and also by his…humanity.

Because as he was standing there looking like a god of cowboy mythology—if such a thing existed—he had also exhibited something more vulnerable and sympathetic than he had before.

He cared about his brother. He was worried about his brother.

And she had a soft spot for brothers like him.

Who cared enough to shift their lives around to make sure their siblings were taken care of.

Because her whole life had depended on that. On her brother Ryder being the way that he was. The kind of man who gave up his dreams, his independence, to make sure his younger siblings could have a stable life.

If not for him… They could have been separated in foster care. Moved around. They would've had to leave Hope Springs Ranch.

She wiggled, shaking her hands out. She didn't need to go thinking about him now. She had too much adrenaline coursing through her system as it was. She didn't do entanglements.

She didn't do…men.

Well, she *liked* men. It was just that she didn't have any experience with them. Somewhat by design. Though, that was getting to the point where it was a little bit silly. But it was one of those things that had just gotten away from her.

Because when you were raised by your overprotective older brother dating was difficult. And then when you became the youngest police officer the city had, and also the only woman, it got even more complicated, and all she had wanted was to be taken seriously.

She certainly didn't need to go pulling over a former

boyfriend or hookup. And now it was one of those things that she had just left a little bit too long.

But not this. You're not going to leave being police chief too long.

Yes. And that mattered a whole lot more than her…

Her *situation*.

A *situation* that felt exacerbated by West Caldwell's body.

She gritted her teeth and put it out of her mind as she walked out of the bathroom and headed down the hallway toward the room where they would be doing the interview.

She knew that it would be a panel of four people including the city manager, the mayor and a couple of council members.

When she walked in, she felt like she'd been hit with a brick, because of course the city council member that was present was Barbara Niedermayer.

And she knew she should feel sorry for Barbara.

For all the reasons Iris had said.

But Rose's words were the ones that replayed in her mind over and over.

She's mean.

"Hi," Pansy said, moving over to the table and taking her seat across from the panel. "Nice to see you all."

"You too, Officer Daniels," said Jeb, the city manager.

"I'm ready," she said.

Whether she meant for the interview to start or for the police chief job, she wasn't entirely sure. But both were true, so it didn't really matter which.

"Any progress on my missing wallet?"

Pansy gritted her teeth. "Not as yet," she said. "But no one has tried to use any of the credit cards. Or produced your ID anywhere. It's all flagged, so if it happens we'll get a notice."

"That's not very compelling," Barbara said, making a note in front of her. The others at the table didn't seem very compelled by *Barbara*. Which made Pansy feel better.

"It says in your file that you have six years of experience on the police force." That comment came from Mayor Lana Ramirez.

"Yes."

"And your father was police chief."

Pansy nodded. "He was."

"But he was thirty-five when he took the job. Do you feel that you have the necessary maturity to handle the responsibilities inherent to this position?"

"My father was thirty-five," Pansy said. "And he also had the responsibilities of a ranch and a family. My life is Gold Valley. I'm devoted absolutely to the community and to the people here."

"And what are your feelings on the school being run at the Dalton ranch?" This question came from Barbara.

"My feelings on it? I don't really have any. They met all the legal requirements to be able to do so."

"So you don't think it's a problem that they're bringing juvenile delinquents into town."

"There hasn't been any trouble."

"One of the boys went missing last year and the search and rescue effort cost the city a substantial sum of money. Additionally, there was the break-in at my home."

"Two incidents don't make a trend," Pansy said. "We are very fortunate in Gold Valley to have a low incidence of crime. But that doesn't mean there won't be issues. The town is populated by people. No matter where they come from, people aren't perfect."

She imagined that she should pander a little bit more, but she really didn't know how. All she knew was honesty. Being straightforward. She looked up and she caught Lana's eyes. The other woman seemed to approve. And maybe this was the strategy that Pansy should use anyway. Because it was proving that she could handle opposition. She didn't know what else to do.

The questioning went on, and Pansy answered everything to the best of her ability. When it came to facts, she was completely certain of herself.

When it came to her qualifications, she was confident.

And when it was finished, she shook hands with the panel and walked out of the room, feeling energized.

She was going to be able to do this. She knew what she wanted. She knew that she was qualified.

And all of her concerns about West faded away because when it came to her work, she knew exactly what she was doing.

Then, her radio squawked. It was dispatch.

"Daniels."

"There's been a break-in at Buttercloud Bakery."

Buttercloud was a small family owned bakery just off Main that had cakes and bread you could buy by the slice or as a whole, and served biscuit sandwiches all day. It was a fairly new business and was becoming popular with locals and tourists alike.

"I'm on my way."

By the time Pansy arrived, the owners were there, surveying the broken windows.

"What was taken?" Pansy asked.

"The register was pried open, but we didn't have more than fifty dollars inside. That's gone. And mostly... A lot of bread. And Twinkies."

Pansy shook her head. "I don't understand. I mean, that window is more expensive than what was taken."

"At least insurance will cover that," said the owner.

"Yeah. Well. We'll check for prints and all of that." And when she was finished, and they ran them through the system later, she was not terribly surprised to discover that they were the same fingerprints that she had found on Barbara Niedermayer's car.

They had a *very* petty serial burglar on their hands.

IT WAS A nice day and West was ready to blow off work and take a trail ride. Really, when you owned the land, it was still working, in some ways.

He tacked up and got on the back of his horse, remembering the night a few months ago when he had gone to ride at the Dalton place. Before he had bought his own land, he had been keeping his horses at the Dalton ranch.

He'd gone for a late night rides out there often. He'd been having trouble sleeping then.

It was a holdover from those years in prison. Years he didn't much like to think about.

It wasn't like the movies. No one had cut him with a shank or made him their bitch. Though, he would have put up a pretty decent fight if anyone had tried. But there were factions, and a hell of a lot of ugliness. Fights broke out all the time. And there was something…dehumanizing about it. Being kept in a cage. Cut off from the world. It had made him forget all the things that made him a man.

He hadn't looked forward to the taste of food, because it was the same monotonous crap. He hadn't looked forward to the day for the same reason.

Prison jumpsuit, the same four walls, the same fenced yard. Day in, day out.

He had forgotten sexual desire for four damned years because there was no excuse or reason to think about it. It was the last thing on his mind. He just wanted to get through.

The act of riding his horse out in the sun… It was something that he had taken for granted.

He had forgotten what he'd come from.

When he had escaped home and gone to the rodeo he had tasted freedom, and he hadn't looked back.

He'd taken it from Oregon to Texas, from poverty to riches. And he'd felt free. Free from what he'd been born to, what he'd been raised in.

Then everything had fallen apart, and he had lost all that he'd built, and he would never take for granted the ability to do what he wanted ever again. He maneuvered his horse up a trail that led up a wide-open grassy hilltop, and from that vantage point, he could see another horse and rider down below.

Pansy.

He hadn't taken note, but he also hadn't seen her horse in the stables, which meant that she was taking advantage of the nice weather the same as he was.

He urged his horse into a trot. "Behind," he said.

She looked over her shoulder, jumping slightly. "Oh," she said.

"We both have the same idea."

"Apparently."

He couldn't help but notice the delicate indent of her waist, the flare of her hip and her heart shaped ass. She was a damned gorgeous woman.

An inconveniently gorgeous woman.

"I haven't been out in too long," she said, clearly begrudging his presence.

"Me either."

"I've always liked to ride." She seemed to surrender to the fact that he was there, and decided to go ahead and make conversation.

"I learned at my first job. I got work mucking stalls at a ranch when I was thirteen. I got paid a little bit of money, and they let me ride the horses. Couldn't ask for better."

"I grew up on a ranch," she said.

"So you mentioned. A cattle ranch?"

"Yeah."

"But you never wanted to run the ranch?"

"Well, my uncle ran it mostly," she said. "He and my dad owned the ranch. The property. Together. And my dad went into law enforcement, helped support my uncle if he needed backup during busy times and contributed financially."

"Makes sense."

"Since he's the oldest, Ryder was the one who ended up taking over everything when they died."

"I always wanted a ranch," he said. "But by the time I had money, I was managing a big financial office. So, it didn't make a lot of sense. We had some horses, some land. Kind of a dream, I guess."

"What happened?"

"I guess that depends on who you ask."

"Like?"

"If you ask my wife's lawyer, then she would tell you that my wife is the real victim. That she tried to make a life with a man who didn't love her. That she felt trapped. Utterly and completely. That because of my relationship with her father she felt like there was nothing she could do and no one she could go to. And if you ask her directly… Well, she'd say that I didn't leave her any choice. I wasn't the man that she thought she married. I didn't do things the way she wanted, and I didn't care about giving her the life that she expected. So while I was still thinking we were happy, she was plotting to frame me for fraud. And succeeded." He took a breath. "You know, you come to a certain acceptance of the fact that life isn't fair. I mean, when you have a beginning like I did, you don't have a choice. But there's also an idea in the back of your mind that the American dream is available to you. If you work hard and stay the course, you can become whatever you want. We see it in movies all the time. Rags to riches. And I did that. So at some point I figured maybe I was safe. But I was wrong. Life is always there waiting to punch you in the teeth."

Pansy made a musing sound. "As a kid who lost her parents I get that. I knew life wasn't fair in the beginning. A deep dark fear I didn't even know I should have was realized when I was ten years old. I became an orphan. But you're right, even with being an orphan you're trained to think it'll all be okay. You watch enough movies... Scrappy orphans can overcome anything, right?"

A sad smile tugged at the corner of her lips. "I had read a series of books about brothers and sisters who lived in a boxcar after their parents died. They lived by themselves, and they survived that way. It seemed like an adventure. But when it really happened to us... It didn't seem like much of an adventure. It was just sad. And we didn't have a rich grandfather who came to rescue us. We had a ranch instead of a boxcar. But... I guess to an extent sometimes I think everything is supposed to be all right now because I already paid into all that. My... Good Luck Bank or whatever."

He chuckled. "Yeah. I figured I had spent all the bad luck I could possibly have in a lifetime. But no. I ended up in jail for something I didn't do. And honestly, as bad as that is it was worse that it was because of my wife."

"You must've loved her a lot," Pansy said, sounding much sadder for him than she should.

He shook his head, looking out over the rolling hills that led to the base of a tall, craggy mountain blanketed by jagged pines.

"No," he said. "I loved the idea of making a life that looked a certain way. I loved the idea of being the kind of man who had a wife like her. A house like mine. A job like I had. With a desk and an office. A view. I felt like I beat the system somehow with it. But you don't. I guess that's the lesson there. You don't really beat the system." He regarded her closely. "I suppose *you* became the system."

"I know that doesn't protect you," she said. "I mean it didn't protect my dad."

"I don't suppose."

They rode on in silence for a while, neither of them saying anything as they continued on down the grass covered hills. Purple flowers bloomed all around them, with sprays of pink and yellow interspersed throughout. The mountains looked like pieces of green velvet layered over each other. A natural collage, the pines all torn edges.

It was the kind of beautiful that made a man's soul ache.

Gold Valley might be getting in his bones now.

He had let himself forget how beautiful it was in Oregon. Let himself forget who he was for a while because it had been better to think that maybe he had started in Texas. That he was somewhere else and someone else, and all the things that had come before didn't matter.

Coming back to Oregon, coming to find the Dalton family, had been the opposite of that.

Leaning into finding out where he came from and what he was built from.

If he was stitched together with rodeo glory, the scent of the forest and personal failure.

Because he had a sense that he might be.

Just like Hank Dalton.

He'd tried to be something else, after all, and that hadn't worked out at all. No. Not at all.

"I haven't ridden this far before," she said, when they came to the edge of the trees. There was a trail that blazed on through.

"It continues along the base of the mountain," he said. "Goes to a small pond."

"Should we go?"

"Sure," he said.

He wasn't quite sure when it had transitioned to the two of them intentionally riding together, but it had. And he didn't mind.

She was a funny thing, this woman.

This woman who represented so many things he didn't like. An adversary in many ways who had been gouged by life. Who'd had things stolen from her the same as he had.

He'd lost four years of his life. Had never had parents who'd cared about him. She had lost the sense that life was safe and certain when she was just a girl.

They were completely different people. At cross-purposes half the time. But they both knew what life could take from you.

They were both there, living proof that no matter where you started, you weren't necessarily safe.

Not the most comforting of realizations, at least not for some people.

West found it oddly comforting. Life was going to do what it did. His response was to just keep saddling up.

As they wound their way up the trail, he saw a tree that

had been scratched bald. He stopped and stared at it for a moment. "Is that just a rub?" he asked, meaning a spot where male deer went to scrape the velvet off their antlers during a particular time of year.

"It doesn't look like one," she said.

"Weird," he commented. His eyes went past the tree, to a space just off the trail. There, he saw a bag full of trash, and what looked like a fire ring. "Looks like I've had a camper."

"Looks like," she said. Her horse pranced in place, and Pansy tugged on the reins, keeping her locked in place. "My sister was telling me that my brother thought someone was in our barn the other night. Considering all the things that have been going on lately, this is a little bit strange."

"Guess so," he commented.

"There was a break-in at Buttercloud."

"Buttercloud?"

"It's a bakery."

"Okay," he said.

She got off her horse and went toward the fire ring. It was the bag of trash she took hold of, opening the top of it and looking inside. "There is in fact a bread bag from Buttercloud here."

"So your bread thief has been here."

"It would seem so." She sighed heavily. "Probably a drifter. And with any luck, he'll move on soon."

"You think so?"

"I mean, if I were not tied to any one place, and I was in the position where I had to steal to get food, yes, I would move quickly. I wouldn't want to linger and keep stealing from the same place, because then you're at risk of the police actually finding out who you are.

"I'm going to take this," she said.

"The bag of trash?"

"It's evidence."

"I guess it is."

"Just more of me trying to do the right thing," she said dryly. "Building up my defenses against life."

"Life doesn't care," he said, flashing her a grin. "I keep hoping it might start to."

She got back on her horse, and they turned around, heading back toward their houses.

He looked at the stubborn line of her jaw, the straight set of her shoulders. She was tough, this woman. Even out on a trail ride, she had stumbled on something she had to inventory.

"What's it like to be a police officer where you grew up?"

He didn't even like to go back to Sweet Home as a *regular* citizen. Too many people knew him, remembered him being a troubled kid. There was too much baggage for his liking.

And then, when Dallas had gotten to be the same he had left there too.

She had been here all of her life, as far as he could tell.

"Complicated," she said.

"But you do it anyway."

"I want to be police chief," she said. "I want to… I owe it to my dad's memory."

He wasn't going to argue with her. Both of his parents were alive, but when they weren't he didn't think he would feel inclined to do anything in their memory. Since they hadn't done much for him in his life. He couldn't argue with that kind of loyalty. If anything, he envied it.

"Do you think you would have wanted to do anything else?"

"No," she said, in that same stubborn tone. "I think this

is who I was meant to be. You can't ask what-if about things like this. You'll go crazy. Because then you start asking questions like what if the plane had left five minutes later? Or the day before? Or not at all? You start… You start seeing everything as a little bit too much of a coin toss. And it makes you too scared to do anything. To decide anything. I can't live like that, not in my line of work. I have to make choices. I have to do things. So… I just figure, this is who I am. Fate or destiny, or whatever you want to call it."

"Probably a good way to look at it."

"Do you believe in fate?"

He shook his head. "No. I chose to make a different life for myself. Monica chose to blow that life up. Because I had money I was able to fight it, and keep on fighting it. Make sure I had good legal counsel. Make sure that we were able to continue questioning evidence and examining everything, making sure that my lawyer got into things that the police missed. But all that was because of choices. No hand of fate or anything like it. Nobody made Hank Dalton cheat on his wife. Nobody made my mom raise me the way she did. Life moves around you. And it'll do good and bad with you, that I believe. But where I'm standing is because of me."

She nodded slowly. "I guess it's all whatever helps you sleep at night."

"Sex and alcohol mostly," he said, his tone dry.

Her cheeks went pink. It surprised him that she was blushing over something that basic. But then, with the way she had been looking at his mouth the other day maybe she couldn't hear the word *sex* without thinking about it with him.

Truth be told… He wasn't neutral on the subject when it came to her.

But he didn't believe in fate. There was no greater power that had tossed the two of them together. It just was. And what he did or didn't do about it was up to him.

She was an impractical distraction, and not worth the hassle. And that was the beginning and end of it.

"I have to go," she said when she dismounted the horse.

"I can put her away for you if you want."

"Oh, that would be…helpful. I need to go down to the station. I want to handle all this myself."

"Works for me."

"Thank you," she said, looking somewhat surprised that he was being a decent human being.

"Not a problem."

She paused.

"Officer," he said. "What helps you sleep at night?"

He shouldn't have stopped her. Shouldn't have poked at her.

She gave him her sternest expression. "Knowing that I had another successful day following all the rules."

"Sometimes it's fun to break the rules," he said, those words bending themselves around and turning on him. Because hadn't he just been thinking that he was in command of himself? And wasn't she a new rule that he had just put out there?

Like waving a red flag in front of a bull.

"I'm not a rule breaker," she said.

And then she turned and left him standing there, holding two horses, and feeling like everything he knew about the world had just been twisted and turned around by a giant hand he didn't even believe in.

CHAPTER SEVEN

PANSY WAS NOT big on going out and drinking after work, in fact she never did it. But, she had spent the day going over plastic bread bags, of all things, making a return visit to the campsite and feeling fairly certain there was a connection between the occupant of the barn, the person staying on West's property and the break-ins that had occurred.

So consequently she found herself doing the very uncharacteristic thing of walking into the Gold Valley Saloon in her plain clothes that afternoon.

It was already packed full of people, most of the tables full, and the barstools too. There was a collection of women around the jukebox giggling and talking to a tall, broad man with a cowboy hat. When he lifted his head, Pansy saw that it was Logan. She felt instantly irritated. Because it was almost the same as coming to the bar and running into her brother.

Really, she couldn't escape.

She took a step into the room, and heard someone from the bar call out, *"The cops are here, everyone behave!"*

She turned her head sharply and couldn't see who had actually said it. This was why she didn't go out. It just wasn't worth it. She thought about turning around and leaving when the door opened again, and in walked West.

Now she was officially beset.

"How did your investigation go?"

She was so taken off guard by the sincere question that she froze.

"That good, huh?" he asked.

"Just fine," she returned.

"Hey," he said. "There's somebody parked in the loading zone outside."

She narrowed her eyes. "Is it you?"

"No. I wouldn't be that careless."

"I'm off duty," she said.

"Somehow, I don't think that would preclude you from giving me a ticket."

"It wouldn't," she said.

"Can I buy you a beer?"

Again, she was completely taken aback. "Why?"

"Because I want to."

She turned and looked over her shoulder at Logan, who hadn't even noticed that she was there. What would he think if he saw a man buying her a drink? Would he think anything about it at all? There was a time when he would have. He was as overprotective as Ryder. But, she was twenty-seven. All around her, people were flirting. She had never flirted a day in her life. Not really.

She looked up at West and he was…well, he was gorgeous.

Seeing him shirtless yesterday had nearly knocked the wind out of her, and when he had come upon her on the ride earlier today she'd thought she was going to fall off the horse.

She couldn't pretend that she didn't think he was handsome.

He was also the epitome of a bad decision. Everything that she had never wanted to be drawn to.

It kind of made sense in a way. She was under an immense amount of pressure right now. Maybe that was the problem. She was having some kind of psychotic break in the shape of a broad-shouldered cowboy. For the first time, suddenly, she understood why people made bad decisions where handsome men were concerned.

Yes. I'm sure that West Caldwell would be very inter-ested in the idea of you testing out your sexuality on him. That he wouldn't find that boring at all.

The idea made her cringe.

He was already on his way to get her a beer, and she was sure that he wasn't pondering her or her sexuality at all.

She burned.

And it made her angry. She was used to being in charge. Of herself, and of the people around her. Sure, sometimes it made it weird to be the person in authority.

To walk into a bar and have someone say *audibly* that they had to stop having fun now. But there was something about it that she liked too, and the fact that West made her want to connect in some way, the fact that he made her feel lonely, galled her.

This was already far too much contemplation to be hav-ing over the offer of a beer.

Normally, though, she found being on the outside com-forting.

It allowed her to maintain the control that she wanted. It allowed her a sense of safety. A bubble around her and everything that she was.

He made her feel lonely. Incredibly conscious of how long she went without being touched by another person on a given week. Months. If she avoided her family...no one touched her. And her brothers were not overly demonstra-tive physically. Iris and Rose hugged. Though, not as often as Sammy, who seemed to touch people as easily as she breathed. But it was all dependent on whether or not she saw them, and she didn't really have anyone else in her life that breached the bubble.

By design.

The reminder didn't help.

West returned with the beer, and she made a concerted effort not to let his hands touch hers. Because every time they had passed beer back and forth between them they had touched, and it was accumulating on her skin. Like the impression of him was there and she couldn't do anything to make it go away.

"Look," he said. "There's a table. Want to snag it?"

"Why?"

He looked at her, those blue eyes making her stomach feel a little bit shaky. "Same reason I bought you the beer. Because I want to."

"But why?" She was persistent in this, because she knew that there was always an angle. Always a catch. That was life in a nutshell. It was never straightforward. It was never simple. You might think one thing was happening, then life would turn around and clock you in the face.

She didn't much trust anything, least of all this far too good-looking cowboy who should be the last person in the room that wanted to talk to her, but wasn't.

"I don't know," he said, not taking his eyes off hers, and it was that admission that made her follow him over to the cleared-out table for two in the far corner.

She could feel people watching her.

She glanced over at the jukebox and saw Logan had noticed her finally. She didn't want him to come over and talk to her. And when she looked up at him she decided to try and give him an expression that said exactly that. His response was to lift a shoulder and one eyebrow.

She didn't know what that meant.

"Did you make any progress on the bread bandit?" West asked.

"No," she said. "I mean, it's all the same person. But I don't know who that person is, and even on the spectrum of small town police work, this feels pretty small."

"But you have to investigate?"

"No question," she said. "If I don't then I'm negligent. And anyway, I want…you know, the police chief thing."

"Yeah," he said, looking around. "Everybody knows who you are, don't they?"

"Yes," she said. "They do."

"Must make dating tough."

He had no idea.

"Doing anything in a small town you grew up in is a whole thing. It was always going to be tough for me because my father was the police chief. But then he was dead, my mother along with him, so I received a fair amount of pity in my life. Then I became a police officer too, and people are a little bit afraid of me. Or, if not afraid then…" She thought about the guy who'd said loudly that the police were here when she walked in. "It's either that or dumb jokes. And it's not everyone, obviously, but I've always been closer to my family than to any friends. It's just that they're the ones that *know*. You know, they get it."

"I can understand that. I think that's one reason I came here. I don't have anything in common with Gabe or Caleb or Jacob, not on the surface. They grew up with money. With a mom and a dad. But they're the only people that know what it's like to be part of this particular ragtag band of half siblings that we are. This *thing* that we all are."

"It's not shared blood for us necessarily. It's the shared upbringing. The shared loss." She flicked her eyes back toward Logan. "He's one of my brothers. You know. More or less."

West followed her gaze. "I guess I'd better be careful then. He looks like he could put up a pretty good fight."

"He'd probably beat you up," she said.

"I doubt it," West said. "I already knew how to fight, but I honed that in prison pretty well."

"Oh," she said. "Were you in a lot of fights in prison?"

"I don't know what the benchmark is for *a lot of prison fights*. I mean, on the scale of prison fights."

"I guess I don't either. What we have basically amounts to a couple of holding cells."

"Very different experience doing police work here than it is in a city, I imagine."

"Yes," she said. She looked down. "I like to think that we would have done a better job for you. That we wouldn't have made the same mistakes the police who handled your case did."

"It's all complicated," he said. "It's not just the failure of a police officer, but the presence of good lawyers and bad lawyers, of bias in the jury. Complicated."

"I suppose."

"My ex-wife was one of them. You know, someone with money. Someone like me, someone who got ahead in life, who got ahead of their station naturally look suspicious to those with generational money. That's the kind of thing that people shouldn't be able to do. On the one hand, we all say we believe in the American dream, right? But when it actually happens we tend to be a bit suspicious of it, and if it appears to crumble all around somebody then I think we figure that's about fair enough. If I'm a criminal, then it makes sense that I was able to jump up in station. Nothing else really does. We have our narratives, we don't like them being disrupted."

"I've never thought about life in terms of money, which I suppose is how you know we've always had enough. There was life insurance money from my parents, plus we were well-off in terms of the land. It doesn't mean we haven't struggled, we have. It's definitely not a…not a situation where we never have to work a day in our lives, but we had enough. For a bunch of kids who went through what we did I think we've had it surprisingly easy."

"I didn't think about anything else but money for most my life. How to get more of it. How to make sure I *kept* more of it. I was so damned envious of what other people had. I figured I could get myself some security. I could make my problems go away." He chuckled. "Not so much."

"I think your circumstances were pretty…unusual."

"Maybe," he said.

Her eyes fell to his hands, the way they wrapped around the beer bottle. They were scarred, rough looking. Workingman's hands.

"When do your cattle come?"

"Next couple of weeks," he responded. "Just about got my fence ready."

"Good," she said.

She didn't know what else to say.

Suddenly she wanted to say more. She wanted to touch him. She wanted to put her hand out and cover his.

She wanted to find a connection between the two of them that was more than just words.

He cleared his throat and knocked the rest of his beer back. "Enjoy the rest of your evening, Pansy," he said, standing up.

"Oh," she said. "Are you…"

"Just figured I'd let you get on with it. You didn't come here to talk to me. See you around the homestead."

He tipped his hat to her, and walked over toward the jukebox. Someone had put a few quarters in, and Garth was singing about the friends he had in low places, which was bringing people up from the tables and out onto the little makeshift dance area.

A couple of the girls that had been talking to Logan broke away and went toward West, one of them reaching out and brushing her hand over his chest.

Pansy's ears burned.

It was easy for that girl to touch West. She just reached right out and did it, and Pansy sat there frozen, her hand welded to her beer bottle like it was a claw.

He took hold of the girl who had touched him, and she giggled as he pulled her up against his body and spun her out onto the dance floor. Pansy looked at those big hands holding the other woman's hips and something burned in her heart that she didn't feel all that often, but she recognized all the same.

The ache to be held by arms she knew would *never* hold her.

It was so different this time than it had been when she was a girl. So much so that she felt guilty calling it the same thing. But it was.

She felt lonely. Bitterly so. Sitting in this room full of people, watching West touch that other woman so effortlessly. Watching her touch him back, smiling big and bright and easy, not at all worried what people might say or do if they saw her with him.

Isn't that just an excuse at this point?

She gritted her teeth against that internal comment.

It was a valid enough excuse. Things were different for

women. And things were different for her because she was local. She had to watch what she said, and watch what she did. She had to be mindful of everything all the time.

But right about now the only thing she was mindful of was the deep ache inside of her chest. Blinking hard, she got up from the table and walked out of the bar alone. Going out drinking had not been a very good idea. She was leaving in worse shape than when she'd arrived, and she didn't know how to untangle all the emotions inside of her. And she wished to God that she just could make them all go away. That she could find a way so to just not have them.

But she had wished that off and on since childhood, and she had yet to find a way to make it so.

So she would just do what she always did.

Find a way to deal with it herself.

Because eventually that ache would fade. That loneliness. It wouldn't go away, but it wouldn't be the only thing she felt, not for too long at a time.

So she would find solace in that. Since she wouldn't allow herself to find solace in West.

WHEN HE LOOKED up again she was gone. He had walked away from her for good reason. Because sitting at that table in that quiet little corner, it had been easy for him to forget all the reasons he wasn't going to go there. Most especially with her brother—or whatever he was—in the room. But then he had gone over, and the touch of the woman he was currently dancing with had failed to spark even a quarter of the interest that a mere glance from Pansy managed to conjure up. And he didn't know what he had expected her to do, but he hadn't expected her to leave.

"Thanks for the dance," he said to his partner. "I gotta go."

"Why?" she asked, looking petulant.

Well, he felt pretty petulant, come to that. Because if he could have contrived to get some physical interest in the little beauty currently holding on to him that's what he would have done.

He hadn't touched a woman in four years. To say that he was hard up was an understatement. And damn but he would like to break his dry spell. But apparently his body was only interested in one woman.

Since when had he become a connoisseur of any kind? Typically, he was a buffet man. Before prison he'd liked sex readily available, plentiful and right there for the taking. Offered up. He didn't want to work for it, he didn't want any of that.

And yeah, he had been married for a few years. He had no trouble being faithful when he took vows. He wasn't picky. That was the thing. He liked women, which meant that attraction should be that simple. But he was having some kind of weird ass chemistry situation with his uptight policewoman, and he didn't care for it.

He could spin whole fantasies out of a brief touch of their fingertips, out of the searing tension that came from sitting in a corner with her.

It made him feel like a boy.

Because only *boys* got excited over things like that. Stolen glances, accidental touches and the indrawn breath of *what-if*.

Grown men didn't deal in *what-if*. It wasn't about possibilities. It was about honesty, simplicity.

Except, here he was, bidding farewell to a sure thing to look for *absolutely not a thing*.

He couldn't credit it, except that he couldn't credit much of anything to do with his own behavior since he had gotten out of jail.

He wasn't the same man.

A hard realization. Because he'd wanted to be. He'd wanted to go back to who he had been before Monica. He didn't want to be changed by her or what she'd done to him.

But he was.

He was rootless, and he was adrift, and he had been looking for something to anchor him since he'd left Texas.

Pansy Daniels felt like an anchor, and he didn't know why. But when he talked to her, he felt like she might understand half of what came out of his mouth, and *he* didn't even understand half of it.

Or maybe that was all justification. Justification because he was horny, and for some reason only for her.

He wasn't sure he much cared.

He pushed open the saloon door and went outside into the balmy evening. The sky was a deep blue, dotted with stars, streetlights not remotely powerful enough to begin to wash them out. For a moment he thought he'd missed her completely, but then he saw a flicker of movement head off Main and down the cross street.

Toward the police station.

He kept his pace, moving quickly down the sidewalk, and when he turned the corner, he called her name. "Pansy."

The slim little shadow stopped.

"Don't shoot me," he said.

"I'm not carrying my gun," she responded. She turned around. "What are you doing?"

"I don't know," he said, the second time he had given her that answer in the space of a half hour. Because he didn't know. He didn't know why Texas was dead to him and he was drawn to Gold Valley. He didn't know why he couldn't get excited over the things that used to excite him. He didn't know why he wanted to talk to this wound up little police officer and not to a woman who had made it plain as day that she was happy to play the part of buckle bunny to any cowboy she could find.

He didn't know why he was standing out on a darkened street instead of getting drunk inside that bar. He could make a whole list of all that he didn't know right about now.

"You were dancing," she said.

"Yeah," he said. "I was."

The darkness felt like a layer of protection. Against prying eyes, against his own better judgment. And he was all for it.

"You should probably go back and dance with her," she said.

"Why?"

"I don't know," Pansy said, clearly mimicking his tone.

"I think you *do* know," he said.

"Well, if you're looking to get lucky, you should definitely be dancing with her. And not out here talking to me."

Get lucky.

That was the furthest thing from his mind. Not sex, sex was very much on his mind, but wrapping it up in the term *get lucky* just didn't work for him right now.

Because there was nothing lucky about the fact that he only wanted this woman. And there was nothing lucky about the fact that she was a walking entanglement.

Maybe this was the problem. Maybe the problem was that *difficult* was what he was into. That *wrong* was what he was after. Because after everything that he'd been through maybe he was just tired of butting up against brick walls and having them stand.

Maybe you want to knock some down.

"Officer Daniels, I don't think there's much of anything

lucky to do with the fact that I would rather be out here with you than in there with her."

He couldn't see her face, but he could feel her posture go rigid even from ten feet away. He walked toward her, strung out like a wire. "And I had the feeling that you walked out of there because you didn't want to see me with her. Am I right?"

"I… I don't care who you're with, West."

It was the first time she'd ever directly addressed him. The first time she'd ever used his name.

"Pansy," he said. "I think you do."

"I don't," she said. "I'm trying to get a job as the police chief. And I'm not going to mess around with… I'm not going to…"

"But you want to."

"I want this job."

But he had seen her. Seen the way that her lips parted softly when she looked at him, the way that she looked at his mouth when he took a drink of beer. He had seen how she looked at him, and he knew the way that it made him feel. It was too damned late for her to pretend that he hadn't.

He reached out and wrapped his arm around her waist, pulled her up against him. He wrapped his other arm around her back and placed his palm directly at the center of her shoulder blades. He expected her to get stiff. Expected her to pull away. But she didn't. Instead, she shivered. Her whole body went pliant against his. All his blood rushed south. He wanted…he wanted her.

He wanted this.

And he was going to take his time, because he hadn't held a woman in his arms since his wife, and every memory of making love to Monica was ruined now. Torn beyond repair.

In the dim light he could just make out her eyes, wide and looking up at his, glittering beneath the moon. He ran his thumb along her lower lip, and found it soft and full.

Inviting.

"Damn you're pretty," he said.

His voice was rough and husky, a stranger's voice. He didn't know if he could recall a time when the potential for a kiss had made him feel this way. So damn hard he couldn't see straight. So damn hard it hurt.

And then she did something he hadn't expected at all. She went up on her toes, bracketing his face with her hands, and kissed him.

Her mouth was so soft.

Damn.

And she tasted like that beer that she just been drinking. And it all went to his head. He tightened his hold on her, angled his head and took the kiss deep, parting her luscious lips with his tongue and tasting her.

It was his turn to shiver.

Desire shot down his spine like a lightning bolt. Need gathered low in his gut as he kissed her and kissed her, luxuriating in the little sounds that she made as he licked into her mouth. Nipped her lower lip.

He felt rooted to something just then. To her. Grounded in ways he hadn't been in years. Maybe ever. She was so petite it would be easy to pick her up and carry her over to the side of the building where he could put her up against it and grind his desire against hers. Have her quick and hard on a darkened, empty street, with no one any the wiser.

The two of them could burn through the need that was eating them up. Except...

She wouldn't like that. It would be against several laws, first of all.

And second of all he knew that she didn't want to be a spectacle. Knew it. Felt it in his bones.

He cared enough that he wouldn't do that to her.

But hell, they were in the perfect situation for someone who didn't want rumors to fly about an affair. They both lived on Redemption Ranch. They couldn't even be faulted for their cars being left anywhere overnight. It was their living arrangement. He moved his mouth away from hers, and her breath fanned against his cheek in intense, ragged puffs. He kissed her jaw. Her neck. She clung to him, making tiny almost injured little sounds that he knew she wouldn't like remembering having made when she was back in full officer mode.

But she wasn't a police officer now, any more than he was an ex-convict.

He was a man and she was a woman. And they wanted each other. This was a simple, beautiful thing in the world.

Desire.

It was honest.

Of all the things on an earth littered with deceit and betrayal, desire like this was real.

"Come back to my place," he said, nuzzling her ear, nipping her earlobe gently.

"I can't," she said.

Suddenly, she was pushing against him. And even when he released his hold on her, she was still pushing at him as if she hadn't realized that he had let go of her immediately.

"Pansy," he said, his voice measured. "I want you. That's the real answer to *why* I bought you a beer, and why I asked you to sit down. To why I followed you out of the bar. I don't want her. I want you. It's not about getting lucky, it's about getting you. And I'm not a man that does relationships or anything like that. My last one soured me a little bit. But there's no reason the two of us can't…"

"Yes, there is," she said. "I'm the reason. I don't… I can't… It's not me, West. I don't do this. I can't do this. Not in this town."

"No one would have to know."

"They would," she said. "Somehow they would, and I just can't. Not right now. You're…you. You're new, you've been in prison, and I want to be the police chief, and there is no way that I can do that while I'm… I can't."

"You left the bar because you didn't want to see me with her. Because you want me."

"I want a lot of things," she said. "I wanted my parents back for a really long time, but nobody dropped them on my doorstep. I wanted to feel normal, and I wanted to have friends, but I felt like an alien swimming outside of my body, and outside of people and society for most of my life. Because nobody but my siblings could ever understand what it was like to be me. I can't have everything I want. I already know that. So I'm choosing to have this one dream. I can have this job. I can… I can make him proud. I was such a…such a terror when I was a kid and he never got to see how I grew up. And I'm not going to screw this up. Over…over a man. I'm not going to do that."

She turned and almost ran away from him, headed toward her car. He hadn't moved. He wasn't chasing her. And he knew that the real truth was that the woman was running away from herself. Not from him.

Damn it all.

She got in her car and drove away, leaving him standing there with unsatisfied desire that he was just going to leave unsatisfied. He wasn't even going to try to make it better. Not with the woman inside the bar, and not with his right hand. Because the only thing that would satisfy him was Pansy, and she'd said no.

He would have preferred it if she'd left him with another ticket, rather than this. Because that at least he could have paid.

This…this, he didn't know what to do about.

And he didn't like feeling helpless.

He had known that touching her would be a bad idea. He just hadn't foreseen it ending like this.

CHAPTER EIGHT

PANSY HAD CONSIDERED just not going to the family dinner on Sunday. But she had already skipped last week and it was going to be far more conspicuous than she wanted to be if she skipped again.

So she had managed dinner with everybody, and had even managed to talk about her pursuit of police chief somewhat normally, and all she could do was hope that she didn't have *I got my first kiss and it was with the absolute least suitable man alive* written all over her face.

Even more terrifying was that somehow Sammy would find a way to wiggle it out of her without even knowing what she was wiggling.

Sammy was uncomfortably perceptive. She always had been.

When she'd come into their family she'd been a breath of shocking air. They had been so isolated since the deaths of their parents.

And then Sammy had appeared one day, like a fairy from the woods.

She'd been sixteen and all constant chatter. She had brought things like new sheets for the beds, chipped dishes with flowers on them.

It was strange that they'd lived next door to each other for years and never met Sammy. And then she'd pulled her little camper onto the property and taken up residence like she'd always been there.

Whatever her relationship to her parents, Pansy knew it was flawed.

She could sense Sammy had come from some darkness. There was a reason she was part of them. Part of Hope Springs. A reason she'd used this place for a refuge.

But for all the world to see, she was sunshine and light.

Also, nosy.

"Who was the guy you were with last night?"

Logan.

She'd been so focused on Sammy she hadn't looked to the obvious problem.

She should have known that he was going to make this difficult. That he wouldn't be able to let go of the fact that she had been sitting at the table with the man he didn't know.

"My landlord," she said, opting for directness, because the shadier she was, the more Sammy would ferret.

"Your landlord?"

"Yes. He just bought Redemption Ranch. He's been doing some work on my house. We were just talking about that. Sorry to disappoint you."

"It's just the way that you warned me off of coming over there I figured you were trying to hook up."

Ryder looked at Logan and scowled. Logan looked back. "What?"

"Do you need to say things like that?" Ryder asked.

Sammy tapped Ryder on the shoulder. "Calm down. She's an adult woman."

"Sure," Ryder grimaced. "But that doesn't mean that *I* need to know about anything."

"There's nothing to know about," Pansy said.

"You had a beer with West Caldwell?" Iris asked. She had half a mind to dive under the table and bite her sister on the leg.

"And his broad shoulders?" Rose asked, an impish smirk on her face.

"Rose..."

"Why are we talking about some guy's shoulders?" Ryder asked, looking appalled.

"Sorry you don't have your boys' club right now," Sammy said, looking cheerful. "You guys are outnumbered very handily with Colt and Jake being out of town."

"I don't like it," Ryder said.

"You don't like anything," Sammy said.

"Not true," he said. "I like having dinner uninterrupted by conversations about my sister's dating life."

"There's no dating," Pansy said.

The subject died after that, but once dinner was over and Ryder and Logan had vanished Sammy rounded on her in a flurry of blond hair and flowing skirts. "So what happened with Mr. Broad Shoulders?"

Iris and Rose looked at her keenly. Because they knew as well as Pansy did that if there was anything to say Sammy would be able to badger her into saying it.

She had a decision to make. Whether or not she was going to resist Sammy's relentlessness or if she was going to accept the inevitable.

"I kissed him," Pansy said, deciding on surrender.

Iris and Rose made very loud sounds, and Pansy looked worriedly toward the living room. She did not want to draw Logan and Ryder's attention.

"You made that almost too easy," Sammy said, looking disappointed.

And the only joy that Pansy could get out of any of this was that she felt she had perhaps mildly defeated Sammy.

"Well, I knew you were going to figure it out," Pansy said. "I'm a terrible liar and I always have been. And *you* are absolutely shameless."

Sammy grinned. "It's true."

Sammy was the biggest source of sex ed for Pansy. Sammy was the one who'd given Pansy a vibrator on her eighteenth birthday, which Pansy had immediately hidden in a drawer.

She'd never used it. The thing terrified her.

But that didn't mean she'd never…that she didn't know her way around her own body. But unlike Sammy she could never be so open about it. So free and easy.

The emergence of her sexuality had been scary for her. Caught between the desire to follow rules, to pursue her goal, and the very real burgeoning of her hormones, along with the fear of caring for someone outside her family, had kept her pretty paralyzed on that front.

And now West, and whatever West made her feel, seemed to sort of…circumvent a lifetime of caution and… well, keeping sexual feelings to her damn self.

"I knew it," Rose said. "I knew you liked him."

"I don't *like* him," she said. "I don't… I don't know what I am."

"Normal?" Sammy asked, lifting his shoulder.

That word diffused it. Made it feel like it must not be that big of a deal. And Pansy wasn't sure how she felt about that, because it had felt earthmoving and singular, and like a gigantic mistake that she shouldn't have committed. And Sammy was acting like it wasn't any of those things.

"Well," Sammy said. "If the world came to a halt every time I kissed a guy we wouldn't get anything done."

She thought back to how she'd felt watching that other woman touch West. How easy it was for her. How casual.

It just wasn't like that for Pansy. She couldn't be casual about a touch. Because all of this had been built up to be so big in her mind.

She couldn't be casual about a kiss.

"Pansy…haven't you…" Sammy suddenly looked very concerned. "Oh no. You've…*dated*, right?"

She had a feeling this was Sammy trying to be delicate about whether or not Pansy had slept with a man.

"Not really," Pansy said.

"Oh, Pansy," Sammy said. *"Date him."*

"He doesn't want a *date*."

"I didn't mean date," Sammy said. *"Bang him."*

"Sammy!" The admonishment came from Iris.

Rose was looking on with deep interest.

Pansy realized that she had covered her mouth like a maiden spinster.

"What?" Sammy asked. "There's no law that says you have to take every physical thing that happens with a man deadly seriously. If you're into him you should do something about it."

"I can't," Pansy said. "I need this job, and I need to make sure that I don't rock the boat until I can have it. It's a bad time to try anything new."

"Why would he compromise your job? Maybe a little bit of fun is what you need to be able to focus on *getting* this job. You work harder at being good than anyone I know, Pansy. Don't you know it's not bad to be with someone?"

Pansy looked from Sammy to her sisters. It was clear that the opinion was divided on this particular topic. She could see that to her sisters the suggestion of a casual relationship was shocking.

"I think Ryder might kill you if he knew what you were advocating," Pansy said.

"Well, he can feel free. I would take him to task for being a judgmental asshole. He...does what he does." She waved a hand. "It's not like he's chaste for all that he wanders around looking grim and forbidding all the time."

Pansy grimaced. "I don't really want to know about his love life any more than he wants to know about mine."

"You have good instincts," Iris said. "If you don't think you should be with him, then don't be."

Pansy hadn't meant to turn this into a kiss by committee. But she should have known that there would be no going back home, no seeing her sisters and Sammy without it turning into this.

For the first time she wondered if they didn't talk about men only because nothing like this had ever happened to any of them.

Sammy excluded.

She did feel like Iris was a bit more secretive, but for all of Rose's big talk, Pansy was sure that she'd never even kissed a man.

If she had, they all would have known.

Rose didn't have the capacity to keep secrets.

"He's out of my league," Pansy said.

"He kissed you," Sammy said.

"I kissed him," Pansy said, belaboring the point. "And I just mean...he's been married and divorced. And...you know, he's not exactly the poster child for good behavior."

"You're worried that he's more sexually experienced than you?"

"This loaf of bread is more sexually experienced than I am," Pansy said, picking up a chunk of sourdough from the counter.

Rose hooted out a laugh. Iris and Sammy just exchanged glances.

"I would embarrass myself," Pansy said.

"So what?" Sammy pressed. "If it's like you say it is, and for him it's super casual, and he has lots of experience, then what does it matter? He's a guy anyway. A bottle of lotion and a lingerie catalog would do it for him. Not much is required of you. And you can benefit from his experience."

Pansy felt horrified to even be discussing this, let alone considering it. "I'm out," Pansy said, tapping the table. "Literally tapping out."

"Why?" Sammy asked. "We're sharing."

"I'm done sharing. I can't do this. I mean… I can't… have this discussion. I don't know what I feel about him. Except…he's good looking. But…"

"But what?"

"But," Pansy said, resolutely.

That put an end to the conversation, at least for a while. And they spent the next couple of hours in the living room together chatting until Pansy started to yawn.

"I'd better go," she said, pushing herself up so that she was standing.

"I'll walk you to your car," Iris offered.

It was warm out, the night sky clear and sprayed with silver stars, crickets chirping a steady rhythm that ran beneath the music of the wind rustling through the trees. "You kissed him," Iris said.

Pansy hunched her shoulders up by her years. "Yeah."

"I think that's pretty brave of you. Even if Sammy can't understand why."

But Iris did. Because she knew what it was like to be a forced member of their fierce, isolated little clan.

Sammy was like a butterfly that flitted through their

garden, and had decided to land on a flower. She fluttered off sometimes in her caravan, traveling for a bit selling jewelry before coming back. She came from a different place. From a different background.

It wasn't the same for her because she'd chosen Hope Springs.

Hope Springs had chosen the rest of them.

"She means well," Pansy said. "But she…she's not the same as we are."

"No," Iris said. "She's not. But I don't think it's…quite as easy as she pretends it is."

"She always seems…like whatever she's doing is easy."

Pansy had watched Sammy flirt effortlessly with men in bars over the years. Not that she had a clear idea of who Sammy did or didn't go home with, but she seemed at ease and able to laugh off just about anything.

"I think it's just casual for her," Pansy said.

Iris shook her head, stubborn. "I don't think so. It's not… it's not a handshake or a dance around a bonfire or whatever it is Sammy pretends. But she's hurt, Pansy. A lot more than she ever lets on. I don't know what went on in her home before she came to us but I don't think it was good. I think she likes to get physically close to men without having relationships because for her it's the emotional closeness that's scary."

That idea made Pansy feel hollow. "I don't understand why she does it if it hurts her."

Iris shrugged. "Well, the alternative is being alone."

Pansy had been alone all this time, so she didn't really see why that was a problem. But then… Sammy hugged all the time. Touched all the time.

Sammy *alone* would be like putting a butterfly in a jar

and cutting off its air supply. Making it so it couldn't fly. Couldn't breathe.

And if Sammy was a butterfly then Pansy was a lone polecat.

One who'd kissed her ex-convict landlord…

"I don't think I can be casual with him," Pansy said. "I don't think I even know what that means."

"You have to do what's right for you, Pansy. No one can tell you what that is. No one else is you."

"I know," she said. "But…" She thought again of the way it had felt to have his mouth pressed to hers. "I never understood what it was like to be tempted."

But a memory pushed into the front of her mind.

When she'd been young. Before her parents had died. She'd been tempted all the time. To steal the cookies out of the cookie jar that she'd been told were for after dinner.

To run when she was supposed to walk.

To try to ride the big horse even though she was supposed to wait until she was older.

To go out riding by herself even though she was supposed to wait for her father.

And she could remember his quiet disappointment every time she had given in.

"Pansy," he said, his voice measured. "You can't just go around doing whatever you want. You can't just follow your heart. You have to follow what's right."

But she'd found it so hard, because her heart burned for things that she wasn't supposed to want.

Her innate nature was selfish. And yes, she'd been a child when she'd behaved like she had, but her dad had worried she'd stay that way, and she really thought she probably would have.

Been the kind of kid she spent a lot of her job dealing with.

Reckless driving, drunk driving, disorderly conduct. Breaking them up having sex in cars by the river.

There were big and great divides in life. People who cared about right, about rules, and people who didn't.

She'd been born as one type. She'd worked to become another.

After her dad had died she'd tried to change. She had forgotten temptation. What it was and what it could be, but somewhere in there she'd forgotten passion too.

She had duty, and a sense of purpose, but until her lips had touched West Caldwell's, she had forgotten what it was to burn.

"I'll see you around," Iris said.

"Yeah," Pansy said, and she wanted to hug her sister.

But then her eye caught a shaft of light coming from across the field, uneven and shaky, before disappearing behind the barn.

"I think your visitor's back," Pansy said.

"What?"

"You can go get Ryder. I'm going to get my gun."

She unlocked her service weapon from her car and holstered it before making her way toward the barn. She had a feeling that everything would be all right, but she needed to be sure before she discounted the need for a weapon.

She moved silently across the grass, and made her way up to the barn, looking through the cracks in the wood as best she could.

She could see a flashlight beam moving around in there. Movement.

The flashlight was set on the ground, a pool of light stretching across the floor. She could hear two sets of feet moving around, but only one of them sounded heavy. The other sounded animal. A dog, probably.

Then she heard a low whisper.

"Sit boy," the voice said.

A young man's voice. Not a *man*. She went around to the door of the barn and pushed it open.

There was a loud curse, an explosion of movement and the figure tried to run past her. He bumped into her shoulder, and she reached out and grabbed on to him, and they both went down to the ground.

"What the hell?" Ryder appeared, and reached down, his strong arm grabbing the back of the trespasser's clothes and hauling him to his feet.

"It was an accident," Pansy said. "He was trying to run away."

"Get the fuck off me!" the boy said, and she was even more certain now that he was practically a kid. "Don't touch me."

"You're trespassing," Ryder said.

"I'll leave," the kid said.

Iris had gone into the barn, and had just returned with a flashlight, which she shone on the kid.

He was young, but tall. Wiry, with sandy blond hair. He had a dog next to him that looked almost as worse for wear as he did, scruffy and thin, his back end going wild as he wagged his tail.

"Some guard dog," he said.

"Who are you?" Pansy asked.

"None of your fucking business," he said, looking at her with defiance, each word used as a weapon. As if an f-bomb was going to scare her off.

"I'm a police officer," she said, calm and firm. "It is my business."

"Where's your badge?"

"I'm off duty," she said. "We can wait for me to get my

badge and you can tell me who you are then, if you like. I can haul you down to the police station. I suspect that you've been involved in some of the theft we've had around here. Am I right?"

"I don't have to tell you anything."

"We can do this the hard way if we have to. But if you've got parents that I can call…"

"I don't have parents." He spat out that last word like it was dirty.

"I don't have parents either," Pansy said.

The kid struggled, but Ryder was still holding on to him.

"I would rather we have a conversation," she continued. "I don't really want to chase you and tackle you. And I don't want to have to take you down to the station tonight. So if you could just tell me who you are so I can figure out who I'm supposed to get in touch with…"

"There's nobody that cares about me," he said. "You'd be wasting your time."

"Your name," she said.

"Emmett," the kid said, finally. "Emmett Caldwell."

CHAPTER NINE

WEST WAS SETTLED in for the night with takeout he'd gotten earlier from Mustard Seed and a beer on his TV tray, when there was a knock at his front door.

Pansy.

He hoped it was Pansy. Come to finish what they'd started outside the saloon the other night. He'd done nothing but think about her ever since then. His body had been persistently hard, which was irritating because he couldn't remember the last time he'd been so het up over a woman. The one woman who didn't seem to be all that into him.

He went over to the door and jerked it open. The first person he saw was Pansy. And the second...

"Emmett?"

"Yes," Pansy confirmed.

Emmett didn't say anything. Pansy all but marched the kid into the house.

"Go sit down on the couch," she ordered.

And in spite of the surly expression on his face, his half brother complied.

"What the hell are you doing here?" West asked.

"What are *you* doing here?" Emmett asked. "Came here to live with your fancy rich family?"

"I came to get to know them," West said, his voice measured. At least, as measured as he could manage.

"Well, you might have remembered about your other

family," he said. "Instead of just…coming straight to them after you got out of jail."

"I asked your mother where you were," West said. "Over and over."

"*Our* mother? You abandoned her too. You don't give a shit about us."

"I give several shits about you, you little asshole," West said, knowing that was probably not the way you were supposed to talk to kids. But he wasn't a damned kindergarten teacher. "I was looking for you. And you've been here the whole time?"

"And responsible for a few break-ins," Pansy said.

West stared hard at his kid brother. "You stole that woman's wallet. And you broke into the bakery." Pansy slipped something out of her pocket, and it took a moment for him to realize it was the missing wallet. She opened it, and he saw a license inside that said Barbara Niedermayer. He shook his head. "Kid, I thought you knew better than this."

"You're going to lecture me?" Emmett scoffed. "You're the one that spent four years in jail."

"For something I didn't do," West said.

"Maybe I didn't do it either," Emmett said, lifting his chin. "Same as you."

"I *really* didn't do it," West said.

"I have to… He's under eighteen," Pansy said. "I don't know if Carl Jacobson from the bakery or Barbara are going to want to press charges. I'm going to recommend that they don't, and that he engage in community service instead."

"He's young," West said. "He shouldn't be…he shouldn't be punished for the crappy life we've had."

"But he did those things," Pansy said, her voice shot through with steel. "And I feel bad about it, but…"

"Pansy," West said. "Please. Work with me."

"I will. The question is if Carl and Barbara will. I have to uphold the law, West."

"Oh, because of your fucking police chief position?"

"Yes," Pansy shot back. "Because of that, and because of what's right. I don't get to just choose when to care about what's legal and what isn't. It's my job to care about it all the time. It just is."

Throughout their argument, Emmett was quiet.

"I'm not going to be able to make this go away, kid," West said. "It's not up to me."

Emmett looked at him. "Am I going to go to jail?"

"For this?" Pansy asked. "Probably not. If so, not for long. But there will be some consequences."

"Are you going to send me back home?" Emmett asked, this question directed straight at West.

West sighed, and looked around the place. His other half brothers happened to run a school for troubled kids. An alternative school. And, on the one hand, the idea of his half brother being around kids who were no less trouble than he was, was a little bit concerning. But then… Emmett was trouble, so it was fair enough.

"I'm not going to send you home," West said. "Unless you *want* to go home."

Emmett looked skeptical. "Really?"

"Emmett," West said. "I was looking for you to find out if you wanted to live with me. From the minute I got out of jail. But Mom didn't know where you were."

"She didn't care where I was," Emmett said. "She never called me or anything."

"You have your phone?"

"Yeah, but it's not hooked up to anything anymore. I was on her plan. She quit paying for it a couple of months ago."

So she could have let the police track her son's phone,

and she hadn't done it. Probably even could have done it through the cell phone company, and hadn't done it.

She had just cut him off. Quit paying for his phone, because it was convenient for her.

West knew that it shouldn't be a surprise to him since he had been raised by the same woman. Since he knew what kind of parent she was.

Still. It damn well shocked him. Because when he looked at Emmett he saw a kid. He might be fifteen, but in West's eyes he was a child.

And the thing that crashed in against him, crushed down on him like a ton of rocks rolling off the side of a mountain, was the fact that his mom didn't seem to look at him and think the same.

That she hadn't looked at West and seen the same.

Or if she had, that she hadn't cared.

She had been young when she'd had West. A kid herself, at eighteen, and he'd always cut her a certain amount of slack because of that. But she wasn't young anymore. There was no excuse. He'd been a kid left behind. One that had fallen between the cracks. He couldn't go back and fix that. Couldn't make their mom a better mother. But…he remembered what Pansy had said.

That he was trying to be the family for Emmett that no one else had stepped up to be for either of them.

He had to be that.

"You can stay here," West said.

"I can?" The question sounded cautious, and not exactly optimistic.

West nodded. "Yes. There's plenty of room here."

"Well," Pansy said. "Then I suppose there's the small matter of…"

She turned and walked out of the room, and left him standing there with Emmett.

"Was there more to that sentence?" West asked.

Emmett shrugged. The two of them just looked at each other until Pansy returned, with a dog following behind her. "He was waiting in the car," she said. "He's a good boy."

"You have a dog?" West asked.

Emmett lifted a shoulder. "I found him. He was a stray. And I guess…" Emmett squared his shoulders. "Well, so am I, I guess."

"Not anymore," West said. "You can stay here. So can he."

His brother blinked twice. Hard.

And if West were a different man, he might have attributed the shifting sensation in his chest to emotion.

"Do you have any clothes or anything?"

Emmett shrugged. "Some. I took a few things with me. Not a lot."

"Have you been camping this whole time?"

"No. When the weather was really crappy I stayed with some friends. But when I came to Gold Valley…yeah."

"So you've been in the barn at Hope Springs, and you've been out here."

"Yeah," Emmett said. "I camped a few other places too. It was nice if I could find a barn, because I felt a little less worried that I was going to get eaten by a cougar. But the dog helped with that too."

West regarded the dog. It was looking at Emmett, like Emmett was his master. His expression didn't hold any concern or worry at all. Just a kind of steady watchfulness. It reminded West of the dog he'd fed all those years ago.

And West had the oddest feeling that he should thank the dog.

For keeping an eye on his kid brother. For being there for Emmett so he wasn't so lonely and scared.

But that was ridiculous.

"Do you have any of the money from the wallet?"

"Some," the kid said. "I used it to buy food, but I was saving the rest."

"Well, hopefully if we return everything we'll get Barbara on our side." Pansy sighed. "I assume your brother will pitch in what's not there. You chose an incredibly unsympathetic target, kid. Not the best choice."

"I'm not exactly out here making historically awesome choices," Emmett said. "I mean. I would have thought that much was obvious."

Pansy shook her head.

"Are you hungry?" West asked.

"Starving," Emmett said.

West looked down at his reheated burger. "I haven't started that yet."

"Can I have a beer too?" he asked, far too hopefully.

"No," West said, emphatically, even though he was sure his younger brother'd had multiple beers in his lifetime. That wasn't the point. He wasn't going to allow it. "Eat," West said, picking the beer up. "Can I talk to you?" He directed the last part at Pansy.

Pansy nodded and the two of them walked out of the room, then out the front door onto the porch.

It was strange, because even though they were outside, they were alone again, and the night air seemed to wrap itself around the two of them like a blanket. Suddenly, it all felt a lot more intimate than it had a few moments before.

Your street urchin of a half brother is in the house eating your soggy french fries. And you're thinking about getting Pansy naked?

Yeah, he was.

"I don't want him in any trouble," West said.

"*I* don't want him in any trouble either," Pansy returned. "But I'm going to have to handle this like I would handle this for anyone. Whether I'm sympathetic or not."

"Right. Just like you had to write me a ticket for being in a loading zone."

"I'm under scrutiny," she said.

"Yeah," West said. "For a job. This is his life."

"My job is where I spend forty hours a week. It's what I poured *my* whole life into. Why do you think it's a separate thing? I learned before I was his age that I had to behave myself. That I was going to have to behave differently than the people around me if I was going to have the life I wanted someday. The one I needed. He's going to have to do the same. And if he has to learn the hard way that's nobody's fault but his. He broke into that store. He got into Barbara's car and took her wallet. I don't have control over what they decide to do with that."

"Pansy…"

"No. The only one who had control over it was him."

"Oh, come on," West said. "You're not that rigid. Not that rigid that you can't see that he's had it tough. That he has it different than other kids, that he wasn't able to make the same choices that a kid like you was."

"I went through enough," she said, stubborn.

"And you *had* enough," West said. "He was out here surviving on nothing. He had to feed himself and the dog."

"Why didn't he come straight to you?"

"I imagine he was afraid of getting rejected," West said. "And you might scoff at that, but you have to remember that you had a family that took care of you this whole time. Our own mother didn't particularly want to take care of us.

I don't think Emmett took it for granted that I would just take him in. It's what he wanted, but he didn't think he could ask for it. So he was skulking around in the woods being pissed. I don't just relate to that, I *over* relate to it."

"I'm not trying to be mean," she said. "But I have to follow procedure. And I have to follow the law."

"You know what," West said, something wild and angry firing through his blood. Through his vision. "Fuck your rules."

And then, somehow, she was in his arms again, and he was kissing her. Kissing her like he might find answers if he searched the deepest parts of her mouth. Kissing her like he could melt her bones and her propriety and her adherence to the *rules*.

Kissing her like there was nothing else to be done, because as far as he was concerned there wasn't. Then somehow, he called upon all the strength in himself to grab hold of her arms and lift her up, setting her away from him.

She took a step back. "Don't," she said. As if she had been the one to stop the kiss, when they both knew full well she hadn't been.

"Then don't kiss me back like you're dying for it," he said.

"This has nothing to do with…your brother. Or my job. Or procedure."

"No. It just is. And I think that's just how sex works sometimes."

Even in the half-light from the porch he could see color mount in her face. "There won't be any sex."

He shrugged, the gesture casual while he felt anything but. "Suit yourself."

She squared her shoulders, all business again. "I need you to bring him by the station tomorrow morning. I need you to do that. Otherwise… I'm going to have to come here."

"I'll bring him by," he said.

Pansy nodded, and then she walked down the stairs. It was only the rhythm of her feet on the boards that told him her footsteps were unsteady.

She got in her car and drove away.

And left him.

That was when West Caldwell realized that not only did he have a kid brother to take care of, he also suddenly had a dog.

CHAPTER TEN

PANSY HAD WRESTLED with herself all the previous night. Not because of the kiss, and not because of what she had said to West, but because of the fact that she had left him.

That she had simply left Emmett and his dog with the command for them all to come to the police station tomorrow.

She felt like she should have done more. But she would have left the kid in any other circumstances, especially when the adult taking care of him was more than fit. She would have handled it the exact same way if it had been anyone else, and only the fact that it was West made her feel like she should have stayed. Like she should have done something to make him feel not quite so alone, when West had never indicated he had any such issues.

She thought about going over in the morning.

She didn't.

Instead, she drove straight to the police station, the scenery around her a blur of green, the red brick of the small town blending together into a seamless background of familiarity. It was easy to make the drive, even while distracted, because it was so familiar.

She shouldn't be spacing out like this. She knew that. She was the first to lecture people up and down about safe driving, but her brain felt foggy, and her body felt restless. She would have actually relished a run this morning.

And she was in luck, because when she got in to the station Chief Doering forced them right back out to do a jog.

She did the run and enjoyed the punishment, not taking in the scenery there either, just enjoying making her body hurt because it deserved to be in pain. When they got back to the station she showered in the women's locker room—which only ever contained her—then changed into her uniform then went to her desk, which was relatively uncharacteristic of her. Normally, she went straight back out to patrol. But not today.

She took out all the files related to the theft cases and stared at them. And hoped that Emmett and West would be in soon. She sighed heavily, then called Carl. She explained the situation to him, how they had found the culprit, but that he was a young kid who was down on his luck.

"I would be willing to let him work off the damage," the older man said.

"That's really nice of you," Pansy said. "And I'm grateful for that, because it's what I would recommend for him. He's not really a hardened criminal. He's just a kid."

Barbara, she knew, she'd have more trouble with.

"I'm expecting Emmett and his guardian soon if you want to come meet him and explain what you're going to expect of him. I think that would be a good idea," Pansy said.

She got off the phone with Carl, but hesitated in calling Barbara.

Finally, she did, and the other woman made no such offers of allowing restitution of any kind that came from anything but the kid being punished to the fullest extent of the law.

"I'd like you to come down to the station."

"Why?"

"I have your wallet. And hopefully I'll have most of the money as well."

"Then I'll be there."

She hung up and Pansy sat impatiently at the desk, drumming her fingers on the top of it. Finally, the door opened, and her heart zipped up into her throat.

It was West, tall and broad, coming through the door with a sullen looking Emmett behind him. She was thankful for the distraction of Emmett and for the safety of her desk, and the police station in general. Otherwise she would have died of a combination of embarrassment and heat stroke remembering their kiss.

As it was, she found she could temporarily put her focus on other things. She could tell the two of them were brothers, even though Emmett was a few inches shorter than West. She had a feeling that he would grow into those lanky limbs and large feet, that he would end up looking a whole lot more like West than not. But for now, he was like a puppy, loping along, not even realizing all that he hadn't grown into yet.

She imagined that he saw himself about the same as West, who had broad shoulders and a deep chest and the lines that evidenced the years he'd lived on his face, evidence that he'd lived the sort of years that made a man interesting.

West gestured toward her desk and Emmett shoved his hands into the pockets of his red sweatshirt and slumped down into the chair across from her.

"Do you have the money that you took from Barbara's wallet?" she asked, keeping her voice measured.

He nodded, and pulled his hand out of his pocket, producing three hundreds and a collection of twenties. He had about $365, most of what he had taken. She still had a feeling Barbara was going to make an issue out of all of it.

"Carl Jacobson is going to be in soon, and he's going to talk to you about how you might be able to make it up to him. He's not interested in pressing charges, but he does want you to do some work for him."

She found herself looking up at West to check his facial expression. It was neutral.

She looked back at Emmett, who nodded. "Okay."

"I don't know what Barbara's going to say. I'm just going to warn you now, she's a tough customer, and she's not going to feel sorry for you."

Emmett tilted his chin up, his lips turned down into a frown. "I don't want anyone to feel sorry for me."

"Well, maybe you should. Because it would probably help you out in this situation if you would play up the fact that you're a little bit pitiful."

He scowled. "I'm not pitiful."

She glanced back at West, who was deliberately looking away from his brother, a small smile tugging at the corner of his mouth.

"I'm glad that you came this morning," she said. "Because this is what I would like to do. I would like to handle it without involving charges or the system at all."

"But you brought me in," Emmett said.

"I did," Pansy said. "Because you have to face up to what you did. And I can't control whether or not the consequences are more severe than either of us would like. I just have to do the right thing. And so do you."

He snorted. "Why?"

She felt like she was standing on the edge of something. A moment that was given to her by her father's memory.

Where maybe she could change Emmett, the way her dad had changed her.

"Because it matters," she said, her dad's face swimming through her mind. She could hear his voice echoing inside of her as she spoke those words. "Because the world can take everything from you, Emmett. Your money, your status, your home. Your job. Your family. But there are a few things in your soul that the world can't have unless you give it up. Your hope. Your faith. Your integrity. That's the measure of a person. Those things that can't be taken and how hard you hold on to them. You've made mistakes, but it takes integrity to come and own up to them."

Emmett looked down, his arms folded, his legs out in front of him. It would be easy to take offense to the posture. Assume it meant he wasn't listening. But Pansy had a feeling he was, and that was why he found it hard to meet her eyes.

The door to the station opened again, and Carl came in. When he met Emmett, he shook his hand, then he sat down in the chair next to him and started to have a talk with him. About the kind of work he could use help with.

The way that he talked to the kid made Pansy proud of the community. That a man who had been wronged the way Carl had been would treat this kid, a stranger, with such kindness and forgiveness.

She was glad that he had come first, because she knew that this was not going to be the scenario with Barbara. Barbara was difficult on a good day, but she had worked herself up into a lather over this. She was one of those people.

Barbara was on the City Council because she was organized. Detail oriented. Because she understood the way that things worked and was often the most capable person to set them in motion.

She was lonely, and Pansy felt some sympathy for her personal life.

But Barbara also didn't know when to stop pushing for things. Didn't know there were times she should sheathe the unerring verbal knife she had the power to wield. Didn't know that sometimes it was best not to cut someone to pieces with your tongue, just because you could. She had no moderation. She was Barbara, all the time.

When Carl left, he shook Emmett's hand. They sat and waited, and then Barbara blustered into the police station. "This is the hoodlum that stole my wallet?" Barbara gave a sidelong glance to West. "He has something to do with you?"

"My half brother," West said.

"I might have known that. You're Hank Dalton's son, aren't you? I've heard about you. The one who was in prison. Seems like the apple doesn't fall far from the tree."

Pansy bit back uncharitable commentary on apples and trees. It wasn't fair to throw her son's situation in her face, but honestly, it was like the woman didn't hear the words that came out of her mouth.

"Well, he's my brother," West said slowly. "So technically I'm not the tree. But we might be the same kind of apple."

Barbara was not amused by West's commentary, but Pansy thought if Barbara didn't want comments she shouldn't make quite so many statements.

"As you can see," Pansy said, her voice measured, "Emmett is a kid. He made a mistake, but he has your wallet, and most of the money that was taken."

Pansy slid the wallet and the money toward Barbara. She grabbed them, and looked fiercely through the wallet, and then counted the money. "There was $500 in the wallet."

"I know," Pansy said. "And Emmett will need to make it up to you."

"He doesn't need to be out on the streets," Barbara said. "He needs to be in prison."

"He isn't going to be out on the streets, and honestly even if you press charges he's not going to go to prison," Pansy said. "Not realistically. But what you are going to do is tie up the court system and give this kid a record he doesn't need. I feel like we can do better than that here."

"That isn't your job," Barbara said. "Your job is to enforce the law."

That ate at Pansy, because in many ways she agreed. But she also felt like there were gray areas and places for leniency, and when it came to fifteen-year-old kids who were wild like the animals that roamed the mountains, and in bad need of support, and needed the adults around them to be the adults and step up and fill in the gaps left behind by parents that hadn't been there for them, then she felt they should do that. That was the point of community, after all.

Community wasn't about *fair*. Not about everything being divided up into equal spaces, or seeing the people around them in a black-and-white fashion. It was about bearing each other's burdens when you needed to. Having a neighbor you could lean on if you ever found yourself unsteady.

That was how her father had done his job for the town. He had done *right*.

Right in a deep and real way, not *right* on paper. And when their parents had died, that was what the community had done for them.

She was committed to doing the same.

"Barbara," Pansy said, trying to keep her voice measured. "I want you to think about what you're advocating for here."

"I'm through with this discussion," Barbara said, "I want to press charges."

She stormed away from her desk, and went right back toward Chief Doering's office.

Pansy pinched the bridge of her nose.

"This is fine," she muttered.

"What's the issue?" West asked. "Because I'll write her a check for the difference. Hell, I'll write her a check for the whole $500. She can make money on this deal."

"The issue is that she's decided to make it one," Pansy said. "Because that's who she is."

Pansy got up and stormed after her. Because she would be damned if she was going to sit back and let this woman intimidate her or run roughshod over her.

Barbara was ranting over Chief Doering's desk when Pansy walked in. "Everything that she was missing is being returned," Pansy said. "West Caldwell is acting as the boy's temporary guardian, and he has offered to pay the difference in the missing money. He can add more for pain and suffering."

"I'm going to tell you right now," Chief Doering said. "This is a case that isn't going to go anywhere and it's going to cost the city a lot of money. If the kid gets anything it's going to be a fine, that might cover the cost of taking this to trial, but that's it. Especially given that Carl Jacobson is not going to press charges. You just don't have a whole lot here. I'd let it go."

"So this is how you run the department now? We're supposed to feel safe?" Barbara was verging on hysteria now, which shouldn't really surprise Pansy. Not given that she was the sort of person who seemed to revel in her own hysteria.

"Yes," he said, keeping his tone solemn. "Because you should know that if your son was ever in this position I would behave the same, and I assume Pansy would too."

She blinked, and then she went on as if he hadn't spoken. "The quality of people who have been moving in to town is a problem. That school out at the Dalton ranch, and the brother of those Daltons is connected to the hoodlum who stole my wallet. It's not a coincidence."

"Barbara…"

"You will *not* have my support for position as police chief," Barbara said. "I will voice dissent on the committee."

"Go ahead and do that," Pansy said. "And when it comes time for you to run for City Council again I will make sure that the entire town knows that you advocated for throwing the book at a fifteen-year-old boy who stole something that you got back. A homeless boy who has no one in his life to care for him. That's who you are. Don't you threaten me. I'm proud of who I am and what I've done, and I'll stand by it. If you think that you would be able to do the same, and if you think that the citizens of this town would like to hear my take on your actions, then go right ahead."

"You can't make me vote in favor of you."

"I can't," Pansy said. "I wouldn't ask you to. Frankly, I don't want a vote of confidence from someone like you. But, I'm not going to have you poisoning other people against me."

The whole situation went flat, and Barbara grabbed her purse and stormed out of the office in a huff.

"You handled it well," Chief Doering said.

"It doesn't much matter. I'm in the middle of a tempest

in the world's smallest teapot. She's going to make an issue out of this no matter what."

"That comes with the job. But then, it comes with this job on every level."

"I can handle it."

"I know you can," he said.

She wasn't sure how empowered she felt at the moment, but it also didn't really matter. Because she was going to see through what needed seeing through and she was going to behave in a way that would make her father proud.

West and Emmett were still sitting there at her desk when she exited the chief's office.

"Is she going to make trouble for you?" West asked.

"It doesn't matter," Pansy said.

"It does," West responded.

"No," she said. "It doesn't. She can do whatever she wants. I don't have any control over her. I don't have control over *you* either." Pansy turned and addressed Emmett. "But I'm willing to stick my neck out for you, so I hope that you don't disappoint me."

She stared at the kid, and he stared back. She didn't know if he had ever been challenged like this before. She wondered if his mom had ever done anything with him. Or if she had simply left him to his own devices.

She couldn't say that her childhood had been perfectly well-ordered. Though Ryder had done his best.

Their lunch had been a peanut butter sandwich every day, until Iris had gotten tired of it and started preparing real food. And they hadn't always looked the best. But the boys had done what they could. They had all taken care of each other. And no one had been left to their own devices. Not ever. It just wasn't how they were. And it wasn't how she was going to be with Emmett. She knew that West wasn't going to be like that with him. If they did the right thing now they could make a difference. And that was… that was the point of all of this. It was easy for her to lose sight of that.

But it was the point.

"I have work," she said. "If anything else comes up I'll let you know."

"I guess I'll see you back at the house," West said.

"Yeah."

"Is she your girlfriend?" Emmett asked.

She and West looked at each other and Pansy exploded with a denial. "No. I live at the ranch. He's my landlord."

"You have a *cop* living at your ranch?"

"Yeah," West said. "What's the big deal?"

"You."

"I told you," West said. "I didn't do it."

"Have a good day," Pansy said, walking out of the police station and leaving them there. She needed to get away from West. She needed to get out. Most of all she needed to try and figure out how to get her head on straight. Because in the last twenty-four hours things had gotten very strange and she didn't know how she was going to set them to rights again.

CHAPTER ELEVEN

"YOU WANT to stay here?"

West posed the question to his half brother as they drove out of town toward the Dalton ranch. He was still wrapping his head around the whole situation and what he was going to do about it. But the first thing to do was to establish what the hell the kid actually thought was happening.

"Look," Emmett said. "I'm not about to stay where I'm not wanted. But I wanted to see what the hell you were doing. You were in that fancy mansion in Texas, and you talked about me coming to live with you."

"I know," West said. "And I got sent to jail. I'm sorry about that. I know that you were mad at me, because I know that you blame me a little bit. I blame me too, hell. Mostly because it was my own bad decision making when it came to wives that led me there. But I didn't break the law. It's not my fault that I got put away, and I didn't mean to put off having you come stay with me."

"Your wife didn't want me to come."

"I know. And I was going to override her on that. You're family."

"Isn't a wife family?"

"I guess. But mine wasn't really. She didn't have a lick of loyalty to me. That's for damn sure. I might not have known that at the time, but it turned out to be true. I've been looking for you. I promise you that. I filed a missing persons report and everything."

"You've been out for months."

"I know." He maneuvered his truck effortlessly around the sharp corners of the two lane road, his tires hugging the yellow double line. "I don't really know how to do this whole family thing. Not any more than you do. You think Mom was any more interested in raising me than she is you? She wasn't."

"You have this whole other family," he said. "But I don't."

"Yeah. Well. You probably do have another family somewhere. Who the hell is your dad anyway?"

Emmett shrugged. "I don't know. I'm not sure she knows."

He remembered vividly when his mother had told him she was pregnant. He'd been eighteen, and it had been a hell of a shock. He'd already been in Texas, and as a result he hadn't had a whole lot of opportunity to get close to Emmett.

"Yeah. I didn't know who my dad was either. Not for a long time. But she knows. You could ask her."

Emmett snorted. "I don't think she wants me to know."

"Well, if he had money she'd want you to know. I mean, she would've gone and asked him for it. She got a payoff from my old man's wife."

Emmett said nothing for a moment. "And you...you speak to them?"

"Yeah. We're about to go talk to them now."

"Doesn't that make you mad? That his wife paid Mom off?"

"No," West said. "She was protecting her own. It was Mom's job to protect me. Tammy Dalton just did what she felt like she had to do. Hank's the one who behaved badly."

"Hank is...your dad."

"Yeah. He's not a bad guy. I mean, not really. They're all pretty decent for a collection of rednecks."

"Aren't *you* a redneck?" Emmett asked.

"I suppose. I figure I'm pretty decent for one too." West took a breath, then drummed his fingers on the steering wheel. "They've got a school there."

"I don't want to go to school."

"Tough shit," he said. "If you want to live with me, there's going to be some expectations of you. Look, the school at the Dalton ranch is different. There's not a lot of homework or anything like that. There's some physical work. You can learn a trade. There's art..."

"I don't want to do art."

"Well, you don't have to. You can figure out what you like. You can go to a regular school if you want. But I thought this might be a good chance for you to get a little bit more."

"Why can't I just work on your ranch?"

"Because." He didn't really have a better answer than that, even though reasons moved around in his head. No one had cared what he did. Not at all. And he knew that that didn't help you get on any kind of good path. But he had the opportunity to get more. To get better. All the things that West had had to fight for, he could help Emmett get.

"You been doing a lot of camping, right?" he asked.

"Yeah," Emmett said.

"Right. Well, how many times did you come up on a trail that was all closed in and overgrown?"

"Lots of times."

"You can get through those paths, but isn't it easier to go through a spot that's already been forged?"

"I guess."

"I *was* you," West said. "I know you might find that hard to believe, but I was. And I had to walk a trail that was all overgrown. I had to find my way through all that stuff. I knocked it all over for you. I cleared the way. I can show you how it can be easier, and I can help you. But you have to let me."

Emmett frowned, but didn't say anything more. When they arrived at the well-manicured Dalton ranch, all white fences and even the clipped green lawn, Emmett looked a little bit stunned.

"They have a lot of money," West said.

He'd had nothing. And he'd also had an excess. Now he was somewhere in the middle, but even still, the Dalton family spread was pretty impressive. The house even more so. It was tacky rich. Gilded trailer park living, and he had to admit that part of him loved it.

When West found financial success, he'd done his best to assimilate. To blend in. He had been looking for a kind of suburban normalcy with his success. Hank Dalton obviously had no interest in normalcy, and there was quite a bit of him that respected the hell out of that.

He looked out at one of the arenas and saw his half brother Gabe out there, with a few of the boys from the school, his wife, Jamie, riding a horse in the arena, likely demonstrating something. Jamie was not wholly unlike Pansy, he thought. Small and determined, and stubborn as hell.

He didn't know why he was thinking about her right now.

Except that he was appreciative of her stubbornness, because she had gone to bat for Emmett today and he was grateful for that.

As they approached the house, he looked to the left and

saw Hank Dalton sitting in his big chair underneath the giant gazebo that overlooked the lawn. "Come on," West said. "Let's go meet Hank."

They got out of the car, and West walked Emmett over to where his dad was sitting. It was strange to him, to think of this man who had his same eye color as his dad. But he could see it. It was the oddest thing. To recognize his own features in the face of a stranger.

"Hank," West said. He still didn't call him dad. Probably never would.

"What can I do for you?"

"I want you to meet Emmett," West said.

"Is he your boy?"

West looked at Emmett, and realized that there would be nothing at all strange to Hank about the possibility that Emmett was his son. Not that West would had to have been eighteen when he was born. Not that he wouldn't have brought him by to meet Hank until now. That the kid didn't live with him. No, none of that would be weird to Hank.

"My half brother. *Other*...half."

Hank laughed. "Shit, boy. Had me worried for a second that it was another one of mine."

As far as West knew, Hank had given up his philandering a while back, but he didn't know how long ago that while was.

"My mom's kid," West said. "He's going to come live with me for a while. I was hoping he could...come to school here."

"That depends." Hank met Emmett's gaze. "Are you a troublemaker?"

Emmett shifted. "I think so."

"Good," Hank said. "We only have space for troublemakers here."

He could tell that Emmett and Hank would get along just fine. The thing about Hank was he never had trouble getting along with people. It was controlling his behavior, and not doing anything terribly selfish and hurting people with his thoughtlessness, that was the real issue.

"I suppose I need to talk to Gabe," West said.

"Probably," Hank said. "Though, this place is still mostly mine."

"Gabe runs it as far as I can tell," West said.

"I reckon so," he said.

"So that's Hank," West said. And then he turned back toward the arena. "And now we'll go meet my half brothers."

"This is so weird," Emmett said.

"Yeah?" West asked as they walked toward Gabe.

"Your half brothers, your dad. And we're half brothers, but they're not related to me."

"Yeah, that is the thing about being half brothers. I have a half sister too."

"Geez," Emmett said.

They went over to the arena, and Gabe turned. The boys did too, but they immediately turned back toward Jamie, who was now whipping through a barrel course in the arena. "I think I have a new student for you," West said.

"You do?" Gabe asked.

"Yeah," West said. "This is my half brother. Emmett."

Gabe stuck his hand out. "Pleased to meet you."

Emmett shook it, giving him a slight side-eye as he did. He imagined that he hadn't been treated with this much respect by adults in a long time. If ever.

That had made a big difference in West's life. Getting a job on the ranch in Oregon when he'd been young, and then when he'd been eighteen and going out to Texas, finding more men who had treated him like *he* was a man too.

Like he was worthy of respect, rather than a boy who was just in the way.

He'd always had that burning desire for independence in his chest. And who wouldn't, with the childhood he'd had? But he hadn't been able to find that kind of respect in his own home. Other places, he found it. And it had shown him the kind of man he wanted to be. He could do that for Emmett. And all these people would too.

"Your mom's kid?" Gabe asked.

"Yeah, your dad had to verify that too."

Gabe huffed a laugh. "Does your mom know you're here?"

"No," he said. "She doesn't know where I am."

Gabe met West's eyes. "I am going to need some guardian stuff."

"I'm his guardian."

"Legally?"

"No," West said.

"Well, you're either going to have to do that, or get your mom to sign some things."

"She'll sign anything," Emmett said. "She doesn't care about me. She just wants me out of her hair."

West would have loved to argue with that, but it was true. She didn't want them around. She wanted to be able to do her own thing. She loved to talk about her kids when they were doing well. But that was it. She did not like to take care of them. She didn't like to deal with their failures.

She wanted them to be convenient accessories. Evidence of the fact that maybe she hadn't just wasted her life on men who didn't much care for her, and the endless grind of jobs that she hated.

They were a double-edged sword for her.

Incontrovertible evidence of the passing years, but also

a potential reminder that she'd done something that had mattered.

But whatever they were, it was only ever when she felt like it, and on her terms. That was just a fact.

"Well, today, Jamie is demonstrating some riding techniques. We ride a lot of horses around here. You ever ridden a horse?"

Emmett shook his head. "No."

West felt that like an echo of failure down through his soul.

"You're going to learn," Gabe said.

"What is this?" Emmett asked. "Cowboy school?"

"Might as well be." Gabe grinned. "Join the other kids."

"Okay," Emmett said, taking a step toward the other boys. They jostled, and moved slightly away from him.

"Are they going to be dicks?" West asked.

"For a while. But then they'll get over it."

And that was true, West knew that it would be.

He stuffed his hands in his pockets, not quite willing to leave just yet. And shocked that he wasn't. That he was nervous for his half brother. Emmett could find a place here, if he wanted to.

West just had to hope that he would want to.

CHAPTER TWELVE

ANOTHER DAY, another panel interview, this time with more people. Pansy was entirely unimpressed with the timing of the event. And she knew that Barbara would be there, raising hell.

In fact, it went even worse than Pansy could have ever imagined.

It was clear that Lana was on her side. And there were obviously a few people who appreciated the route she'd taken with Emmett. But Barbara wasn't the only one that had concerns over her leniency.

It made Pansy want to scream.

How could so many grown people who had benefited from having a support network in their lives not understand that a boy like Emmett needed a community to come together around him, not shun him?

They kept saying that by *not* punishing him she was going to turn him into a hardened criminal, but Pansy had a fair idea of what made a criminal, and in her mind it was more things like *this*. Desperation and a lack of hope. A lack of accountability. If nobody cared about you then you didn't care about anyone in return.

The kid needed to feel a sense of responsibility to the community. To the people in it. Carl Jacobson was going to help with that. By having Emmett work off his debt,

Carl was going to make Emmett feel a sense of responsibility for the place.

People like Barbara would make him feel poisoned against it.

She had said as much, and she knew that the people who liked her anyway thought it was great.

And those who didn't were yet more skeptical.

The ultimate decision lay with the city manager, but, the way that all of it went, each panel meeting and the final community meeting would bear weight.

She didn't know how Officer Johnson's panels were going. But considering he could show up and be a man she imagined it was all going well.

He hadn't made a controversial decision, recently or ever.

And his *general* normalcy was going to serve him well.

He looked like every police chief they'd ever had. He did things the same as everyone else. Or at least, people could assume that he did things the way they wanted because they didn't know how he did things, because he didn't do much.

She was feeling surly by the time she dragged herself back to her house. But some of the surliness abated when she pulled up and saw Emmett working on digging fence postholes with West.

"I didn't know I was getting a new fence too," she said.

"I figured you might as well. I had extra supplies," he said.

"Well that's…nice."

"I am pretty nice," West said. "Once you get to know me."

"Pity I don't have a reason to get to know you," she shot back.

He gave her a half grin, and a kick of something she didn't want to acknowledge made her stomach feel fluttery. She liked sparring with him.

But she felt down and *crispy* after her day, and there was something about flinging herself at him that made her feel something. Something better. Something better than stale and sad and alone.

"No," he said, that grin sliding into something wicked. "No reason at all."

"Are either of you hungry?"

She asked the question to avoid having to deal with the heat that was coursing through her body. Because feeding people was as decent an answer to unpleasant emotions as anything.

Why feel something unwanted when you could eat cheese instead?

A reasonable question as far as Pansy was concerned.

"No that's all right," West said at the same time Emmett said, "Sure."

"I'll do grilled cheese," Pansy said.

She went inside the house, and began to cook, and it occurred to her as she was midway through flipping the second grilled cheese that she had never really taken care of anyone before.

She and her siblings had depended on each other. They had created a home, a life, had taken all their broken pieces and glued themselves back together so they could go on. It had been survival. Cheerful and raucous at times, but survival nonetheless.

There were things they'd done for each other—punch a bully in the nose if he dared pick on someone in the family.

There were things they'd done for themselves—pack lunches, do their own laundry. And no one had ever cleaned their rooms.

When it came to dinner, Iris and Sammy had taken

on the task. Transportation, discipline, signing teacher's notes…well that had all been Ryder.

She was one of the younger kids. And the position of the younger kids in the family was quite clear. West had taken care of himself primarily, as far as she could tell.

She wondered if he had ever taken care of anyone else before, or if Emmett would be the first.

Maybe his wife.

But, she hadn't heard anything about his marriage that made it sound like…that made it sound like they really did things for each other in that way.

One of her early memories of her parents was her dad coming home after a long day of work and telling her mother to go sit down because she had been on her feet all day. As if he hadn't been.

But they had been like that with each other. They had checked in with each other. They had cared for each other. They hadn't kept score when it had come to who had been carrying what share of the load.

At least, they hadn't done it in front of the kids.

So Pansy knew that marriage could be that way. Good and balanced. *Real.*

And even though she hadn't really made a space for marriage in her own life, she knew that it *could* be good. West's marriage didn't sound good.

Framing him for fraud aside.

She went back outside with the grilled cheese sandwiches, and a beer, plus a bottled water.

She set all of the things down on the picnic bench and table right out front of her house. Because she was not handing West anything. Not again.

They needed to not touch.

She was too confused about all of that to add another

spark to the fire that was making it feel like her body wasn't her own.

"Barbara has requested that you do some service at the Community Center. She'd like you to come help weed and plant flowers."

Okay, maybe *like* was overstating it. But she had agreed to allow him to do that, and Pansy hoped that the opportunity to use the young man for free manual labor would make her a little bit easier to deal with in general.

And maybe, eventually, she would even understand the point of all of this.

Though, Pansy doubted it.

She'd had a lot of years to become thoroughly set in her own ways and Pansy didn't imagine she was going to magically become forgiving and generous now.

But if they could come to some sort of…truce.

Pansy didn't need Barbara on her side for any of this to go her way, but she didn't like the resistance.

"Okay," he said. "I'm going to school, though."

"Good," she said. "You can do that too."

Emmett looked at West. "Don't look at me," West said. "I want to keep you busy. Because I don't want to have to deal with you and your idle hands becoming a devil's workshop."

"Are you ninety?" Emmett asked, clearly bristling under the authority West was doling out. Authority Emmett wasn't used to, but Pansy could tell he desperately wanted.

She related heavily. To being lonely. To missing something from your life like that. And while she'd had no problem letting Ryder be there for her, she'd watched it play out differently with the others.

Sometimes you resisted what you needed because of how much it hurt.

"No. But I do remember what it's like to be your age.

And, having caused my fair amount of trouble, I can tell you right now I don't want to have to clean up after you."

"My mom doesn't care."

"No, our mom doesn't care," West said. "But I do. That means I'm not going to let you run around like a hellion. I'm not going to let you make a mess of your life."

"Who said I was making a mess of anything? It just is what it is."

"Nothing *is what it is*, unless you let it be. You can have different. I know you can."

"Says the guy who ended up in jail."

West shook his head. "Finish your food, go work on the fence."

Emmett stuffed the last of his sandwich into his mouth and got up, walking away from the table and back toward the work site, where he got back to the task at hand with an almost dramatic flare.

"So it's going well," Pansy said.

West crossed his arms, the corners of his lips turned down. "I miss the simpler days. When I would park in a bad spot you would write me a ticket. When I wasn't taking care of a surly teenager."

"I'm glad you found him," she said.

The alternative was too sad. Just thinking about Emmett out there all alone… No one should ever be alone.

West shrugged. "*You* found him. Not me. I'm thankful for that. Don't get me wrong. Doesn't mean that it's easy."

Pansy nodded. "Well. As far as I can tell there's very little about life that's easy. He needs you, though, whether he can show it or not is another matter. And there are certain things that good people do. And one of those things is… be there. When your family needs you. You're doing that."

"I think you just came perilously close to calling me good."

Pansy was never spontaneous, but as she looked at West she said just the first thing that popped into her head. "I suspect you're about as good as you are bad."

Their eyes caught, and his mouth curved into a smile that made the word *wicked* echo inside of her.

She didn't know anything about men. But she knew that she liked kissing this one. Knew that the parts of him that were bad called her maybe even more loudly than the parts of him that were good, and that scared her.

Because it reminded her of when she was young and she had a restless, wild spirit that she'd made a concerted effort to change.

West called to that spirit inside of her, the one that she had shut down deep. And it was tempting. *So* tempting to just not control it anymore.

To throw caution and everything else to the wind and explore what was bad in him.

That, she had a feeling could be very good.

She didn't know why she had that feeling. Maybe it was a host of tangled up bad boy stereotypes and TV and the fevered fantasies of her own body, which currently seemed to be reminding her that she had left the whole virginity thing far too long.

It was the silliest, most trivial thing to be thinking about. While she had the concerns of the new job hanging over her head, and West had the concerns of his half brother to deal with.

But she was thinking about it anyway.

It was amazing how the curve of that man's lips could twist her thoughts.

Could tie her stomach in a knot and make her feel like a foreign entity unto herself.

"That's probably the highest praise anyone has ever given me," he said.

"Well, it's not very high praise," she pointed out.

"I don't suppose."

She pushed an anxious breath out of her lungs, hoping it would ease some of the tension in her. "If it weren't for my siblings… I would have ended up in foster care. And that can be good. I mean…it's not ideal. But… I wouldn't have been able to grow up on my family ranch. I would've lost my parents and my home. It's not a small thing that you're doing. Stepping in for him like this. It could change his life. Utterly and completely change his life. Knowing that someone cares about you enough to sacrifice for you changes everything."

"I hope so," he said. "I hope it's enough to change him. I made it through without anyone. More or less. I don't want him to have to. I don't want him to have to make the mistakes I did. You can come back from pretty much anything. I'm a walking testament to that. But you know, I don't recommend getting married to a person who would get you sent to prison."

"Well…yeah, solid advice," she said.

"There's a certain amount of resilience that you get in life because you go through things that are out of your control. But I'd like to soften some blows for him."

There was something about the glint in his eye that made her breath catch in her throat. She wanted…she wanted to reach out to him. She wanted to touch him. It occurred to her that only a couple of short weeks ago this man had been a stranger she'd pulled over on the roadside and given a ticket to. Now his face was so familiar she could close her eyes and trace it in her mind.

She had kissed him.

She swallowed hard.

"If you keep looking at me like that, Officer Daniels, I'm going to think that you're issuing invitations."

His voice went all low and husky, and she could feel it echoing inside of her body.

"Neither of us have time for any parties," she whispered.

He chuckled, the sound warm and husky, rolling through her bones. "But I give such good parties." He shook his head. "How much time do you think it would take?"

He was offering an express trip to sin, and lord she was tempted.

"Too much," she said. "Too complicated."

"Doesn't have to be."

She could think of nothing more ridiculous than instigating a physical relationship for the first time in her life when she was in the middle of such a critical moment.

"We both have a lot on our plates," she pointed out.

"It'd be nice to have something there that wasn't terrible, wouldn't it?"

She looked away. "I don't know."

"Pansy…"

She jumped up off the bench. "I just remembered that I forgot to get something from town."

"Liar."

"I'm a police officer. I don't lie."

He looked at her, too long. Too hard. "I think you do. To me. But mostly to yourself."

"I need milk."

"Go get your milk." She nearly fled, stumbling away from him and back to her car, and it was only when she was almost the whole way back to town that she could admit that he was right. That she was lying because she was afraid. Because she didn't know what would happen if she took that step.

It was silly. And she couldn't banish the panic that fluttered in her breast. Instead of figuring that out, she went into the community center, hoping that she would find Barbara there. She wasn't disappointed.

"Emmett agreed to your plan," she said. "He's going to come and do community service for the next few weekends."

"Good. It doesn't change the fact that I'm unhappy with how this was handled. I'm not going to give you my support."

Pansy only just managed to stop herself from rolling her eyes and opened her mouth to say something, but Barbara interrupted her.

"Your father was a good man, Pansy. And he honored the position that he had. But you've lost your way. You are not the person that this town needs. It doesn't matter how hard you try, you won't be. You're the wrong fit."

Pansy had managed to stand strong in the face of everything this woman had thrown at her up until now. She had been able to stand up to anything, everything, except for this. Except for her saying that her father was fundamentally different than she was.

That she could never be all that he was.

Because deep down, she believed it.

Because it was true.

West had tested that thing inside of her that was so wild, and he had woken it up.

She wasn't going to do what her father had done, because she couldn't be the steady, perfect person that he was.

She didn't know what to do about that. It was a crisis point in her chest that burned.

Failure.

Was this what failure was? It wasn't about the job. It was about…her. She wondered if there was something broken in her that other people could just see.

Or maybe Barbara is just a horrible person?

She gritted her teeth. "Fine," she said. "I'm not like him. I won't ever be. There's no way. But I'm not going to let you ruin that kid's life. I just won't. So yeah, maybe that doesn't make you happy. Maybe I failed as far as you're concerned. But I hope that I helped him. And I hope that you can find it in yourself to treat him like he's a human when he's here. He has been failed by every adult in his life. Don't join that list. You're right. I'm not my dad. But I do know what it's like to grow up without a dad. Just like Emmett. He's nothing but a fatherless child. Give him a chance. Show him that he can come back from a mistake. Punish me if you need to. But don't punish him."

She turned and walked back out of the Community Center feeling deflated. More upset than she should.

She had come to town to run away, to find solace in the familiar. And she hadn't been able to do it. She hadn't been able to make herself feel fixed.

West.

West was to blame for all of this. Anger burned in her chest, doing something to cover up the pain. The uncertainty.

She drove. Just to drive, and when it got dark she finally headed back toward her house.

She still didn't want to go inside. Didn't want to go to bed. So she headed out toward the barn.

Maybe she would find some clarity there.

But the light was already on. And it wasn't clarity she found inside.

It was West.

CHAPTER THIRTEEN

WHEN PANSY CAME storming into the barn, West knew that one of two things was about to happen. Either she was on the verge of hauling off and punching him in the face, or she was on the verge of flinging herself in his arms.

West knew which one he would prefer.

Instead, she stopped herself short, standing in the center of the room, anger and uncertainty radiating off of her tiny frame in waves.

"Fancy meeting you here."

"I didn't mean to," she said.

"No. But you have something to say to me. That much is clear. So you might as well."

"You're ruining everything," she said. "Absolutely everything. Before you came here everything was fine. But you brought *you*… And you brought Emmett, and now I have a one-woman wrecking crew trying to destroy my campaign for police chief."

"Technically you don't get elected, do you?"

"Not in a technical sense, but I'm being chosen with the help of this very specific panel. And she's an influential part of this selection process. And she…she told me that I was never going to be like my dad. You know what? She's right. But before you came, I wouldn't have believed that. But you…you make me realize that it's true. I'm not my dad. I'm not ever going to be. I don't have his dedication to law and order. I'm too soft, and I'm too… I'm weak. And the harder things get with this job the more I notice it. But that's because of you too. Do you know what I was thinking about last night before I went to sleep? It wasn't my job."

"I hope it was me," he said, heat igniting in his gut.

She hated him either way. So if she wanted to blame him for a little bout of self-destruction that was fine by him. But he wanted her. He wanted her, and he was damned tired of fighting it because he wasn't a man who had ever engaged in much altruism in his life, but here he was trying to do his best to take care of his half brother, and he couldn't resist her on top of it.

Yes. She was an entanglement. Yes, she was a hell of a lot more trouble than he wanted to get involved in, but she woke up places in him that had been sleeping for a long damned time.

Places that he thought irreparably damaged by the betrayal of his ex-wife. The years of prison he thought had damaged him beyond repair.

Because the West who had gone into prison wouldn't have come straight out and looked for his father. He would've come straight out and looked for a hot, willing woman to take to bed.

But everything had gotten twisted up somehow. His life, himself and somehow as little sense as she made, Pansy felt like a solution in the middle of it all.

Like a return to what he'd been, and he was hungry for that.

Hungry for her. So if making her angry brought her closer, made those eyes glitter, made her face flush, then he would go ahead and poke away, because he had a feeling it was the way to get that mouth back on his. And he wanted it.

"You did something to me," she accused, her brown eyes furious.

He'd have laughed if he could breathe.

"It's called attraction, Pansy. And I wasn't looking for it any more than you were, but there it is. Why do you think I was parking my truck in all those spaces? So that you could get mad at me again. Because you make sparks inside me, darlin', and I've been cold in there for a long time. You put men in prison, do you know what it's like? It's not fun. Your day gets ground down to a tired routine. You forget that you're a man. Hell, you're lucky if you remember that you are human and not an animal. I never got wood the whole time I was in there. Dead below the waist. Why? Because there's nothing to get excited about. Because there's no point dreaming about a woman or a cheeseburger or soft bed, because you're not going to get it."

He took a step toward her. "You…you make me hard. You make me want. And I didn't want to be into some prissy cop who's everything I hate in the world, but maybe that's why. Maybe that's why I want you. Why I want to push you up against this wall right now and tear your shirt off. I want to see what color your nipples are. See how wet you get between your legs when a man touches you there. Tastes you there. That's what I want. You. Mindless and naked and mine. And it doesn't make any sense. Because I could go out to a bar and have a woman I didn't have to work for. But I don't want any woman. I want you. All hell-fire and angry, biting me while you kiss me." The color had risen high in her cheeks, her breath coming in short, harsh bursts. "Maybe that's the thing. Like you said about me. I want it as good as I want it bad. I want it to hurt. I want you to dig your nails into me while you come around me."

She shrunk back. "You shouldn't say things like that to me."

"Should I go say things like that to someone else?"

That seemed to be it. The challenge that broke her.

She growled. Like a feral cat before she launched herself across the distance between them and grabbed hold of his face, kissing him with a hell of a lot more fury than finesse.

But fury was fine with him.

Fury was the substance of his being, and being able to hold it like this, female and soft, small enough to wrap up in his arms and big enough to arouse him more than he could remember ever having been aroused, was all right by him.

She did bite him. Her teeth sinking deep into his lower lip. He wrapped her ponytail around his fist and pulled her head back, separating their mouths, exposing her throat so he could kiss her there. Then he worked his way back to her lips, moving his tongue deep and tasting her.

"You're a hot little piece," he growled. "Damn hot."

"I think that's insulting," she said, panting.

"Is it? Because you're the only one I want. The only one that's done a damn thing for me in the last four years. You tell me if that's insulting."

It was going on more than four years since he'd been with a woman. Ridiculous. And he'd been married about five years before that. A decade since he had a woman other than his ex-wife in his arms.

And he couldn't even fantasize about the sex they'd had, because she'd ruined it. He was a damn sight past even finding the idea of hate sex with her hot. She had him sent to prison. He had no forgiveness for her in his body.

Pansy wasn't a fantasy. She was real. She was fire in his arms. He reversed their positions, pressing her against one of the barn walls, then he grabbed her arms and trapped them up over her head, wrapping one hand around her wrist as he continued to kiss her.

She arched into him, those full breasts pressing into his chest. He grinned against her mouth, because he couldn't help it. Then he bit her right back.

She whimpered, her pelvis moving restlessly against his. He knew exactly what she wanted.

He flicked open the button on her jeans, dragged her zipper down and pushed his hand right down between her legs, right where he'd been fantasizing about touching.

She was wet.

So damn slick and perfect. He stroked her, moving his fingers through the seam of her folds, paying extra close attention to the sensitized bundle of nerves that he knew would bring her extreme pleasure. She gasped, moving against his hand, each little noise that she made in time with his strokes like a plea for more. And he answered that plea. He shifted his hand, pinching her gently before pressing his palm against her as he explored her deeper, pushing one finger inside of her. She pulled her mouth from his, letting her head fall back against the wall, her eyes wide, her mouth dropping open in shock.

"You okay?" He was barely able to ask the question. He didn't know what the hell he would do if she wanted to stop.

Well, he'd stop. But he'd have to go jump in a cold river and put his balls on ice.

"Good," she panted.

But there was a strange and wild look in her eyes, something that seemed to sit on the edge of pleasure and fear. But then she leaned in and kissed his mouth, and he figured he would believe the lady when she told him it was good.

He worked his finger in and out of her body, and she wiggled her hips in time with the movement. Suddenly, she planted her palms against his chest and pushed him backward. He slipped his hand out of her jeans and let her move him away.

She was strong, and there was a lot of sexy, tight muscle under that smooth skin of hers, but she was no match for him if he decided he wasn't going to be moved.

But then she planted her hands on his stomach, let them drift down as they crept beneath the hem of his shirt. She blinked rapidly when her fingertips made contact with his skin. Then she bit her lip and pushed her hands farther up, pushing his shirt up and exposing his stomach and chest. He grabbed the bottom of it and pulled it up over his head. She put her hand in the center of his chest, the expression on her face one of awe as she stared at the place where her palm rested against him.

"You're beautiful," she said.

He didn't think a woman had ever called him beautiful before. "Not much to do but work out for the last few years."

"Thank you," she said, letting her fingertips drift over his muscles. "Really."

"Officer Daniels," he said. "I think you're a little bit of a bad girl."

She blinked. "Me?"

"You sure make me think bad things." He lifted her hand from his chest and brought her fingertips to his mouth, biting the tip of one gently. She shivered. He took her by the hand and led her back to the tack room. There was a couch in there. Not the most civilized space, given that there were harnesses and crops hanging all over the walls.

Though, to be honest, he could think of a few things he wouldn't mind doing with the crop and Officer Daniels's pretty backside.

But, that conversation could happen later.

Next time, maybe.

He slammed the door closed behind them, just in case Emmett ended up wandering around. He was pretty sure the kid was occupied playing some game on his phone— or looking at things West didn't want to think about him looking at—and wouldn't be leaving the house. But still.

He moved to Pansy, pulling her T-shirt up over her head.

She was wearing a sensible sports bra that didn't do a whole lot to show off her curves. But he didn't care. He pushed that up too, making quick work of it and flinging it onto the floor.

A blush covered her cheeks, spreading down lower, over those pretty breasts.

And they were pretty. Barely a handful, but with hard, dark pink nipples that he wanted to taste.

He pulled her up against him, her bare breasts against his bare chest, and kissed her, bringing her down onto the couch, onto his lap. They were both in only blue jeans, her thighs spread wide.

Then he moved his hands down her back, down to her ass, and jerked her against him so that she could feel the hard length of him.

The denim kept them both from getting as much stimulation as he'd like, but the tease was fun in its way. She gasped, letting her head fall back, and he scraped his teeth along her neck, kissing a path down to the plump curve of one breast before drawing a tightened bud deep into his mouth. Her hands went to his shoulders, those nails digging into his skin just like he had said he wanted.

That sweet pain a counterpoint to the intense pleasure that he felt tasting her. He moved his attention to her other breast, tracing her nipple with the tip of his tongue before sucking her in deep. He teased her like that until she was wiggling against him, until she was panting, whimpering.

He lifted her up and set her so that she was sitting side-saddle on him. Then he pushed her jeans down her hips, pulled them off along with her panties in as fluid a move-ment as he could manage in that position.

That left the good officer naked on his lap, the whole of her pretty body exposed to him. She breathed in and out, the muscles on her stomach visible as she did. Her arms were toned, and so were her thighs. He liked the look of her. Like a pint-size warrior who could kick his ass as readily as she could turn all soft and pliant and willing in his arms.

That pretty patch of curls between her legs made his mouth water. Made him so stiff he hurt.

Her skin was the most brilliant, beautiful shade of pink he'd ever seen, a flush spreading over her and getting deeper. He moved his hands slowly over her curves, care-ful not to miss an inch.

Then he shifted, setting her beside him on the couch so that he could get his wallet that was in his back pocket, and make quick work of his own boots and jeans so that he could be naked. Skin to skin with her. She was looking at him, her eyes darting everywhere but right to the part of him that showed how much he wanted her.

It was sweet to be with a woman who was a little bit coy. He didn't have any experience with that. He liked them brazen and bold, and if he and Pansy were to do this again, he had a feeling that she would get a hell of a lot more bold. But, he was kind of enjoying that expression on her face now.

Because it was something between awe and reverence and he couldn't remember the last time anyone has looked at him like that.

Maybe never.

And maybe that didn't say great things about his ego, but his ego had taken a pounding over the last few years, so he would take it.

She lifted her hand and reached out, fingertips brushing against where he was hot and hard for her. He sucked a breath in, pleasure skittering over him like lightning.

"Did I hurt you?"

"Almost," he said. "But in the best way."

She sat there, unmoving.

"Touch me," he ground out.

She did, wrapping her fingers around him, testing him, squeezing him. And then, she devoted her full attention to him. Her mouth fell open slightly, those pink lips parted and when she licked them he felt the echo of that slick tongue stroke against his length.

"You're so sexy," he ground out. "I want to be inside you."

He was a liar.

He didn't *want* it.

He *needed* it.

She rose up onto her knees, still holding him in her hand, and she kissed him. She was getting bolder with her kisses already, her tongue delving into his mouth to explore him without hesitation. He planted his hand on her ass, slipping his fingertips between her legs and teasing her damp opening as she continued to squeeze him. She gasped, and he pushed his finger back inside of her, then a second, glorying in how hot she was. How wet.

How good she would feel when he pushed his way inside of her.

This was just teasing.

He was ready for the real thing. He grabbed his wallet and pulled out a condom, tearing it open and rolling it onto his length.

Sure he hadn't been with a woman in years, but he made sure that he had the necessities just in case.

He was a man who didn't take chances. Especially not anymore.

He grabbed hold of her again and positioned her so that she was astride him on his lap again, pulling her close so that he could push his hardness through her slickness.

She shuddered and he gripped her chin with his thumb and forefinger, parting her mouth and kissing her deep, gripping her tightly with his other hand. Teasing her relentlessly between her legs.

Then he moved his hands to her hips and lifted her slowly, pressing the head of him to the entrance of her body and bringing her down slowly, achingly slow, onto him, inch by excruciating inch. She whimpered, she wiggled, a harsh sound rising in her throat as he arched his hips upward and thrust all the way home.

She went stiff, and when he looked at her face he saw that she was not having very much fun.

"What?" he asked, doing his best to form words, because his brain wasn't working well at all. She was so tight. So perfect, and he hadn't been inside anyone in so long. Even then, no one had ever felt like her. Not like this.

She was a revelation. Having to think while buried inside of her was not easy.

"It's fine," she said, but a tear escaped the corner of her eye, and he knew it wasn't fine.

"What's wrong," he asked, moving to pull out.

She put her hand against his wrist. "No," she said. "I want to."

"I'm hurting you," he said.

"It's getting better."

"*Why* does it hurt?"

"I've never… I've never done this before," she said.

He cursed, and lifted her away from him, laying her down on the couch. "Pansy…"

"No," she said fiercely. "Don't leave it half done. Don't just give me the pain. This was supposed to be something wild. Don't make it something sad." She reached up, curving her fingers around his neck, her eyes meeting his. "I've had enough sad."

He couldn't resist that. He let her pull his face down to hers, kissed her. She parted her legs for him, and he slid himself between them, pushing inside of her again. This time, she gasped, but she didn't cry out. He pressed his thumb where he knew she needed him most and stroked her as he moved in and out of her slowly, as gently as he could. He did that until she was making those same movements with her hips she'd done when he was just touching her. Did that until he was sure he had brought her back to the peak of mindless pleasure instead of to that space where they were both thinking too damned much.

Then she gripped his shoulders, her fingernails digging into his skin again. And he lost it. He braced himself against the couch and withdrew slowly, then thrust back in hard.

This time, when she made a sound, it was definitely of pleasure.

His control unraveled, then released completely. And he could do nothing but lose himself in the deep, primal rhythm he established between them.

She lifted her hips, meeting him thrust for thrust, her lack of experience lost in the way they learned each other. In the way they each followed their pleasure.

Her mouth was soft, and she kissed his jaw, his chin, his

lips. Soft kisses that joined with those sharp nails. Pleasure and pain, perfect from her.

It had been inevitable. From the moment she pulled him over, that they would end up here. That he would take her like this.

He was just damned glad that they'd finally accepted that inevitability.

And when it was over, he was going to have to deal with the rest. With the practicality.

But not now.

Hell no, not now.

"West," she whispered his name, lifting her hips and grinding herself against him as he thrust deep. She shuddered, her internal muscles getting impossibly tighter as her orgasm wrenched through her, deep and intense, judging by the way she squeezed him.

And then, he was gone. Utterly and completely gone. His every thought turned to fire, each brain cell turning into a nerve ending, capable of only registering one thing. White-hot pleasure.

She surrounded him. That tight, beautiful body, her soap-scented clean skin that smelled like sweat now because of him.

This good girl. A uniformed police officer. Naked and panting and dirty because of him.

He gritted his teeth, his orgasm rushing over him like a tidal wave. He came on a hoarse growl, pumping into her hard as he spent himself. Then he lowered his head, pressing his forehead to her shoulder, trying to catch his breath as reality began to set in.

He had just screwed the very last woman he should've ever touched.

His tenant. A cop.

A damned virgin.

He pulled away from her, draping her legs over his lap as he pushed into a sitting position, leaning his back against the couch.

"Why didn't you tell me?" he panted.

"I didn't want it to matter," she said. "Hell, I didn't even want it to be true. I wish I'd been with someone else first. So that…this was easier. Because I really wanted this. And I have a feeling that it would've been…a lot simpler if I'd done it before."

Perversely, he found that on a primal level he was glad he'd been the first. But maybe it all tied in with whatever the hell made her so irresistible to him.

That good girl, bad boy thing.

That desire to take someone like her and bring her down to his level.

"Nothing was ever going to make this simple," he said.

And of all the things that he knew in that moment, he knew that best of all.

"Don't…don't worry about it," she said, moving away from him and looking for her clothes. Even with things the way they were, he couldn't help but admire that pretty, toned body of hers.

He was only a man, and simple enough after all.

"Do you want me to walk you back?"

Her body went stiff.

Everything in him said that he ought to, because it was the gentlemanly thing to do. And while he might not be a gentleman in the classical sense, he certainly knew how to play the part.

"I really don't," she said.

She wanted to be alone. And he supposed that he should respect that. Supposed that he should take the hint.

But he wasn't the kind of man who had ever been good at taking hints.

Or, outright statements, really.

"It's dark," he said, moving to dress himself. He discarded the condom in the wastebasket next to the couch and began to get dressed.

By the time they walked out of the barn she looked like she was ready to fold in on herself. So he walked next to her, with a healthy amount of space between. But he just felt like he should be there. The dark offered a little bit of privacy anyway.

Of course, Pansy Daniels would laugh if she knew that he was walking her back home with half a mind to keep her safe.

He had a feeling she was sure and certain she could protect herself and didn't need any interference from him. And fair enough. She was a tough woman. And she had gone up like flames in his hands.

But she had also been a *virgin*. And he was under the impression that was a big deal.

He'd felt a little bit raw and confused after his first time, granted he'd been younger. A lot younger. But he imagined that it was the same no matter what age you were.

Hell.

He felt a little bit raw right now. It was the first time in a long time for him, and the first time with a new lover in longer. And as much as he wanted to pretend that nothing affected him, this did.

She did.

He was no kind of hero. Never had been. He needed to figure out how to be a little bit more of one. He had Emmett living under his roof, and he had stripped Pansy naked and been the first man to be inside of her.

They might need different things from him, but they both needed *something*.

And he couldn't recall ever having been needed by anyone before.

His wife had liked his lifestyle and his money, but she had come from that. Took it as her due. And he hadn't taken care of her in an emotional sense. Not at all.

He'd been the kind of husband a woman like her wanted to have. Tall and good-looking, with the means to keep her in the lifestyle she was accustomed to.

Likewise, she'd been just what he'd wanted. Pretty, polished, a gateway to a certain part of society.

They'd had a decent sex life, and he'd imagined that had meant something to her.

Except it hadn't been enough.

Whatever he'd been, it had never been enough.

His mother didn't particularly want to take care of him, his wife had seen him as an easy scapegoat.

Yeah. He was going to have to figure out how to be a hell of a lot more to get through all of this.

When they got to the edge of the drive that led up to her house she stopped. "Okay," she said. "We're here."

He turned to face her, and wanted to find something to say. He failed at it.

"What?" she asked.

"Did anybody ever tuck you in at night?"

He didn't know why the hell he'd asked that question.

"Is that a… Are you…you hitting on me?"

"No," he said. Though, now that she mentioned it he wouldn't mind tucking her in. "It was a question."

"No," she said. "Not after...not after they died."

He nodded slowly. "Me neither. Sleep well."

And then he turned and walked away, not sure what he should have done differently, but sure it should have been something.

CHAPTER FOURTEEN

PANSY WENT INTO her house slowly, and stripped off her clothes as quickly as she had put them back on at the barn.

A little bit faster than she had stripped them off the first time with West.

She felt numb. Numb and buzzing all at the same time.

She stumbled toward her bathroom on feet that felt like they weren't quite connecting with the ground and turned on the hot water in the shower. She stood in front of the mirror and stared at herself.

Her ponytail was wrecked. Her eyes were red, but she hadn't cried. Her lips were swollen. It made her mouth look funny. Like *not* hers.

She touched it, pressing her index finger down on her lower lip.

She wanted to hide. And she wanted to talk to someone.

But she couldn't talk to West because they didn't have an actual relationship.

They'd just had sex.

That made her eyes feel scratchy.

She got into the shower and let the water slide over her skin.

She wasn't washing him off. It wasn't like that. It was just that her body felt sore and strange, and she thought if she could be somewhere familiar it might make her feel grounded.

It didn't.

She wondered if she would have talked to her mother about this.

Something turned over inside of her and she had the sudden realization that it was possible she had put it off for so long because she knew she would have *wanted* to talk to her mother about this.

Her mom had been free and easy. A contrast to her father and his uptight, brusque demeanor.

He had been constant certainty. Her mother had been the laughter.

How would having her for longer have made Pansy different? Would she have made all this seem easier?

Would Pansy have lost her virginity at seventeen instead of twenty-seven? And would her mom have held her and told her it was going to be okay? That it was part of life and she was a woman now, or something like that?

Maybe that would have happened after she got her period for the first time. Her sister had tried, but she'd been awkward and embarrassed because she was barely used to the whole thing herself.

There was a sudden rush of milestones going through her head. All the things that she'd missed. She didn't think about her mom as often as she thought about her dad. It was a side effect of following in his footsteps.

When she put on those standard-issue shoes every day, she was quite literally walking in those footsteps. She thought about making him proud a lot, and it hit her then she had never thought about making her mother proud.

Because she already had.

Her mom had been proud of her from the beginning and she had always known it, a constant, easy love that she had taken for granted until this moment.

Even when she'd misbehaved, even when she'd had to scold her, her mom had picked her up after and held her.

And told her she loved her.

Tears filled her eyes, and one rolled down her cheek, joining with the shower water.

It was an easy place to cry.

Because *she* could hardly tell. Except that her chest felt like it was splitting apart.

She had just tried so hard, so very hard not to do this. Not to show weakness. Because each and every one of them had been going through insurmountable pain when their parents had died. Because Iris and Rose were in their own kind of pain, and Ryder had done his best to take care of them, while being in the exact same position of grief they all were.

So no.

She had never asked anyone to tuck her in. They had all been missing those people from their lives.

They'd had each other, but it had been different.

It had to be.

But all she wanted right now was her mom.

And to be tucked in.

She got out of the shower and wrapped up in a giant towel, then fell down on her bed. She lay there for a moment, swathed in terry cloth and still damp with tears, before she grabbed her phone. She looked at it for a long moment.

She could call Sammy. Sammy would tell her it was okay. Sammy would tell her it wasn't a big deal.

In some ways, Sammy was a lot like her mother. Though, her mother would never have used the kind of language that Sammy did.

But Sammy wasn't judgmental. She was relaxed and

happy and smiling and she would be the one to make any feeling Pansy had feel normal.

She had a feeling Sammy would suggest they dance out under the moon or something to commemorate the experience.

She decided *against* calling Sammy. She could call Rose. And Rose would crack a dirty joke and ask for details, and then start scheming ways for Pansy to end up married to him or something.

The thought made Pansy cringe. She didn't want to share details.

She wasn't even ready to go back over details in her head.

Iris would let her talk. But Iris might judge her little bit.

She decided against calling anyone.

She crawled underneath the covers and West's question echoed in her mind.

Did anyone ever tuck you in?

She had just done the most intimate thing she'd ever done with another human being.

He'd been inside of her.

And somehow, it had left her feeling impossibly lonely.

More lonely than she'd ever been.

Or maybe she was just crushingly aware of it.

Of what she'd lost. Of what she wished she had.

She wondered what it would be like if West had come home with her.

If he'd gotten into bed with her.

What then? What would it be like to fall asleep in those strong arms?

That was the last thought she let herself have before she went to sleep.

But in her dreams, she was alone.

WEST WAS UP with the sun the next morning, and he made sure that Emmett was up with him. It was his first day at the school on the Dalton property. And West figured it was as good a time as any for him to go and spend some quality time with his brothers.

The ass crack of dawn, after a night spent not sleeping, which as far as he was concerned was pretty damned unfair considering the strength of the orgasm he had.

He was a man who'd been dead below the waist, for all intents and purposes, for the last few years. You'd think that he would've been able to hijack the benefits of his climax. But no.

He'd been worried about her. All damned night.

He couldn't remember the last time he'd been worried about another person other than Emmett.

But hell, he was worried about her.

He had a feeling, though, that him showing up at her house unannounced in the middle of the night wouldn't have been taken too kindly.

So, he left her alone.

He'd tossed and turned for a while, then gone downstairs and got a beer and sat up, watching TV till he fell into a half sleep on the couch that had lasted until about 5 a.m. And now, he and Emmett were just pulling into the ranch property.

"Are we early?" Emmett grumbled.

"Yep," he said. "You sure are. But, it's good to be early on your first day."

"Is it?"

"When I was a kid I used to stay up late and watch these old reruns on the Disney Channel. There was stuff from… I don't know, the nineteen fifties, probably. They used to talk a lot about work ethic. Show up fifteen minutes early at least," West said. "I took that to heart."

"We are more than fifteen minutes early."

"Maybe," West said. "But I don't think the literal time is as important as the concept. You want to set yourself apart. You want to make sure that you work harder."

"Why would I want to work harder?"

"Because nothing in life gets handed to you, Emmett. No one is standing around waiting to give kids like us a handout. So we can either stay in the exact same place our parents put us, or we can figure out how to do something different."

"I'm not better than where I came from," Emmett said. "I expect you think you are."

"I don't know that *I'm* better, but I *want* better. What kind of life do you see having?"

"I don't know," Emmett said.

He knew what that was like. To be afraid to think too far ahead. When you were a kid whose life was governed by the adults that were supposed to take care of you, you didn't the hell know what might come next.

But until you got past that, until you could get to a place where you could dream... You were stuck.

"You're being given an opportunity here," West said. "Make something of it."

"Why do you care?"

He didn't know. He really couldn't answer that, because in the grand scheme of things he didn't care about much that wasn't him.

Except...

"Because nobody was there to help me. And if I can make things easier for you I damn well will, kid. You should recognize that as a gift."

"Thank you for the gift of yourself, West. Where would I be without my big brother that I barely saw until recently?"

"That's not what I mean. It's a gift of resources, dumbass. Grab hold of it. Learn something while you're here. Figure out what you want to do with your life and then do it."

"That simple?"

"What do you think Mom wants?"

"I don't know."

"Neither do I. As far as I can tell a man to share her bed and give her life a little bit of drama, a couple of packs of cigarettes a day and what else? She just wants to survive. I don't want to be her. Do you?"

"No," Emmett said. "Mostly because I don't want a man to share my bed."

West shot the kid a look. "You know what I mean."

"Yeah," Emmett said reluctantly. "She said if she could have married your dad she would've been rich."

He snorted. "Yeah. Sadly for her my dad was already married."

"She's hoping someone else will save her," Emmett said.

West was surprised by his younger brother's insight. "Yeah," he said. "I guess she is."

"I never figured anyone would save me. Not her, not anyone."

"So you figured what? You figured you'd just scrape by on your own?" West asked.

"Yeah. I don't need much."

"All right. Maybe you don't need much. But how about letting yourself want more?"

A sly look came over Emmett's face. "Does that mean getting up this early?"

"I expect that'll come into it."

"Shit," he said.

West chuckled and parked the truck.

Caleb, Gabe and Jacob were all there, standing out in front of the house drinking coffee. Caleb didn't work on the ranch, so he was surprised to see him there.

"What are you doing here?"

"I dropped Ellie off," he said. Caleb's fiancée was one of the teachers at the school. "And Amelia. She's spending the day with Tammy."

Amelia was Caleb's future stepdaughter. Though, she called him dad. Amelia's own father, who had been Caleb's best friend, had died before she was born. Caleb had been a constant in Amelia and Ellie's life, but it had taken some time for Ellie to come to terms with her feelings for Caleb.

West had been part and parcel to fixing that.

And try as he might to deny it, it did make him feel slightly closer to Caleb.

"For those of you who haven't met him," he said, clapping his hand on Emmett's shoulder. "This is my half brother Emmett."

"Welcome to the half siblings club," Caleb said.

"I'm not *your* half brother," Emmett said.

"Still," Gabe commented. "This place is pretty lousy with them."

"That's what I hear," Emmett said.

"We practically have a baseball team of half siblings," Caleb said.

"Not that many," Gabe said, deadpan. "That we know of."

"I can help you get started on some chores," Jacob said. "And we can discuss the art class you'll be taking today."

West had a feeling that Jacob was really just going to tell the kid that he better be nice to the art teacher, who was Jacob's wife, Vanessa.

Emmett looked at West.

"Go," West said. "Learn stuff. Make the most of opportunities. Seize the day."

"Fuck you," Emmett said, but followed Jacob off toward the barn.

"So you acquired another sibling?" Caleb asked.

"I did. I mean, I knew about him. I've been looking for him, actually. I wanted him to come live with me here. But then it turned out he was causing some mischief locally. Hanging around. He's angry at me for some things. Some justified, I guess. Some not. But when you're his age and the world is full of asshole adults you just pick your targets where you can."

"Yeah," Gabe said. "We know a little bit about asshole adults."

"Sure," West responded. "But it's not the same. I mean, I know you had stuff. But Emmett and I had to actually worry about whether or not we were going to get taken care of. We didn't have a fancy house to cushion the blow."

He looked at his brothers, standing in front of him, so... so similar to him in looks. It was weird. For a guy who had never put much stock in family, or blood connections, having so many people out there in the world who shared his DNA was a little bit strange.

Especially because that link was what brought him here.

That link that never mattered much to his mother, and sure as hell didn't change the way she treated him... It was why he was here.

It was why he cared about Emmett. Because otherwise he sure wouldn't care about some snot nosed fifteen-year-old.

Obligation. Blood.

That's what it was. These made-up reasons you were

supposed to care about each other, when you had come from such different circumstances.

Though it felt like more than made-up stuff now. It felt like…it felt like something deeper.

He and Emmett, for all that they were of different generations, had more in common.

His half brothers here… Yes, their father was a problem. A philanderer. Someone who had sown his seed indiscriminately and left a whole lot of pain behind.

But he also seemed to open his arms and his home easily enough. He had treated them like he cared about them—each and every foundling that had come into the place. He had given them a space in this family.

Emmett and West couldn't much get the mother who'd raised them to do that.

"I suppose that's true," Caleb said slowly. "But you look at our parents now and you see them with things kind of held together. For a while there…it was held together with duct tape. It might've been gold duct tape, but duct tape nonetheless. We kind of had to be the adults. Because they couldn't seem to manage it. They were always fighting and screaming and lighting things on fire."

"You mean that as a figure of speech, right?" West asked.

"Hell no," Gabe said. "Tammy Dalton lit her share of things on fire. And she smashed in Hank's truck with a baseball bat. Pretty sure Carrie Underwood writes her songs about Tammy."

"Well okay, that is something," he said.

"It wasn't all easy stuff growing up here," Gabe said. "But we made it through. And we're…family. For whatever that's worth."

"I guess it's as good a reason as any to band together."

"Sure. But this ranch…the boys that are here… The family is expanding, and that feels good too."

"You know…our friend who died, Ellie's first husband," Caleb said. "He was part of our family even though we weren't blood related. And I think because of him this school exists. Because of him, because of McKenna. Because of expanding our ideas of what it meant, and who we might feel responsible for. Our dad was irresponsible, and he did a whole bunch of stuff that my wife would divorce my ass for. But I think from that we've made something good. And I guess that's the thing. You can let bad things take hold, take over. Or you can decide who you're going to be and why. I think we all damn well decided."

And because of that they were helping Emmett.

Because he had come here. Because he had reached out. It was all a decent enough endorsement for the idea of family. In whatever shape it came.

Well, he was grateful for it when it came to Emmett, anyway.

"I figured I'd help give you a hand this morning, if you were all right with that."

"Sure," Caleb said, draining the last of his coffee. "I'm not staying long. I gotta get back to the ranch."

"Why?" Gabe asked. "Time to feed the Christmas trees?"

Caleb took plenty of crap for running a Christmas tree farm. It had been so lucrative for him, that while his plans had been to expand into beef, he had ended up sticking with the trees.

"Yeah," he said. "Something like that. You know, I work my own land, Gabe, not just something that Dad built."

"You're an ass," Gabe said.

"Yeah," Caleb said. "That's well established. And the only person in the world I really care about doesn't mind."

He winked and Gabe rolled his eyes. Then the fight seemed to be over.

So this was having brothers.

It was weird.

But he didn't mind it.

"Let's get to work," Gabe said.

They did, and West allowed it to drown out thoughts of Pansy, and the fact that he wanted to call even though he was pretty sure she wouldn't want him to.

And that he was also pretty sure he was damned if he did and damned if he didn't.

But there was ranch work.

And ranch work was a good thing to have when you didn't want to think about your problems.

CHAPTER FIFTEEN

SHE WASN'T A VIRGIN.

As Pansy sat at her desk at the police station she could only think that phrase over and over again.

She was no longer a twenty-seven-year-old virgin.

She had dealt with it handily in the arms of West Caldwell last night.

She kept having to remind herself, because it seemed so strange. Like she was having an out-of-body experience, except her body *felt* so many things.

She'd had a small breakdown last night. Curled in on herself and felt utterly wrecked from the inside out. But, she had found herself this morning.

What she had done was kind of a big deal. But she could finally also understand what Sammy had said about it *not* being a big deal.

She was realistic. She knew that she and West did not have a future. She didn't want a future with West. Her future was here at the police department, and on Hope Springs Ranch, and in general the life that she had planned out for herself didn't have room for a man in a permanent sense at the moment.

Maybe someday.

And when that someday came she would be grateful always that she'd had West to give her that experience.

It wasn't hearts and flowers.

It was a dusty old couch in a barn. And there was something fitting about that too.

She was glad that he hadn't handled her with too much delicacy. Glad that he hadn't treated her like she was fragile or breakable, because life had done a good job of breaking her as it was.

She'd pieced herself back together a long time ago and found a life that made her proud. A life that felt like it had purpose.

A life that had been affected suitably by the death of her parents and had given that loss purpose.

She had allowed it to make her better. To make her stronger.

Because if she didn't... There was no point to anything.

Because of that she'd been made strong. And she hadn't wanted romance and all that anyway.

She didn't need it. She wasn't that kind of girl, not really.

It was okay. She didn't want to be or need to be. What he'd said to her before she'd gone into her house had stuck in her head.

Had anybody tucked her in at night?

No. But then she remembered that she'd survived it. And, there was no point being upset about what you didn't have. It didn't bring it back. It didn't fix what was broken.

You just grew into the kind of person who didn't need it. He should know that as well as anyone.

So yeah. A little bit rough, a little bit careless on a couch in a barn, completely unplanned, seemed about right for her first time.

She wasn't going to regret it. Life was too short for that. And while she clearly wasn't the kind of person who rushed out to have experiences just for the sake of them, now that she had one, and it was decent enough, she wasn't going to waste any time feeling upset about it.

Anyway it was difficult to feel upset about it. Rough and careless, yes. Totally out of character, yes. And completely and utterly mind-blowing, possibly *because* of all that.

She stood up from her desk and finished the paperwork she was going over, then headed out the door to her police car. It was a beautiful day.

A beautiful day to not be a virgin.

She felt slightly giggly and decided that she deserved a drink from Sugar Cup. After all, a little bit of celebrating herself didn't seem like a bad idea. Not after that.

She was really doing this. Owning it. She felt very un-Pansy about the whole thing, and she was really quite cheered about it.

She was normally so rigid, so *concerned* with everything going a certain way. To have found some sort of relief from that in the aftermath of such a reckless and huge decision was welcome. She diverted herself away from her car and headed toward the coffeehouse, pushing open the door and stopping when she got inside.

Because who was in there, but West and Emmett.

This was her deepest fear. That if she hooked up in a small town, she was going to have to continue to run into that person whether she chose it or not. And it was all well and good to be casual about the whole thing when West was a memory and seeing him again was theoretical. It was quite another to be casual when he was right *there* and it was in public, and she was having to see him for the first time since she had gotten naked with him with *other people* around. With his half brother around.

She was just about to back out the door when he looked up over his coffee cup and his eyes collided with hers.

"Pansy," he said. "Why don't you join us?"

"I'm on duty," she said, indicating her uniform.

And when he looked at her his eyes were full of heat. He took a leisurely tour of said uniform, and all the places it clung to her body. And it made her face hot.

"I can stay for a second," she said.

She walked over to where he sat and crossed her arms. "Aren't you going to order a drink?" he asked.

"Oh," she said.

"What do you want?" he asked.

"I usually get a Big Hunk."

"Emmett," he said, handing Emmett a five. "Can you get Officer Daniels a drink?"

To her surprise, Emmett rushed off to do just that without giving his half brother any back talk. "He likes you," West said. "Probably because you were against him going to jail."

"Oh yes," Pansy said. "I find that does tend to make a person popular."

"Why don't you sit down?"

"No," she said. "I'm not going to stay."

"I'm happy to see you," he said.

"Yeah," she said. "It's…good to see you."

"How are you?" he asked.

She ignored the feeling of pressure behind her eyes, in her throat. "Are you…asking after my health? As if you might have broken me?" She gritted her teeth to try and keep from blushing. She didn't know that would actually help to stop a person from blushing, but she had to try *something*.

But if he was going to bring it up…if he was going to try and take control of it in some way, well, she wasn't going to let that happen. She would go ahead and face it head-on, if she had to.

"It seems like the thing to do. Like the kind of thing a gentleman might do. Which I can only sort of speculate about." He shrugged. "All things considered."

"I'm fine," she said.

"Good to know. Good to know that I left you feeling… *fine*."

She looked over and saw Emmett was still standing near the counter, waiting for her drink. "It was good," she said, not quite sure of the protocol to all of this, but she knew that men had somewhat fragile egos so she supposed that she ought to tell him that it was *good* rather than *fine*.

"Oh I know it was good," he said. "Women don't come apart like that if it's not. It was good for me too. Thanks for asking."

"Oh." Well maybe his ego was healthy enough he didn't need the affirmation. And she hadn't thought it could be… less than good for men. She hadn't even wondered what he'd thought of it. Why should she, anyway? He'd had lots of sex, presumably.

It was her watershed moment. Not his.

"I hadn't been with anybody since before I went to prison." His eyes flicked over his half brother. "I just wanted you to know that." He met her eyes then, that startling blue that had captivated her from the first. Apparently it was a moment for him too. She had no idea how to process that. "It's been a long time for me, and I don't want you to think that's just something I do. It *was*. A long time ago. But then I got married. Then I went to jail. And I never wanted anybody. Until I met you."

She hadn't expected that. It made her feel…not quite like she was the only inexperienced one. It made her feel like her initial thoughts about the whole thing had been turned on their head.

Because if he had felt like she was different, then maybe it really was different. Maybe it wasn't just her being a virgin. Maybe it was true.

And all right, maybe it was a little bit sad that she wanted to think that. And Sammy would probably tell her it was a failure at being casual.

But surely, she could be casual while wanting to think that she mattered a little bit?

"I never met anyone I really wanted," she said, the words making her throat tight. She questioned herself when she said them. Questioned if she should have spoken them out loud. But she had. So it was too late to get all wound up about it.

"How?" he asked.

She floundered for a second, because she didn't really know the answer to that. Not when being with him had felt so right. So easy. When her attraction to him hadn't been something she could control. She couldn't claim any kind of superior willpower. Not when it had never been tested. She couldn't claim she'd never been around a good-looking man. Her house was a stampede of sexy cowboys at any given time.

Obviously, she was never going to look at her brothers or cousins that way. Or Logan, for that matter.

But they were friends with a host of rodeo cowboys, and Pansy had seen a lot of masculine, hot cowboys up close.

So it wasn't like there hadn't been good-looking men.

"I wear a bulletproof vest," she said.

She had meant it as a joke, but it landed somewhat serious, and she couldn't even dispute the double meaning.

He opened his mouth to say something, but then Emmett returned with her coffee.

"Here you go," he said.

"Thank you," she said. "I better go. Have a good day. Both of you."

Then she realized it was probably Emmett's first day of the school. "Oh," she said. "How was your day, Emmett?"

The kid looked stunned, and he just stared at her with his eyes wide. Then he blinked a couple of times. Hard.

"Good," he said.

"I'm glad."

She took one last look at West before turning away and heading back out the door.

But she felt like she had left a part of herself behind, and she wasn't quite sure what to do about that. Wasn't quite sure what to do with it.

But it didn't matter. Because she had a job to do.

And one thing she could not allow was for West Caldwell to become a distraction from that job.

What she really didn't want to do was to prove her past self right, and prove that she couldn't actually handle sleeping with somebody and conducting business around town.

Are you actually going to sleep with him again?

She didn't know. She didn't know if she could handle something this big, that filled her up so completely, dominating her thoughts right now. No. She could not have sex with him, have an emotional breakdown and spend half the day completely preoccupied thinking about him. And that made her sad.

But it was the way it was. And anyway, they'd both had a good time. He'd…broken his dry spell. She'd had her first time. It was good enough.

She took a sip of her coffee and looked down the main street of town.

Her town.

It was good enough.

It had to be.

CHAPTER SIXTEEN

HE HAD ONLY seen glimpses of Pansy over the last couple of days, and he really hadn't expected to see her at the community center that weekend when he showed up with Emmett. But there she was. Plain clothes and pretty wearing a gray T-shirt and a pair of blue jeans that showed off her slight curves.

Her hair was up in that ponytail that she favored.

His hands itched to take it down.

His hands itched to do a hell of a lot of things. But of course he couldn't do any of them, since she seemed to want to avoid it all. Him and everything that had happened between them. The heat and fire that had burned between them.

Hell.

He practically pushed Emmett out of the truck and he got out on his side. And when his eyes were finally able to find a resting place other than Pansy, the reason that she was there became clear.

Barbara Niedermayer was standing there with her arms crossed and a sour expression on her face.

It was clear to West that Pansy had come to run interference.

Not that one sour faced woman was going to be a problem for West. But, being civil might be. So he had a feeling it was a decent thing that the police were there to enforce civil rest. Or whatever.

"Good morning," Pansy said. "We have some tools for you right over here." She gestured broadly toward a rake, shovel and a wheelbarrow. West knew Pansy well enough to know that nothing about this tone was sincere. And he had a feeling that she was doing her best to forcefully steer the way the interaction was going to go.

He'd never met so much intent packed into such a tiny frame before.

Damned if he didn't like it. Damned if he didn't like *her*. She had started out as a burr underneath his skin and she had transformed into...well. Something. If he were a different man he might have attributed some softer feelings to it.

After that, Barbara took hold of Emmett and began to give him instruction. And that was when Pansy turned and addressed West directly for the first time. "Glad you came. Grab a shovel."

"I only saw one shovel."

"There's always an extra shovel, West." Her words were overbright and so was her smile. He didn't trust it. "We are demonstrating our commitment to the community."

"Really?"

She seemed to produce an extra shovel out of nowhere. "Really," she said, thrusting it in his direction.

That was how he found himself digging weeds out of flower beds and turning the soil, trying to get rid of the nasty plants that had taken hold and lain dormant since the previous spring. It seemed like a metaphor.

He'd never liked poetry or anything of the sort, so he chose not to dwell on it too much.

There were no answers in a flower bed. At least...none that West was interested in.

Though he cast a sidelong glance at his sidekick, who was named for a flower, and decided this was a hell of a strange situation.

"When you were in school did the other kids tease you for your name?" he asked.

She looked over at him, some strands of hair from her ponytail falling in her face. She blew them away, and shook her head, digging the shovel down deep. "Of course," she responded, looking at him like he was an idiot. "What *don't* you get teased for in school?"

"Good point," he said. And it was.

"Yes. I got teased for my name. No, it's not why I became a police officer. But yes, it is kind of a handy thing to always be packing heat when your name is Pansy."

He laughed. "I bet. I mean, I'm a cowboy named West. Insert your joke here."

"But you haven't always been a cowboy," she pointed out.

"Yeah, I basically have been," he said. "I might have worked in an office for a while, but it didn't change what I was."

Saying that seemed weird. He could see that man clearly in his mind, but it was hard for him to accept that the man was him.

That man who had left rodeo dirt and arenas behind and had gone into an office five days a week, worked on a computer at home more days than that.

For a long time he'd thought that prison was a weird time-out in his life. A moment when he had stopped being *him*.

But, truth was, he'd stopped being *him* a long time before that.

"I made money that way," he said. "I thought that's what I had to do to be happy."

"And did it make you happy?"

He chuckled and stabbed the end of the shovel into the dirt. "You know how it ends, so…no."

"What if it hadn't ended that way? Would you have kept on doing it?"

He nodded slowly. "Yeah. I would have. I had pretty much made the choice to make that my life. I mean, I married a woman who would have… She never would have accepted anything else. Still, on the weekends I was a cowboy. Not really the life I dreamed of in every way. But I had a big house. I fit in."

"What's that like?" she asked. And he saw that she was looking at him with no small amount of sincerity in her eyes.

"Terrible," he said. "If it's not the space you were meant to fit in to."

She nodded slowly. She pushed the head of her shovel down into the dirt and lifted out a weed, the roots all splayed out and crooked. Detached. Another damned metaphor.

"I've never fit," she said. "I've never fit here in my hometown. I didn't have a ton of friends in school after my parents died because I was too serious. Because no one wanted their kids to come to our house—who wants their kid going to a place where kids are raising kids? Even now, I'm trying to fill a uniform that came before me. I'm not him."

"Did it ever occur to you that maybe you don't have to be?"

She said nothing, the two of them just kept on digging.

They worked until the sun was high in the sky and they were all sweating, and to West's surprise, Barbara bought Emmett lunch.

"If you want to we can be finished. Or, you can go on to Carl's place and work a shift."

Emmett squared his shoulders. "I'm not tired."

West wasn't quite sure where the bakery was, so Pansy walked with him and Emmett down the street toward the place.

"Can I buy you a drink?"

She flashed him a suspicious look. "I don't know."

"You're off duty," he said.

"Yes," she said slowly.

"Have a drink," he said.

They walked back toward Main Street, and he could feel the tension radiating off of her in waves. He wasn't sure what the deciding factor had been that made her stay with him, since she was clearly uncomfortable.

He wondered if it had more to do with the challenge of the whole thing than anything else.

That she couldn't show him she was nervous to be around him. Because that would violate her down to her core.

When they arrived at the Gold Valley Saloon, it was fairly empty, given that it was pretty early on a Saturday. There were a few people in there having lunch, but it was not the best food place in town. People generally congregated there at night to get drunk.

Laz was there behind the counter, and he grinned when West walked in. "How's that Texas whiskey cabinet working out for you?"

"Good. Does your whiskey taste like pine yet?"

Laz laughed. "Of course not. It tastes like kale."

"A Pacific Northwest influence I could live without. I'll have a beer. And whatever the lady wants."

Pansy gave him a look that was comically prissy, considering he'd seen the woman come apart, naked and sweaty in a barn. "It's the middle of the day, so the lady will have a Coke."

"Suit yourself," West said.

"So you two are speaking to each other now," Laz said when he brought their drinks back.

"Sometimes," West said, looking at Pansy's defiant profile. "When the good officer is in the mood."

Color mounted in her cheeks, and West was just childish enough to take joy in that.

"Don't push your luck," she said, popping the top of her Coke can and taking a drink.

"Hey," Laz said. "I have another piece of furniture you might want. Down in the storage area of the museum."

The *old* museum. It was West's understanding that nothing had been in there for a few years.

He set a key on the counter. "If you want to go down and check it out, it's an old bed frame that's up against the wall in the back, behind a couple barstools, I think."

West actually needed the bed frame. Considering Emmett was sleeping on a mattress on the floor, and he hadn't fixed that yet.

"Thanks," West said. "I'll check it out."

Laz left the counter, heading to the back of the saloon.

"You're just in a furniture exchange program with him?" Pansy asked.

"He's my friend," West said.

As soon as he said it he realized that it was a little weird.

All those years in Texas, and he had never made a real friend. All of that had become evident when his life had fallen apart and people had taken a kind of ghoulish interest in the proceedings, while very few people had rallied around him. And then when he was convicted, no one had rallied anywhere.

But here… He had his family. *His family.* Weird as hell.

And there was Laz, who he'd gotten really friendly with. A few other people he saw at the bar frequently enough. Jackson and Calder Reid, who he'd had drinks with a couple of times. Though they were family men, so they didn't come out that often.

He thought back to what Pansy had asked him earlier. If he never fit in.

He wondered if this was fitting in.

Except it had required very few acrobatics, so it didn't seem right to him.

In his experience finding a place had always required that.

"Want to come with me and check out the furniture?"

She wrinkled her nose. "I don't know."

"I might get in trouble if you don't. I'm an ex-con," he said. "God knows what I'll get up to in the basement of an old building."

She rolled her eyes. "Fine. I just need to go to the bathroom first."

"Hey, do you know the deal with the names on the bathroom wall?"

She frowned. "No."

"People who have hooked up in there carve their names on it."

She blinked. *"No."*

She was scandalized, and he'd be damned if he wasn't charmed.

"Yes," he responded.

"Olivia Hollister's name is in that bathroom."

"Yeah. But look who she's married to."

He hadn't had a whole lot of interaction with Luke Hollister, but enough to know exactly what manner of man he was.

Pansy beat a hasty retreat to the bathroom but when she returned, she didn't look flustered at all.

"Okay," she said. "Let's go get your furniture. If you end up getting it you can even park in a loading zone."

"Officer," he said. "There's nothing more I'd like to do than park in a loading zone with you."

WHY WAS SHE still with him? It was a question she asked herself several times as she walked down the street with West toward the old museum building.

She could say that it was because she was curious to go poke around in the old, abandoned museum that had lost its funding several years ago and now sat as a sad storage unit for many of the town's great histories.

She could say that it was because she had nothing else to do and it was more convenient to stay with him than to walk away.

And she could say it was because she was curious to see how everything went for Emmett. But then, she could always go back in and check with Carl if she wanted to know how things went for Emmett.

No, if she was deeply honest with herself the issue was that she wanted to be with West.

She had felt a strange, gnawing sense of incompletion ever since she had…since they had…slept together. Except, the euphemism didn't really work in this case. Because they hadn't *slept* at all, they had just done something rough and hard in a barn that had taken less than an hour and had transformed the very fabric of who she was.

No big deal.

And she had rationalized staying away from him in that regard, but here she was.

She just wanted to be near him.

That she was vulnerable and predictable in that way annoyed her.

She wanted to be stronger than that.

Because life had forced her to be stronger than that.

She knew better than to idealize anything.

She wasn't the kind of person who had ever lived in a fantasy world. She had learned about the realities of life too early.

Her dream—her biggest dream—was to be police chief of her small town. And that was realistic. It was a job she was qualified for, a job she even had a dynastic pedigree for. In her world that was a dream.

There was no room for fantasies about strong, hard, scarred cowboys who were all kinds of wrong and all kinds of bad, and where they might fit into her life.

There was no room for him.

And even if there were, he wasn't the kind of man who would want there to be room for him.

He had stated that openly enough.

And now she was walking with him and brooding. Which was even worse than being with him in the first place.

The old Museum was a two-story brick building with white trim, a broad porch and an American flag waving cheerily from the top.

The building itself was still lovingly cared for, the front lawn cut and manicured. But the inside was dark, and had been for a long while.

"I think this thing is for the door down here," West said, gesturing toward the side of the building.

She walked with him toward the back, where there was a door that was much less grand than the one at the front. He took the key and stuck it into the lock, and it turned.

And for some reason Pansy felt that catch in her chest. But she ignored that. And she followed him into the dark building. They went down a set of stairs that went straight into a basement area that was surprisingly neat and tidy. Items were organized carefully into groups, and everything was spotlessly clean.

"I wonder if Barbara takes care of this," Pansy said, touching an utterly dust free rolltop desk that was pushed against one of the walls.

West huffed a laugh. "She seems like a whole thing."

That was definitely one way to put it. "She is. And it's easy for me to forget that she does care about this town, even if she is rigid and uncompromising. I tend to think of her as someone who's always trying to protect her own position. Her own power. And that's somewhat true. She wants to feel important. And because of that she doesn't really mind making other people feel...you know. But I think she's just sad and lonely. And she does do an awful lot for this town. Granted, I care a little bit more about the future of Emmett than I do about whether or not this desk stays free of dust."

West chuckled. "Yeah, I'm with you there."

West pulled his phone out of his pocket and turned the flashlight on. Pansy laughed.

"What?" he asked.

"It's just funny. Because you look like the kind of guy who would actually have a big, stalwart flashlight on them. Not a cell phone."

In his battered blue jeans, tight black T-shirt and cowboy hat, he looked like a man who had just come in from the fields, who perhaps didn't give any consideration to technology or the modern world at all.

"I like convenience," he said. He lifted the cell phone a little bit higher. "My phone before I went to prison didn't have an official flashlight on it. That was a cool modern convenience waiting for me when I got out."

There was so much buried in such a simple sentence. Time wasted, missed. Stolen.

"I'm sorry," she said.

The image of this man, this rugged man, locked away for years nearly destroyed her.

She knew the justice system was flawed. Every system had flaws, because it was run by people. But staring at someone who had suffered directly from that failure really drove the point home.

"It happened," he said. "I've come to terms with it. More or less. Well, maybe *come to terms with* is a bad way to put it. I'm not sure if I've come to terms with it. But I have figured out where to go after. That's all you can do sometimes."

"Yeah. I know that."

They moved deeper into the space and West's body felt warm and solid by her side, and she did her best to ignore it.

"I bet this is it," West said, finding a small grouping of furniture on a blank wall that matched the description that Laz had given.

Pansy maneuvered so that she was on the other side of it. "Yeah," she said. "You going to need some help carrying it?"

He looked at her, a smile playing at his lips. She could see it, even in the dim light. "You're going to help me carry these?"

"I'm strong," she said.

"I know you are," he said. "But you're small."

She frowned. "So? I can help with that."

"I might wait till Emmett is finished. No pressure."

"You're ridiculous," she said. "A fifteen-year-old boy is not stronger than me."

Suddenly, she realized that he was not looking at her face. Not at her eyes. He was looking at her mouth.

"You're small," he said. "But strong. And damn pretty."

The words felt strange. They twisted in her stomach. West was the first person she could remember calling her pretty. And before that she couldn't remember the last time she had really thought about being pretty.

She worried about her body being serviceable. Able to do its job. She didn't really worry about how she looked. And when she had taken her clothes off in front of him in the barn she hadn't given it much thought either. It had all been a frantic, crazy moment, and she hadn't been insecure about what he saw when he looked at her, but more about what might happen next.

Suddenly she cared—deeply cared—that West Caldwell thought she was pretty.

It made her own mind a stranger. Her own body out of her control.

And that was foreign. Utterly and completely.

Somehow, down here in this basement, the basement of an old museum in the town that she loved so much, she didn't even really mind.

Why was she here? She was afraid that she was here for this. For this moment. This long, steady moment that seemed to stretch endlessly in the dark. Where West was looking at her mouth and she was hoping it was a promise.

He shoved his phone into his pocket, and as soon as he was finished with that, he reached out and touched her face.

She closed her eyes, and she let the particular weakness that took over her when West touched her win.

She let him melt her bones. Let him turn her muscles into jelly.

Let him take that body that had always been about strength, and had always been about serviceability, and turn it into something that belonged to him.

She sighed. As if it was the invitation he'd been waiting for, he caught that sigh with his mouth and kissed her.

It was deep and hard and consuming. Not gentle like the previous moment had been. And she was glad. She didn't want gentle.

No.

She felt like something foreign. An entity that she didn't understand. And right now, didn't want to have to.

Because she could allow herself to get caught up in this.

No one was here. No one would know.

Except for him.

Didn't he already know her secrets? That a man had never touched her until him. Didn't he already know what her body looked like, and what sounds she made?

Didn't he already know that he could make her mindless?

That she felt like she didn't fit anywhere. That sometimes she felt alone.

West already knew all those things, so she didn't have to be afraid.

He had already seen her weakness.

And he was the only one.

What harm was there and letting him see it again?

It was why she had been here. From the beginning.

She could admit that now. Now that his lips were consuming hers. Now that his tongue was sliding against hers, delving deep, and his rough hands were moving over her body, large and calloused, spanning her waist with ease.

He made being small feel *good*.

When before, if it had been anything to her it had only been a detraction. Because she wanted to be a police officer, and you didn't exactly inspire fear in people when you weren't halfway over five foot.

But West, broad and muscular and over six feet tall, made her frame feel lovely. Like it had been created to fit against his. Like she was made to fit right into his arms.

He made her feel like her softness existed to complement his hardness. And there was so much *hard* about this man.

She let herself touch all of it.

His chest, his body lived in her dreams every night. The way that he looked. The way that it had felt to touch that hot skin, those hard packed muscles. That perfect amount of body hair over the top of them.

He was a *man*.

And he made her feel glad to be a *woman* in ways that she had never been aware of before.

He made her understand why that difference was a mystery meant to be untangled without clothes on. Made her understand why being around a pack of large cowboys all of her life didn't really mean anything in terms of being accustomed to men like that.

Because this was a whole different thing. A whole different intimacy. A whole different reason for noticing the differences between men and women.

Before it was that they were tall. That they smelled after a hard day's work. That they weren't afraid to take up space or leave their muddy boots all over.

But now it was about bodies. About the way his sigh

sounded deep and heavy when she pushed her hands up underneath his shirt.

The way he went tense and hard when she licked his lips.

The way he got hard between his legs.

About the square cut of his jaw and the feel of his whiskers under her palm.

About how strength could be overwhelming and controlled at the same time. How she could feel with his every touch that he could easily overwhelm her, and also feel that he was choosing not to.

With that strength, he moved his hands down to her hips and maneuvered her up against the wall, her shoulder blades pressing against that hard surface.

She didn't want to think.

She didn't want to do the right thing.

She didn't want to be responsible.

Life had taken so many things from her.

Why couldn't she have this? This moment of insanity.

This moment that was almost certainly against the law.

For *some reason* that thought only spurred her on. Made her more excited. When West pushed his hand up her shirt, underneath her sports bra and cupped her bare breasts, so that she could feel his rough fingertips moving over her nipple, she gasped, her internal muscles clenching. She was so close to the edge. Just with that.

He teased her for a moment, but didn't strip her clothes off her. Then he undid the button on her jeans and pressed his hand down beneath the fabric, beneath her panties. And he found her, wet and slick and ready for him.

She might have been embarrassed another time. To let him know how much she wanted him.

But this was about her.

Her gift from the universe after she had received blessed little for all these years.

Her due.

West Caldwell and his magic hands were compensation for a life spent lonely.

And she was going to revel in it.

His fingers were magic, and he brought her to the edge, and then tipped her over. She was shocked how easily.

It was never this easy at home alone with her own hands, though heaven knew she was experienced enough with it. You didn't get to be a twenty-seven-year-old virgin without figuring out how to deal with yourself.

But with his hands, she didn't have control. With his hands, she didn't get to choose *when*.

And that made it feel exhilarating. Exciting.

And then, he was pushing her jeans and panties down, midway down her thighs, and he had opened the front of his own jeans, taking his wallet out of his back pocket and quickly sliding a condom over himself.

And then, with West, hot and hard in front of her and the wall uncompromising and cold behind her, he pushed himself in deep.

This felt different than when she had been on top of him on the couch.

It took her breath away.

It didn't hurt like it had done the first time, but she still felt full. Stretched. Like she couldn't breathe for how deeply he had buried himself inside of her.

This time, it was his ride. His rhythm.

Hard and magical and filthy. Dirty.

Bad.

Everything she had not to be for so long. But she gave

it all up. Her perfection. Her ideas of what she had to do and who she had to be.

She surrendered it all to West.

He grabbed her wrists and pinned them up against the wall, and rode her hard, his mouth firm against hers, then skimming over her jaw, her neck. And impossibly she felt her orgasm begin to build inside of her again.

She clung to him, to his shoulders, as ripples of pleasure moved through her body. She buried her head in his chest and cried out, and then he followed, and she could feel him, pulsing inside of her as he found his own release. His heart hammered hard beneath her forehead.

His breathing uneven.

It was the same.

It was the same for him. This magic explosion of color and sensation was something that he felt too. But as soon as it was finished, as soon as the pleasure started to recede, she felt lost.

And that was terrifying.

"I…"

She pushed him away. She started to straighten her clothes desperately. "I have to go," she said.

"Do you?" he responded, straightening his own self and hunting around for a trash can.

She put her hands over her face. "You can't get rid of that here."

"Where else am I going to get rid of it?"

He discarded the protection then. In that wastebasket and she felt…panicked.

"*We* went down *here*."

"And if someone hunts through the trash can and they figure it out that's their problem."

She did not feel that sanguine about it.

She felt exposed.

Like her weakness was just out there for everyone to see. For him to see.

It had been all fine and good to think that was okay while she had been mindless with pleasure.

But her mind had been returned to her.

She sort of wish it hadn't been.

"Well, you didn't think you needed my help to move any of this anyway. So I'm going to go."

She ran. It was even worse than the first time. She was such…she was such a baby. And she didn't know how to handle any of this. She didn't know what to do with herself.

She walked blindly to her car, trying to hold back tears, because the last thing she needed was for people to say that they saw Officer Pansy Daniels weeping openly on the streets of Gold Valley.

That would do wonders for rumors about her mental stability. And…and…everything else.

When she got in her car, to keep from crying, she called Sammy.

"Are you guys around?"

"Yes. Iris and I are making cookies."

"What about Rose?"

"She's working. But…she should be in for lunch soon."

"Are Ryder and Logan there?" Anywhere near Hope Springs, that's what she should have made clear. Not just in the house. She didn't want them anywhere near when she arrived. She didn't even want to see them. Couldn't stand looking them in the face.

"No. They're off getting a new load of cattle."

"I'll be right over."

Maybe she would regret it. But she regretted a whole

lot of things that she had just done, and she needed to sort it all out.

Clearly, she couldn't trust herself to sort through anything.

BY THE TIME Pansy arrived at Hope Springs Ranch Iris, Rose and Sammy were all waiting for her, along with a plate of cookies, a tall pitcher of lemonade and an unidentified cake.

"I didn't know there was cake," Pansy said.

"It sounded like it might be a cake situation," Sammy said, pushing it in Pansy's direction.

"Well, cake is always appreciated." Food was a way Iris and Sammy showed they cared, and Pansy was very into that sort of caring.

"I know," Sammy said. "But to be clear, you sounded like you really needed cake."

"I don't know what that means," she said.

"You had that sound in your voice. Like you were in the middle of a crisis that can only be solved by buttercream."

"That's any number of crises," Iris said, "in fairness."

"Sure. But I'm wondering if this particular crisis wears a Stetson and saunters around broad shouldered and in possession of large hands," Sammy said.

Rose's eyes went wide. *"Does it?"* she asked, her voice going almost supersonic.

"Yes," Pansy said, keeping her voice sure and solid.

Like a criminal bent on confessing.

Because again, she was the one that had come here. She was the one that was submitting herself to this torture, and she couldn't really figure out why. Most of her wanted to run and hide from it. Most of her wanted to pretend that none of this was happening. But... It was. It was, and she wasn't handling it well on her own. Not at all. She had now had sex with the man in two very unconventional places. And she didn't know what to make of that. What to make of herself. What to do with herself.

"It's okay," Sammy said, keeping her voice knowing and authoritative.

"You don't *know* it's okay," Iris said.

Sometimes Pansy thought that Iris might find Sammy's intrusiveness a little bit irritating. They weren't far apart in age, but because Sammy had imprinted on Ryder, Sammy identified more with the way he treated all of them. But Iris was the older sister to Pansy and Rose. And sometimes Sammy took that spot.

"It… I don't know," Pansy said.

Rose was looking at her beseechingly, and she had a feeling that what Rose was beseeching for was physical details and not any kind of emotional update. Iris, she knew, would be concerned with her emotional state.

"I… I had sex with him," Pansy said.

A whole lot of movement happened at once. Rose slammed her hands down on the table, Iris seemed to shrink in on herself. And Sammy wrapped her soft arms around Pansy, bringing her fragrant scent into Pansy's orbit.

"That's good," Sammy said at the same time Iris said, "Are you sure you're okay?"

"I'm fine," Pansy said. "But I'm not exactly ready to wave a flag or celebrate it."

"Why not?" Sammy asked. "You lost your virginity. Which, frankly is a social construct, and not something that you should be worried about anyway."

"It felt like a construct of my hymen at the time," Pansy said, her tone dry.

Iris winced. Rose looked wide-eyed and bemused.

"You know what I mean," Sammy said. "You don't

need to be ashamed of your sexuality just because you're a woman. Do you think any of the guys in this house swan around feeling concerned about how many women they've slept with? About where it might be going when they do? No," she continued. "They don't, because they are blessedly free of those kinds of societal expectations."

"The thing about societal expectations," Iris said, her tone stern, "is that when you violate them it does tend to be noticed. Because they are societal expectations."

"Who cares?" Sammy asked, lifting her hands and turning back toward the oven in a swirl of skirts and blond hair.

"Says the woman who lives in a caravan."

"Yes," Sammy said, turning and glaring pointedly at Iris. "I do. I gaily choose to defy social norms. It makes me happy. And ultimately, that is the point. You should make yourself happy. Because there's no guarantee that there's going to be a future. You of all people should know that."

Rose scowled. "Don't talk about the life lessons we should have learned from our parents dying. Your parents are across the field and you don't know how to have a conversation with them."

Pansy's stomach tightened. She didn't know the whole story about Sammy and her parents, but she never would have gone there.

"Some things are more complicated than you might think, Rose," Sammy said.

Pansy looked from Iris to Rose to Sammy. She would have expected an explosion somewhere along the chain except... Sammy just would never let it get there.

Iris would probably gladly duke it out. Rose would happily start *or* finish any fight. But Sammy never would. She would contort and twist and dance around the expected fight.

It was just who she was. She liked things soft and easy. Diffused. It was nice to have her here as a counterbalance to Iris, who was far too practical.

But who also probably had a better grasp on how Pansy actually felt.

And essentially, Pansy wanted both reactions. She wanted Iris to slap her upside the head and tell her to quit being stupid. And she wanted Sammy to tell her that she wasn't being all that stupid after all. And she wanted Rose to be in awe of her, because *somebody* should be. Because she'd *had* sex in a barn, and then again in the basement of the museum. A public building. And that was a whole lot more daring than she had ever imagined she might be.

"How do you feel about it?" Sammy asked, clearly deciding to take a different tack.

"I've lost my mind," Pansy said. "That's how I feel. I'm always controlled. Always. And suddenly, there's West Caldwell, and I do really ridiculous things. Stupid things. Incredibly stupid things. Like suddenly attacking him physically in his barn and losing my virginity to him. Like… like meeting with him in town and going down into the basement of the old museum together."

"Are you sleeping with him or are you on an episode of *Scooby-Doo* with him?" Rose asked.

Pansy glared at Rose. "Can you not mock my nervous breakdown?"

"I'm your little sister. I feel like mocking your nervous breakdown is basically my function."

"This isn't like me," Pansy said. "You should all yell at me and tell me that it's out of character. Check my pupils. See if I'm on drugs."

"*Are* you on drugs?" Iris asked.

"*No.*"

"Well, I'm not going to tell you that there's anything wrong with what you've done," Sammy said, resolute. "It might be good for you to do something out of character. Because it might be good for you to experience this, and experiment in this way. Because who am I to tell you that your choices are wrong? Anyway. It doesn't much matter. If it doesn't work out, you move on. And you chalk it up to experience."

She had no idea how she was supposed to chalk up something so intimate as having another human being inside of her body to *experience*.

She had no idea how she was ever going to erase the memory of West's hands burning over her skin. Of how vulnerable it made her feel to know that she had come apart in his arms like that. That he had seen her that way. Sammy didn't understand. She didn't understand how exposed she felt. How utterly and completely raw.

The first time the newness of it all had protected her in a way. She'd been able to let herself be consumed by how foreign it was to be intimate in that way physically.

This time, it had been…different. That she'd wanted it again knowing how it was, how intense, how all consuming, made it different. And rather than being able to shield herself even more, she'd been less able to do so.

West had reached down into parts of herself that she hadn't even known existed. And while she had been gasping and panting against him, he had been witnessing a moment of self-discovery that she was almost embarrassed to have witnessed herself.

How was she supposed to go on with her life knowing that that man was wandering around the earth knowing those things about her? How was she supposed to erase what it looked like when he lost his own control from her head? That moment when his face contorted with pleasure and he... *How?*

"Look, it always feels like a big deal at first," Sammy said. "And I know that I said it wasn't a big deal. It isn't. I think someone needs to say that to you. Because it really doesn't have to be. So whatever it is in you that's telling you that you need to make it a big deal because you're trying to be a good girl, or whatever, banish that. But whatever *emotions* are telling you it feels like a big deal, you can embrace those."

Iris snorted. "You don't make any sense. She feels bad, it was a big deal for her. End of story. Her feelings don't have anything to do with it really. Which ones you trust and which ones you discard. What's society, what's her. What does it matter? She feels like crap."

"I don't know," Pansy said. And suddenly, a realization washed over her, all warm and perfect. "I don't feel bad," she continued. "And that's part of what confuses me. I really quite enjoyed myself. I really did. I liked being with him. And... Today I put myself in his path in hopes that it would happen again. I can't deny it. As much as I would like to. But I don't know what to do. I don't know what to do from here."

"Have sex with him again?" Sammy asked.

"If she feels bad how's that going to help?" Iris rounded on Sammy.

"I don't know," Sammy said. "In my experience sex can make you feel a whole lot better."

"And then it makes you confused," Pansy said. "And makes you feel like you're a stranger unto yourself."

"Does it?" Rose asked, round eyed.

"I had sex with him in the museum."

"Oh my gosh," Iris said. "You didn't. I bet that's against the law."

"I know," Pansy said. "I'm sure we violated laws. Decency laws. I am always decent, I am never in violation of laws. Never. And yet… I am. And I kind of didn't hate it. I think what scares me most isn't that I did it with him, it's that I liked it. It's not even that I'm acting out of character, it's that I want to embrace the fact that I'm out of character. I don't know who I am. I'm not sure I care."

"Good," Sammy said. "Have an affair with him. Have a wild, amazing physical only affair with him. Have sex with him in strange places, break rules."

"I am trying to get a job as police chief. I have a ton of things on my plate. It is the worst time in the world for me to try to have…a life. I can have a life later. I can have a life when everything is settled. But I can't have a life now."

"No, the reason you're having a mental breakdown is because you left having a life for way too long. The first hot cowboy you see, and you jump on him."

"That isn't true," Pansy said. "There are hot cowboys around here all the time."

Sammy laughed. "Well, Ryder is your brother."

"And he's your best friend," Pansy said.

"But I'm not blind," Sammy said.

"He has some pretty hot friends, too," Pansy said.

Sammy waved a hand. "Whatever. My point is, the reason that you're losing it and having sex with him in semi-public places is because you never lost it on a milder scale. Give in to this. Give in to this for your health. If you don't, I fear that it's going to turn you into a full-scale nymphomaniac and you're going to start jumping every rodeo guy that comes through town. Maybe on Main Street."

Pansy rolled her eyes. What Sammy was saying was so ridiculous she didn't even find it embarrassing.

"Okay. But seriously, you really think that I should keep doing this?"

Because as ridiculous as Sammy seemed, she wasn't wrong. Maybe the reason this was all so difficult was because she had never done it before. Maybe she was just so very overdue, and the combination of that and the stress at work had made her...well, sex crazed.

"Sure," Sammy said. "It's safe."

"How is it safe to have sex with a man in the museum?" Iris asked.

"Well, technically it was the museum basement."

"A basement," Iris said. "How is *that* safe?"

"Well, in the sense that no one is going to go into it because it's closed, and only certain people have keys... I guess it's safe?" Pansy asked.

"This is ridiculous," Iris said.

"Also we used a condom," Pansy said, flat affect. "So. Safe in that way too."

Iris made a small gasping noise and Sammy smirked.

"It's kind of badass," Rose said. "And why not? You know, all those guys who carved their names in the bathrooms at the Gold Valley Saloon... You should carve your name in the museum basement."

"Am I the only one who didn't know people do that?" Pansy asked.

"Yes," Iris, Sammy and Rose said in unison.

"Well. *I didn't.* And I'm not carving my name anywhere. But maybe...maybe you're right. Maybe it's time for me to cut loose. Just with him. And then I can still get my job, and everything will be okay. But I can... I can be a little crazy. In a controlled environment." She snapped her fingers. "It's like a controlled burn. A controlled burn so that there doesn't end up being a whole giant wildfire. Forestry management. Lust management."

Sammy nodded sagely. "Yes. Yes."

"Controlled burns require experts," Iris said. "Otherwise things get out of control."

"Well," Pansy said. "West is an expert. So I'm just going to have to trust him."

"Trusting the ex-con cowboy?"

"He didn't do it," she said.

Rose shook her head. "You've become a cowboy apologist."

"Well, are you going to be mad at me if I do this?" she asked, directing that question to Iris. Iris looked at her for a long moment, and something in her face reminded Pansy of their mother. Or maybe it didn't. Maybe she didn't really know. Maybe she was being silly. Maybe she was misremembering. Maybe it was just what she thought maternal might look like. Maybe it wasn't their own mother she saw at all. But it still made her think of her. And it made her feel morose.

"I'm not mad," Iris said. "I just worry about you."

She got up from her chair and went and embraced her sister. "I know you do," she said. "You don't have to."

"I know you're a police officer and all, Pansy. And I know that you've been through your share of trauma, and you don't need me to hold your hand. But… I want to."

"And I want to push you out of the nest," Sammy said. "But if you're not ready yet… I'm not going to be mad."

"I don't care what you do," Rose said. "I'm just going to put it out there right now."

"Thanks, Rose," Pansy said.

Her sister was being funny but Pansy's throat was tight.

She might not get to have this moment with her mom, but she had them. These wonderful women who wanted different things, lived life in different ways and loved her.

She loved them too.

They didn't need to be alike, they just needed love. Acceptance. And they had that. Pansy had never really done anything that might test those bonds. She had grown into someone decidedly uncontroversial.

Until this week.

And still she'd known she could talk to them.

She'd been right.

"You're welcome."

"Why not do it?" Sammy asked. "You're already in. Might as well jump in all the way."

She still felt so raw. So fragile. But somehow this all made her feel better. Giving it a reason. Giving it a name. That she'd been looking for a place to be wild while all else stayed orderly. It made her feel less like she was losing her mind.

She looked at the three women that she called sisters. "Thank you," she said.

Her family might not look like very many other people's families. But she had a wonderful family.

And whatever she decided to do about West, she had never appreciated her family more.

CHAPTER SEVENTEEN

CONSIDERING THE WAY that Pansy had run away from him, West's primary concern when he got back to the homestead was that he check on her.

Everything had gone well for Emmett at the bakery. West was impressed with the way Carl dealt with his half brother. He gave him just the right amount of responsibility while offering a certain amount of guidance. It was just what a young boy in Emmett's situation needed. He didn't need to be treated like a kid, no, that ship had sailed.

He still was a kid, though. A kid who'd had to grow up too fast with no guide on how to do it.

But he had grown up in a household with a mother who had never treated him like he needed to be nurtured. Offering it suddenly now would seem strange. Backward. Because he had never, ever been given anything like that in the past. Not when he had needed it more. And he had grown hard and tough in the intervening years, and he needed to be given the respect that he had earned by still being here.

West understood that, because it had been his experience.

Emmett was exhausted by the time they got back to the house. They had gotten a take and bake pizza from the store, and he had put Emmett in charge of baking it and had made no pretense about the fact that he was going to find Pansy. Because Emmett had assumed they were sleeping together anyway. And he was sure his brother hadn't believed their denial. So given that it was true now, West didn't see the point of pretending it wasn't.

He grabbed a beer out of his fridge, then another, and went out the front door, and down the porch, down the well-worn path that led to Pansy's cabin. When he got there, he knocked on the door.

It took a moment, but then it cracked open and he saw one suspicious dark eye looking up at him.

"I came to check on you," he said.

"I'm here," she said. "And I'm whole."

"Proof required."

She opened the door a bit farther, and revealed that she was in fact intact. "A relief," he said.

"Did you think that I had been eaten by wolverines?"

"Not eaten. Maybe just gnawed on a little bit."

Her eyes narrowed. "I don't want to be gnawed on by wolverines."

"Who does?"

"Someone *probably* does. If there's one thing I've learned in my line of work it's that people are weird. So trust me, someone, somewhere out there, really wants to be chewed on by a wolverine. And will probably film it. And upload it to the internet for other people to watch."

"The world is weird," he said.

"No argument from me."

"You ran away," he said.

She drew up to her full height. Which wasn't that impressive. "No I didn't. I went to visit my sisters."

"You ran away from me," he repeated.

She kept her posture, all stiff and huffy. "Well. OK. Fine. Maybe I did."

Her eyes met his and his stomach went tight. What had

happened between them earlier today was burned into him. Every touch from Pansy Daniels was burned into him. Sunk down beneath his skin. He couldn't begin to understand it. Couldn't begin to understand the madness that took over him when her lips touched his. And he wasn't sure that he wanted to understand it. Wasn't sure what was required. It was a good thing, just to be lost in it. Just to be held captive by the excitement.

It was a kind of dirty magic he hadn't known he'd wanted.

"Did I hurt you?"

She shook her head. "No."

He reached out and brushed his knuckles over her cheek, the intensity of the impact of that soft skin against the back of his fingers shocking him. "I don't want to hurt you," he said.

He wanted her and no mistake. But he needed her to know exactly who he was. Exactly what he was. Because he couldn't stand the idea of fooling her, even unintentionally.

If she was hurt as a result of what happened between them it wouldn't be because of his lack of honesty.

"I'm... I went and I played the part of slick sophisticate for a while, but it's not me. I'm a lot closer to the man I was in prison than I am to the man who works in an office five days a week. I'm burned-out. I want to start over, but I don't want that life. Not again."

"That's your way of telling me you don't want to get married."

He nodded his head. "Yeah, basically."

"Right. West, I don't want to get married. But I also... I don't understand what's happening between us. And I don't mean that in the sense of wanting to know where it's going. It has nothing to do with you, actually. It has everything to do with me."

He didn't know how he felt about that statement. He would like for this to have something to do with him a little bit. Because whatever was happening to him… It had something to do with her. She was the one that had been a virgin. Not him.

He had plenty of experience. He knew how to separate sexual desire from actual feelings.

What he was feeling right now was a disruptive level of sexual desire, it was true. But it wasn't feelings.

"I've always followed the rules," she said. Then she closed her eyes. "I haven't always followed the rules. I… I was so bad when I was a kid. I just felt like there was something wild inside of me trying to get out all the time. And I had so much energy and I didn't know what to do with it."

Looking at her, it made sense. She had a lot of hard packed muscle that suggested she spent a frequent amount of time being active. Even now.

She looked down and continued, "When I wanted something… I couldn't help myself. I just took it. I took it because I wanted it. I would steal cookies when they were being saved for a bake sale. And stick my finger in a birthday cake. My parents would get so frustrated with me. Especially my dad. He would say that there are rules set out for us for a reason. And I just…" She met his gaze. "I didn't care, West. I didn't care. All I cared about was feeling good. The day that my parents left for their Alaska trip I ended up eating half the brownies my mom made to bring with them. She wasn't that angry, but my dad… I ran away. I ran away and I hid. I didn't say goodbye to them. And I can still hear him in my head yelling for me. And telling me…that I was bad."

He could sense the enormity of the emotion, vibrating beneath her skin. But her eyes were dry. Her expression stoic. "And then they died. They died on their way to Alaska. The plane went down… My mom and dad, Logan's mother, Colt and Jake's mother and father, they were gone. We were all left alone. And the last thing that my father thought about me was that I was bad. I just wanted to fix it. That's all I've ever wanted. Was to find a way to be good. So that the biggest thing I was…wasn't a disappointment. Wasn't bad. And I've done that. I never drank underage. Even now, I keep it to one beer, one beer just like he did. I have this job. I want to be police chief. And this…this thing between you and me is not like me. It's not like me at all. And I don't know what to do about that. Maybe it's okay. Maybe…"

She looked at him full-on, her eyes meeting his. "Maybe I can just misbehave with you."

The words hit him funny. Because he didn't know how he felt about being a little something bad for this good girl. But then, he was who he was. It wasn't set in stone, he supposed, but it was just the truth of it. The truth of him, the truth of her.

"What if what we're doing isn't so bad?" he asked.

He leaned down and he kissed her. Pressing his mouth gently to hers. He was used to things erupting between them. He was used to fire and passion and heat. But this was different. It was just a slow, sweet taste of her lips. And damn was she sweet.

She whimpered, and shifted against him, pressing her mouth harder to his, but he resisted. He kept it gentle, kept it soft.

"No," she protested. "That's not how I want it."

"Too damned bad," he said. "You'll take it how I give it."

"This is supposed to be my rebellion."

"But it's my redemption, baby," he said. "My first

woman since prison. Don't I get what I want too?" He abandoned her mouth, peppering kisses over her jaw, down her neck. "I can't stay," he whispered.

"Then why did you do that?" she asked, shivering restlessly beneath his touch.

"Because I wanted you to know how beautiful I think you are. How hard it is for me to keep my hands off you. You should know that."

"I don't need to hear things like that," she said, looking up at him with ferocity. "I'm tough. I've had to be. Don't go getting all…sappy on me. Or gentle. Do you think it's an accident that I wanted to have you in…those places?"

"Okay," he said. "So what you're saying is you don't want a bed. You don't want gentle. You want to be on couches and against walls. You want to be out in the barn. Surrounded by all the trappings of ranch life. Those riding crops. You know, I had a thought about one of those riding crops. And how I might use it on that ass of yours."

The color in her cheeks went crimson, but to his surprise, she didn't look disgusted so much as angrily intrigued.

"Whatever you dish out," she said, "I can take it."

Except he had a feeling that wasn't true. He had a feeling that she was trying to make this affair into something very specific because she absolutely *couldn't* handle everything. She had decided that he was a rebellion and she was comfortable with that in her way. But anything else? No, it was anything else that seemed to scare his stalwart officer.

"You don't have to be tough all the time," he said. "You don't have to be brave."

"Yes I do," she said. "I absolutely do. Because the world is going to do what it does, and no one can go through it for me. It just…is. You know. That's how it is."

"You could let me," he said. "You could let me share some of it."

"We don't have that kind of relationship."

"Not in a romantic sense," he said, "but we do have a relationship. You've helped me with Emmett. And I'm damned appreciative. If there's something going on with you, if you feel stressed or anything like that about the police chief position…well, you can talk to me."

She looked up at him like she would rather bite his face than take his comfort.

"I'll see you tomorrow," he said.

"Maybe I'll be busy tomorrow," she said.

She looked so resolute and stubborn, and he might have laughed if looking at her didn't make his gut so tight. Didn't make him hard.

"I don't think so," he said.

"Why not?"

"Because I'm your rebellion. Because you've decided. And I don't think you ever back down on what you've decided, Pansy Daniels."

She gave him a look that seemed to grudgingly say that he was right.

"I've gotta go see to Emmett. You know, I had a thought," he said. "What you were saying about deciding to be good even though it was hard for you. I think there's some kids at the school that would maybe benefit from hearing your story."

She huffed a laugh. "Except didn't I also just make it clear I'm maybe not balanced in that regard?"

"Maybe. But neither are they. It might be inspiring to hear your story." He paused for a moment. "But for what it's worth… I didn't know your dad. And I don't know much of anything about your childhood but the way that you all took care of each other when you needed it, the way you rallied around each other, I think you were raised with a pretty strong sense of family. I don't think your dad thought you were bad. Not really. He might have worried about you, your behavior, but I don't think he thought that."

"How would you know? Your parents weren't anything like mine."

"I know," he said. "But there was a time when I thought I might want to have children. I did get married thinking that. That I might be a father. And when I had that thought, well, I thought about what it actually meant to be a father. I didn't have an example of one, so I really had to ask myself what I thought it should mean. So. For what it's worth, the hypothetical opinion of a man who thought once that he might've had children, but now has no plans to, I think this is the kind of role model stuff kids need."

"Well. Sorry but that's not the most encouraging thing."

"I never am to you. Until I am. And then I'm a whole big problem aren't I, Officer Daniels?"

"You better see to Emmett."

He had to. Because if he was here for another moment then he was going to take her into his arms and kiss her. Then he was going to end up staying the night. He was going to end up giving her exactly what she said she wanted. Hard and rough in a thousand different ways. And he would do that. He would. But whether it was because he was a contrary bastard or for some other reason, he was now obsessed with the idea of having Pansy Daniels in a bed. Wrapped in a blanket, wrapped in his arms.

Slow and sweet.

"Good night," he said. She tilted her face up toward him, like she was expecting a kiss. He looked at her for a long moment. "I didn't think you wanted anything gentle from me."

Her eyes fell. "I don't," she said.

He felt like an ass. And that was a strange thing too. That she had the ability to make him feel bad when she was the one who'd gone issuing challenges. It wasn't his fault if she went badgering him and he set about to put an end to it.

He should be glad she wanted something he'd denied her.

He found he just wanted to give to her.

"Good night then."

Then he turned and walked out of the cabin, leaving Pansy behind. And for some reason he had the terrible feeling that he had left part of himself behind as well.

PANSY COULDN'T HELP but feel that even though the other night had been meant to be about her good girl emancipation, she had somehow come out behind West.

If it were a contest. Or a race. She didn't think it was really either but she didn't know what it was, and it all left her feeling unsettled.

She didn't know quite how that had happened, and she was still stewing about it while she sat at her desk at the police station the next day.

"Phone call for you," Officer Martinez said from the back.

She nodded, then picked up her line.

"Good morning," came the gravelly, husky voice on the other end.

"I'm at work," she said.

"I'm here too," he said, and just as he did, he walked into the doors of the police station.

She hung the phone up clumsily. "What are you doing

here?" she mouthed more than asked as he made his way past reception and toward her desk.

"I just got done at the ranch. The Dalton ranch. I dropped Emmett off for the day and spent a little bit of time with my brothers. And I wanted to come talk to you before I went back home."

"I'm at work," she said again. Realizing that she sounded lame.

"Yes," he said. "That is how I found you."

"Okay," she said. "That's a good point. But obviously you couldn't have found me if I wasn't where you knew I would be." She frowned. "Do you know my work schedule?"

"I'm learning it."

There was an intensity to those blue eyes she thought she shouldn't like. But she did. It made her whole body feel tight, on edge. And she should dislike that feeling too. But she didn't.

"I have another interview today. Last one before the final."

"And you're telling me subtly that you don't want me here?"

"Was that subtle?"

"No," he said. "Not really. But then, you're not a subtle kind of girl, and I like that."

"What's that supposed to mean?"

"It means exactly what you think it means. Also. You're at work. You probably shouldn't flirt with me."

"I am not flirting with you. Do you need me to write you a ticket to prove that point?"

"Honey," he said, leaning a little bit closer, keeping his voice low. "You were flirting with me every time you wrote me a ticket. Don't pretend otherwise."

She felt breathless. It was difficult to think. When he was standing there above her, looking so tall and large, and like the most rock-solid bad decision a girl could possibly make.

And she had decided that he was *her* bad decision. Last night he had talked about riding crops, and then he had kissed her so gently. Today, she wanted to drag him back to the locker room—the women's locker room that only she used—and have her way with him. More than just about anything. Right on the job. She wanted him to strip off her uniform and…

Well, maybe she didn't really want him to strip off her uniform, because all things considered it wasn't that sexy.

The harsh and terrible truth was that her belt buckle was Velcro. And the idea of him undoing her Velcro belt seemed a bit anticlimactic. Then there was all the work of dealing with her flak jacket. Yeah, no, she didn't actually want him to strip her naked at work.

Of course, if he did…

It would be wrong. So *very* wrong…

She squeezed her eyes shut angrily for a moment, an extended blink where she wasn't looking at West Caldwell, and righted herself.

"I'm actually just about to go out and do my rounds."

"Can I do a ride along?"

She opened her mouth and closed it. She really didn't have a good reason that he couldn't.

"There's normally protocol for that."

"Yeah, but is it a problem if I do?"

She knew the general rules about it at the Gold Valley Police Department, and no. There wasn't an issue.

"Before your interview," he said. "Just for a little while. Come on, Pansy. I only ever get to see what you do when you're writing me a ticket."

"Fine," she said. She breezed past him, past Martinez and past the receptionist without looking at any of them. Because if she did then she knew that she was going to see that they were gaping at West. And she didn't need to be dealing with that. With speculation. Because she wasn't going to be able to hold up to speculation. Not when that speculation was true, and likely even more salacious than the speculation was.

They headed toward the police car, and he opened the passenger door, then stopped. "I haven't actually been in one of these when I wasn't sitting in the back."

She would have said something disdainful, but it just made her heart clench tight. And all of her frustration with him seemed to dissolve. He was making a joke, but she felt... She was angry.

Angry that he'd had years of his life taken from him. Angry that he had been painted as something he absolutely wasn't. A man who would steal money. A man who would show such disregard for what other people had built with their own hands. If there was one thing that West seemed to hold sacred it was hard work. And he was...he was incredibly respectful of it. Of hers. He seemed to actually care quite a bit about her job.

And he had been concerned about it when he thought that Emmett and his situation might impact on her. About what Barbara might do. He would never have taken money someone else had worked for. She knew that.

She swallowed hard, then sank into the driver's seat. He followed suit, settling into the passenger's seat and buckling up. She started the car and pulled out of the parking lot, turning right and heading toward Main. She stopped at the cross street, with her right blinker on, waiting for her opportunity to turn. It didn't take long.

Rush hour through Gold Valley was usually the result of ten cars getting backed up behind a tractor.

"So, what do your rounds include?" he asked.

"I do a circuit of the whole town. Go to the outskirts. Some days I park for a while, I'm not above being a speed trap. Especially not on the road that heads up to the lake and the beaches. On the weekends especially people get silly, and they drink. The very worst part of my job is having to tell someone that their son or daughter isn't coming home because they went out with friends, drank too many beers on the beach and hit a tree. So I'm pretty vigilant about monitoring all of that, especially in the summer."

He looked at her, hard. She kept her eyes on the road, on the yellow center line, but she could still feel him. The intensity as he looked at her profile. "I never thought about that part of the job."

She pulled her lips tight. "It's not a fun part."

"Who told you that your father was dead?"

Tension crept up her spine. "I was asleep," she said, "when Chief Doering came to the door."

West nodded slowly. "He's your boss now, isn't he?"

"Yes," she said. "He is. My dad was his boss, his mentor. He loved him. He really did. I remember… I heard that someone was there, and I got out of bed. I saw that it was Chief Doering, and I knew him, so I started coming down the stairs so that I could say hi, even though I thought it was strange." The whole scene was tilted and fuzzy in her memory, but some pieces of it were so sharp and clear it felt like she was living them now. She thought she might have seen it that way even then. That the reality of the moment had faded in and out. But she couldn't be sure.

"He said they were all gone. We were all there at the house, because we were all staying together while our parents went on that trip. I just remember... Ryder made a sound that I've never heard another person make before. Short and guttural. Like he'd been shot. And then he looked over his shoulder and saw me. And everything in him went straight and rigid. And he never shed a tear, not in front of me. He never made another sound like that. He told me to come down the stairs. I don't remember anything else."

"Nothing?" he asked, his voice rough.

"No. It's like I woke up two days later. But I don't think I did. I think I was awake that couple of days. I just don't remember them. It's all right. I don't really want to."

"Does it bring it back? When you have to go and tell someone?"

"Yes," she said. "And for a while I thought that it wasn't really fair that I had to live that out over and over again. But gradually, I've realized that there was no one better to deliver news like that. Because I've had that visit. I've experienced loss like that. That unexpected, jarring kind. The kind you think happens to other people and never to you. And you know, I never get used to it, but I realize that whether or not I'm the one to deliver the news, tragedy will happen. And I can at least be for someone what Roger Doering was for me. What he was for us. He was stalwart, even though it hurt him. And I admire that. You know the streets of Gold Valley aren't mean at all, but the roads are a bitch. Every year we lose way too many people. And that's...just part of my job."

"It's a crime," he said. "The way the world steals innocence from people who deserve to hang on to it for a little while longer."

A smile tugged at the corner of her mouth. "I'm pretty sure you're the one who stole my innocence."

He chuckled, and he didn't challenge her, but they both

knew it wasn't true. The world had taken it from her a whole lot sooner than he had. He had just taken her virginity.

"You don't have time to see to a little bit of personal police business, do you?"

She frowned. "Personal police business? What does that mean?"

"In that it's somewhat personal to me, as it's kind of a favor," he said. "But I do think that it would mean a lot if you would come and talk to those boys. I know that you believe in a sense of community. I think we have a similar opinion on it. The way that Carl Jacobson dealt with Emmett mattered. Because he treated him like a person who still meant something. Treated him with respect. And I know that kids like Emmett, kids like me, kids like the ones at the school…they don't get that. Not often. If not ever. To have a police officer come and speak to them. You know, who isn't trying to scare them straight, but just maybe talk a little bit about responsibility, the community, those kinds of things, well I think it would be really important."

Pansy nodded slowly. "I can come by. Before the interview."

"Excellent," he said.

"Just give me directions."

Which was how she found herself driving toward the Dalton ranch. She'd had a vague idea of where it was, so she didn't need detailed instructions on how to get there. But she had never been there before.

It was a beautiful property with manicured green lawns and pristine, freshly painted barns. Everywhere you looked there were pieces of evidence of Hank's good fortune. From the brand-new ranching equipment to the big shiny trucks on down to the details like sheet metal roofing and specially treated decks and fences that were guaranteed to withstand the weather and had cost thousands of dollars to have installed.

"He's something else," West said. He gave her instructions to pull around to a barn which was apparently near the classrooms, and when they did, they saw his brother Gabe.

When Gabe saw them, his eyes widened. And Pansy realized that it must look weird. Whatever you thought was happening, the situation looked weird. West in the passenger seat of her police car, her pulling up in her police car... So much for keeping things low profile.

She turned the engine off and stepped out of the car, adjusting her belt out of force of habit. West got out, rising high above the car as he straightened.

"Before you ask, if I were in trouble I would have been in the back seat," West said.

Gabe lifted his hands. "I wasn't going to say anything."

"Sure you weren't," West said.

"You got me," Gabe said. "I was totally going to say something."

"Hi," Pansy said, extending her hand. "I'm Officer Pansy Daniels. It's obvious your brother didn't talk to you about me coming by."

"No," Gabe said. "To what do we owe the pleasure?"

"He thought that it might be a good idea if I came by at some point and had a talk with the kids. About...well, about being good citizens, kind of." She winced. "Of course I won't say it like that, because then they'll throw rotten fruit at me and immediately decide that everything I have to say is lame."

Gabe and West smirked. She was struck by how alike they looked.

It was so clear that they were brothers. And yet, given the way that they stood when they were near each other, she could see clearly that they weren't all that comfortable around each other yet. They definitely didn't have the ease of family.

"I think that's a good idea," Gabe said. "Honestly, most of the contact these kids have had with adults has been pretty bad."

"That's what I was thinking," West said. "I was thinking that it would be good for them to deal with an authority figure that didn't treat them like they were a problem."

"I'm a big believer in the idea that we need to provide a support system for each other in this community," Pansy said. "And I... I'm going out for police chief. If I get it, I guarantee you that's going to be a big part of my job. Community outreach. Making sure kids like these, whether they're from Gold Valley or from somewhere else, know that they can always make a different choice. That they're not going to be labeled as trouble based on where they came from, what they look like or even what they might have done in the past. Everybody deserves a fresh start."

She felt like it was something her dad might have said.

Something he might have done if he were here and were able to talk to these kids.

Because of what he'd taught her. About rules and responsibility. Even if he didn't know she'd ever learned it.

And it made her feel warm. Made her feel like she'd found a way to take some pieces of him, of what he'd left behind, and bring them into the present.

"I agree," Gabe said. "It's what I'm trying to do here."

He set about to showing her around the facility, and uncharacteristically, West was quiet during the proceedings. The whole place was wonderful, and by the time Pansy had to leave to get back to her interview, she was feeling enthused. She dropped West off at his truck, and then made her way down to the police station. When she walked in, it was that same, now-familiar panel of people.

Barbara was there, looking particularly pinched.

As nemeses went, Pansy felt that she was a bit of an anticlimax. She didn't particularly love the idea that her greatest enemy was in possession of a collection of bright colored blazers and a single string of pearls.

But as confident as she had felt in every other interaction, this time, she was only more confident.

"And what do you plan to do about the concerns that the Dalton school might bring in more crime?" Barbara asked.

"Outreach," Pansy said. "That's what I plan to do everywhere in the community. We are here to serve the community, and that means doing so in creative ways. I want to make sure that we're visiting schools. That we're making sure the kids here are familiar to us. It will establish a feeling of accountability. And among the kids who don't have positive role models in their lives, we can offer that. And other members of the community can get involved as well, and I'm more than happy to help make that happen. Everyone deserves second chances. Another opportunity to get their foot on the right path."

She had no idea how it all went when it was done. But she felt good.

For the first time, she felt like she knew why she wanted to do this job for herself. Which made it a great time for her to go in for her psych eval, and she was glad she'd scheduled it for today. That part didn't intimidate her. She'd had to do it to get hired on in the first place, and she knew what to expect.

Afterward, she was still reflecting on the shift that had taken place inside her during that interview.

It was strange, because she loved her job and she always

had. But the reason she gave people when they asked why she had become a police officer was her father. Always. Without fail.

Now though, if someone asked, she might answer the same. But she'd have more to say about it as well. It wasn't only that. She could make a difference this way. A difference she truly believed in, not just because she was trying to honor a memory, or make a man proud who wasn't even here. But because it made her proud. It made her feel hopeful.

And it felt like a step. An evolution.

It made her wonder if it had something to do with West. Except, it was probably less West and more to do with whatever was happening in her at the moment. And he was an extension of that, but it wasn't him. It couldn't be. Because in the end, when all was said and done, West wasn't going to stay in her life in this way. So any changes she made had to be about her, for her. And she had to be able and willing to be her own master. The one making all the changes.

That didn't really matter, not really. Because while she might not have a handle on everything, she had a handle on this.

She found a way to give back to the community that had given her a purpose when everything had seemed dark.

And she was going to hold on to that with both hands.

CHAPTER EIGHTEEN

WEST HAD BEEN invited to go out for a drink by his half siblings, and he felt like he should go. Even though what he really wanted to do was find Pansy and make good on the promise that he had left her with the night before.

But instead, he had resisted. He'd gotten Emmett all set at home, and then had gone to the Gold Valley Saloon. When he'd arrived, he was surprised to see it was a whole family affair.

Gabe, Jacob, Caleb and their half sister, McKenna, who they saw less because she was often busy at her husband's ranch.

Easier for West to see Gabe and Jacob all the time since they worked on their dad's ranch, and Caleb was around because his fiancée still worked there, even though he had his own place now.

"Well, if it isn't the ragtag group of Hank Dalton's bastards."

"Only you two are bastards," Jacob said, pointing to McKenna and West.

"That would hurt my feelings if it wasn't one of the wimpiest insults anyone had ever thrown at me," McKenna said.

McKenna had grown up rough. Even rougher than he had. While West maybe *should* have been in a foster home, McKenna had been in several, and while he knew the families she'd been with had been good enough to her, she'd been bounced around a lot and then spit out of the system at eighteen with no support and no real idea of how to make it in the world.

"So, how are things?" he asked.

"Great," McKenna said. "I think this is the first time in my life I've ever been able to say that and mean it. Not a bad place to be."

"I'll get a round of beers," Caleb said, standing up and walking toward the bar.

For some reason, it struck West right then that he was the only one in this group that wasn't paired off. But then, he was also the only one that had been in a marriage that had ended in divorce.

He couldn't decide whether he was the *before* or the *after*. Whether this thing that they'd all found was out there waiting for him, or if he'd already spent his tokens on a bad marriage. A bad life.

No, he had never really thought that he would get married again.

But…

Somehow, love had worked out for all of them.

It was a strange realization.

Jacob, Gabe and McKenna were talking about family life in a way that West felt on the outside, in spite of the fact that he'd been married for a good number of years.

And when Caleb returned, the conversation went to children for a while, since he and Jacob were fathers.

"Thankfully, I don't have to get a babysitter for Emmett," West said.

"Who's Emmett?" McKenna asked.

"My half brother," West said. And when her eyes flew wide he added, "Mine. Not yours."

She chuckled. "Thank God. Honestly you never know with this family. You kick a rock over and find another Dalton."

"Hey, we already know there are more," Gabe pointed out.

"Yeah, we're kind of a tangled mess," Jacob agreed.

A mess he was part of, but they'd let him in anyway. He and McKenna, the interlopers who were just here at the table with them. Like they mattered just the same.

"Well, it's the only real family I've ever known," McKenna said. "And of course the Dodges. They're like family too. Before I came here I never had anybody. My mom…my mom gave me up when I was two. I don't even remember her. And then I came here, expecting to find…well, deep down I wanted to find family. But in reality I expected that what I would find was just people who didn't want anything to do with me. Because that was my experience all my life. I thought family just existed to disappoint you."

The men around the table fell quiet. In some ways they *all* had experience with that.

Caleb, Jacob and Gabe had had some form of stability living with Hank and Tammy, but he knew that it had been a rocky upbringing, and that Hank's behavior had hurt everyone.

"At least nobody knew about you," Caleb said. "Poor West… Our mom knew."

West felt all eyes on him. "I'm not mad at her about that," he said.

"Really?" Jacob asked. "Because I was pretty mad about it."

"I was furious about it when I realized," Gabe said. "And upset about my part in it. Because I knew Mom had turned away other women claiming to have Dad's kids, that she'd paid them off."

"I didn't mean to blame you," Caleb said. "That's not my point in bringing it up."

Gabe shrugged. "I know. But it's true all the same. I knew about them too and I didn't say anything."

"*You* didn't physically turn their mothers away at the door," Jacob pointed out.

"I said I'm not mad at her," West said.

"I don't understand how," Gabe said.

"Because. Because I wish my mom would have done half of that for me. She came after your dad's money, it's true. She did, and so did the other mothers of the other two brothers we don't even know. I can't speak for those women, but my mom didn't do it for me. It wasn't for Emmett. It didn't benefit us. I think she cares about us in her way, but it's not like Tammy does. Your mom fought for you. She fought for that family as best she could. And she didn't give a shit about me. But…why should she?"

"Because it was the right thing to do," Gabe said. "Because you're our family."

"Just because were related by a couple strands of DNA?"

"I'm not really sure what family is," McKenna said. "I mean, in a technical sense. Except I just know it when I feel it. It's not always DNA. But…through no fault of our own we are all tied to Hank. All to each other. The world is a pretty harsh and lonely place, so we might as well band together."

"Yeah, I'm just saying… I don't really blame Tammy for buckling down and protecting her own when she felt like she needed to." He didn't feel like he was being generous. He didn't feel like he was being especially kind.

The truth was, when he had found out about all of it, he

had admired Tammy. He had envied those boys that had her for her mother. He had never really cared much about Hank. But he had been in awe of the woman who had stood firm when three other women came to her door and had tried to extort money from her.

He had always thought that if Tammy Dalton were his mother, things might've been different. That he might've felt different.

He had too much respect for her to try and inflict himself on her even now. She'd done her best to protect her boys, protect her home, and he couldn't forget that he was what she was trying to protect it from.

She'd been cordial to him in every meetup they'd had. Almost friendly.

But he still felt like respect meant giving her space.

"I think your mom is a hell of a woman," West said. "Everyone should be so lucky to have someone who protected them like that."

Gabe shook his head. "In the end, though, I just can't get on board with the idea that she protected me from you. Because you're our brother. And we care about you."

Caleb nodded. "Hell, if it weren't for you, West, I might never have figured things out with Ellie."

"I would've been fine," McKenna said, leaning over across the table and bumping his shoulder. "But, I sure do appreciate having gone from nothing to having all these great older brothers. And a husband. And all my husband's brothers. And his sister."

"I appreciate your husband's sister too," Gabe said, winking.

"He would punch you in the face if he heard you say that."

Gabe had ended up married to McKenna's sister-in-law,

after she'd come to work for him at the Dalton ranch. West had heard that her three older brothers had taken a very dim view on the whole thing initially.

"Hey," he said. "I *married* her."

"Still. Grant's pretty sore about the whole thing. He doesn't think you're good enough for her."

"Really?" Gabe asked. "And what did you say?"

"I told him to watch himself, because he was talking about my brother." McKenna grinned.

Family. He wondered if, a lot like the way Carl Jacobson had reacted to Emmett's misdeeds, versus the way Barbara had reacted to it, family was a lot about making a choice.

More than anything else. A choice to band together.

That was what Pansy's family had done. They had made the choice to stick strong together. Not just her brother, but their friend, their cousins.

And he was included now. Wound up in this thing that he wasn't even sure he understood. But it was what he was here for, wasn't it?

Family.

He'd come back for Emmett, and he'd come back for them.

He'd come back to be part of something different. Bigger than himself, because he'd reached the end of himself when he'd been sentenced to prison and he'd been damned tired of what he was. Of who he was.

It wasn't just Monica's betrayal that made his old life into a fraud, it was the life itself. He'd never loved it, not really. He'd been trying to be something he wasn't. Trying to fit into skin that wasn't his.

He hadn't known for sure he'd find a fit here, but he'd hoped.

And here it was.

He'd been without this all his life, and he knew it wasn't something that could be taken for granted. Sentiment tightened his chest. He'd like to blame the beer, but he hadn't even had a whole one.

"I wasn't really sure why I came to Gold Valley," West said, slowly. "Not at first. Because I would have told you that I didn't care about family. That it didn't mean anything to me. I lived a life that was designed around not needing one. But I came here for this. I came here for you all. And that was hard as hell for me to admit. Even now. Because I don't like feelings. I don't like them at all."

It was the truth. He hated to acknowledge his feelings here. Or anywhere. Even in his own head.

"I'll drink to that," Caleb said. "Feelings are overrated."

"But the whole damned world seems to be put together by them, and no matter how much I want to, I can't outrun them," West said, his voice rough.

Was this what family did to you? An overflow of feelings along with stupid, immature squabbles?

People who understood you. Put up with you.

Sat with you while you vomited all your emotions out.

"It gets like that," Jacob said, looking down, holding his beer bottle tighter.

"I didn't want to need anybody," he said. "Nothing in my life was ever set up for me to need someone. But when I got sent to prison I realized that I didn't have anyone in my life who really cared about me. And that it was no way to live. There was no one to be sorry that I was put away, no one to fight on my behalf. And I suspect just like the boys at the school, just like Emmett needs community, I do too, whether I want it or not."

There was silence for a bit, all around the table as they sat in their mutual discomfort of his sincerity.

"Well, you certainly joined the right family," McKenna said, finally. "None of us were particularly thrilled about having to admit we needed anyone. Least of all me. Grant Dodge is the strongest man I've ever known. And I learned a lot from him about being brave. I learned a lot from him about being strong enough to love someone. He taught me that needing people wasn't a bad thing. Even if he didn't mean to teach that to me. And he resented it for a little bit." She smiled.

"Ellie too," Caleb said, nodding. "She made me believe in things I never did before. Mostly, she puts me to shame with how strong she is."

Jacob nodded. "Vanessa's been through hell in her life. And I figured that if she could be brave enough to love me, I had to let go of my own issues."

"Jamie is made of iron and grit and everything tough," Gabe said. "She lost her mother, she had to be so strong and independent from an early age because she felt responsible for it. All of her life she carried guilt over it. That girl broke me. She changed me. And I think it made my relationship stronger with my family too."

The way they all spoke, with such conviction about their partners, was a hell of a thing. But then, he supposed all he could do was be grateful for his half siblings' partners, because they had clearly paved the way for this evening to happen. Because that they had been changed by love had beaten the path down for him to be here.

Hell, it was his marriage that had led him here. It just wasn't the kind of change they'd experienced.

West chuckled. "Well, all my ex-wife did was send me to prison." He took a sip of beer and shook his head. "But in fairness, it's the reason I'm here."

He was happy for them. That they'd all figured out that it was okay for them to need people the way that they did.

He wouldn't wish his own epiphany on anyone. But it had been that isolation that had shown him that he was going to have to find a way to make a life that included other people or…being out of prison wasn't going to be a whole lot different than being in it.

"Well, we're glad you're here," Gabe said. "Even if we all agree it would have been better if you hadn't come via prison."

He laughed. "Sometimes you don't get to choose."

They lapsed into silence, all taking drinks of their beer.

No, sometimes you didn't get to choose.

But they had gotten to choose. Between family and being alone.

And he was pretty damned grateful that in the end they had all chosen family.

It was Sunday night dinner, and Pansy had been tapped to bring dessert. Which was silly. They did this thing where they spread out bringing or contributing different items. Often, Pansy brought beers. Or chips. Something that didn't require cooking.

She had gone to Sugarplum Fairy because she was not going to bake. Not when Iris and Sammy were goddesses of butter. There wasn't any point. And they knew that, it was about lightening the workload. It was about contributing.

It was going to be a big night, because Colt and Jake had rolled into town. It had been a few months since she'd seen her cousins, and she was looking forward to it.

When the front door to the house opened, the dogs charged out, chaos raining down as they went after a chicken that was roaming around in the front. They wouldn't do anything to the chicken, but they liked to terrorize them.

"Stop it," she said, admonishing the dogs on her way up the steps. The dogs followed her inside, and she knew that Iris would scold them *and* her for it, but she didn't really care.

The house was just as chaotic as the outdoors. Her entire family was already inside. Talking, laughing and fighting over bowls of chips. Colt noticed her first, getting up from his position on the well-worn couch and moving quickly to the door.

"Squirt," he said, pulling her into a hug. She hugged him back, but squinted slightly at the use of her old nickname.

"How are you, Hatchet Head?" She used *his* old nickname, which was derived from the time his brother, Jake, had accidentally pulled his hatchet back without paying attention while he was chopping wood and had driven it partway into Colt's forehead. Which, when she really thought about it, was a bit of a mean nickname.

But she didn't like to be called *squirt*.

He scrubbed his hand over the scar on his forehead, still visible after all this time. "You always were a tough cookie," he said.

"I try," she said.

Then she found herself being lifted up off the ground by Jake, who at least didn't call her squirt. But, he picked her up, which was a cardinal sin akin to the first.

"Knock it off," Ryder said, making his way across the living room to the front door, which he slammed shut. "She's a grown woman, and a police officer. You don't get to treat her like she's a bratty little sister."

That was met with a crack of laughter from Colt.

Ryder scowled. "I do, you don't."

Pansy rolled her eyes. "Or maybe you should take your own advice."

She finally managed to get herself the rest of the way into the house, and she brought her goodies into the kitchen. As usual, Rose was sitting, and Iris and Sammy were cooking busily. Pansy was about to open her mouth to ask if Rose was going to actually make herself useful when Logan walked in. She was struck by something strange about him in that moment. She had known him all of his life, and she rarely took stock of his looks. He was handsome, that was obvious in the way it was obvious that he was tall, or blond.

But for the first time she noticed that his eyes were a very particular shade of blue. It was familiar. It reminded her a lot of West.

But then, it was possible that everything reminded her of West right now. Just thinking of him made her stomach churn. At the way he had been with her the other night. And the way that he... The way that he cared about those boys on the ranch. There was something about it that made her... She took a breath and tried to banish thoughts of West from her mind. She was with her family. And she didn't need to combine West with family.

"Do you need any help?" Logan asked.

"I'm more than happy to put you to work," Sammy said, tossing a dish towel his way.

He caught it, and chuckled, draping it over his shoulder and making his way to the sink. Pansy took a seat next to Rose.

"You know," she said, "you could help."

"So could you," Rose pointed out.

"Sure," Pansy said. "But I brought dessert. I already contributed."

"I brought drinks," Rose said, gesturing toward a bottle of root beer, and a bottle of cola sitting on the counter.

"That isn't helping." Pansy treated her little sister to a withering look.

"Then your baked goods aren't helping, because you didn't make them."

"Everybody likes cake better than off-brand soda," Pansy said.

"That isn't true." Rose turned her focus to Logan. "Logan, which is better? Soda or cake?"

He lifted a brow. "I'm not sure what kind of question that even is."

"Pansy is trying to invalidate my help," Rose said, her tone full of mutiny and irritation.

"What was your help?" Logan asked.

"I brought soda," Rose said.

He looked between Pansy and Rose. "Well," he said. "The soda will be a nice complement to Sammy's homemade meal."

Logan finished wiping up the dishes, then grabbed a stack out of the cabinet and made his way into the dining room.

When he was out of earshot Iris looked at Sammy. "I think Logan has a crush on you," Iris said.

Sammy frowned. "Really?"

"Yes. Because cake is better than soda, but he made that about you. And he came in here to wash dishes. None of the other boys are in here washing dishes."

Sammy blinked for a moment. "I… Maybe he's just being nice."

"He's not that nice," Iris said.

Rose shook her head. "He's really not. I work with him every day."

Sammy huffed. "Men like Logan don't have crushes."

"What do they have?" Rose asked keenly.

"Hookups," Sammy said sagely.

"No," Rose said. "He's way too respectable for that."

Sammy snorted. "You think he's a virgin, then?"

Rose's mouth dropped open, then she snapped it back shut. "No. But..."

"They go out of town, you know," Sammy said archly. "Him and Ryder. They don't like to poach from their own pond, so to speak."

They all just stared at her. She scowled. "Why can't it be any of you three? Maybe he likes one of you."

Rose howled. "*Us?* We're basically his sisters."

"I'm part of the family too," Sammy pointed out.

Pansy thought she might be imagining the note of hurt that wound through Sammy's voice. But then, maybe not.

"Yes," Rose said delicately. "But you did come later. He wouldn't... He wouldn't feel that way about any of us."

Sammy looked stricken by the thought of Logan liking her. It didn't take a genius to figure out why. Sammy wasn't close to her family, not at all. She was an only child, and she had all but moved in with their patchwork clan when she'd been sixteen.

The idea of disrupting any of that with crushes would never be anything but abhorrent to Sammy.

But as for Logan, Pansy had to agree with Iris that it was strange that he had been in here helping out.

"He would be perfect for you," Rose said, getting that sharp look to her she always had when she latched on to an idea. "He's very...and you're so..."

"I banish this topic," Sammy said, waving a hand. "I would burn sage to clear the air if I could."

Rose snorted. "That's dramatic."

"Aren't I always?"

Their conversation was interrupted then by the men clattering into the room, as if sent there by Logan. They began pitching in and offering extra hands, and before Pansy knew it, they were all sitting down to dinner.

Pansy was between her sisters, Sammy next to Ryder. Logan, Colt and Jake occupied the other side of the table.

Logan asked for someone to pass him the bottle of root beer. And Pansy found herself looking at him for a long moment, initially to try and unlock that behavior and if it meant anything. But then just...looking at his eyes again. And letting her mind wander back to West.

It was an easy thing to do, all things considered. Considering that she was currently obsessed with him and the effect that he had on her. It was so utterly different to anything she had ever experienced before.

She was so different.

She sat at the family dinner table, surrounded by these people who had shaped her, made her, and for the first time she felt like she might actually be grown-up.

Really.

Moving out hadn't done it. Getting started on the police force hadn't done it particularly. But having a secret. A salacious, wonderful secret that made her feel alive in a way she never had before... That did something. It really did.

"Pansy here is going out for police chief," Logan announced, for Colt and Jake's benefit, she assumed.

"Good for you," Jake said. "Your old man would be proud."

Pansy felt her throat getting tight. Because no matter how grown-up she felt, no matter how renewed with personal purpose she felt, that would always touch her deep. She wanted her dad to have been proud of her. And maybe he would see, from where he was at. Maybe in heaven you got a front row view to what was happening down on earth, but the fact of the matter was nobody knew. Not for sure. So she didn't know if her dad could be proud of her in the way that she had always hoped. She just had to believe. And hearing Jake say it…

Well, she would never hear her dad say it. This was as close as it got.

She gritted her teeth, fighting against the wave of sadness that enveloped her.

"You okay?" he asked.

"I'm fine," she said, looking down at her roast chicken. "I hope that I do a good job. I hope that I…do his memory proud."

Of course, there was no guarantee she would even get the job. None at all. She might not. It was possible. Barbara still wasn't especially thrilled with her. No matter how good of a performance she had turned in today, there was going to be opposition. And she was still pretty confident that she was going to get the job, but…

Suddenly, she felt overwhelmed, and her eyes felt prickly. And she was filled with a sense of horror. Because she did not do this in front of her family. She didn't do this in front of anyone ever. She just didn't. There was no reason for her to have an emotional breakdown. She was fine. She was with her family.

And they were strong for each other. She wasn't going to have a weird emotional breakdown.

Everything felt tangled inside of her. She had been feeling strong a moment ago, transformed, and now, somehow, she felt weak. She didn't know how to reconcile those two things.

Or maybe it wasn't two things. Maybe it was one thing.

Maybe it was all just her.

Maybe she was somehow more fragile now.

And she couldn't afford that. Couldn't afford to give in. She wasn't fragile.

She was capable. She was the tough one, and that was why everyone at the table was looking at her like she'd grown a second head, or maybe another personality.

"Everything is fine," she said.

"No one said it wasn't," Ryder said.

"But you're looking at me like you're afraid I'm going to freak out. I'm not going to freak out."

"So you're not under stress because of your job?"

"No," she said. "How's yours? I know ranching can be difficult."

"Well," Ryder said. "Sometimes I worry the cows don't like me anymore."

"They don't," Rose said. "They never did. They told me."

"They don't like *you* very much either, Rose," Ryder said.

"I'm fine," Pansy said. "I've been doing this job for a long time."

"Whatever happened with that kid? The one that you took out of the barn the other day?" Logan asked.

"Oh," she said, realizing that she had never actually given her family the whole story about Emmett. "He was West Caldwell's half brother. You know, West. My…my landlord."

She shot what she hoped was a surreptitious look toward Iris, Rose and Sammy. All three of them appeared to be on very good behavior, but that was almost more concerning. Because they were never on good behavior. Well, except maybe Iris.

"That's a coincidence," Ryder said.

"Well, not really. I mean that he was in our barn is, but that he was in Gold Valley isn't. When West came to look for his family, I think Emmett was afraid that it meant West wouldn't have a place for him in his life anymore. I mean, so I gathered. I helped get the kid settled in at his place, and he was…he was behind some of the mischief that's been happening in town. I also encouraged Barbara and Carl not to press charges for the thefts. He's been doing community service."

Ryder frowned. "Do you think that's a good idea?"

It didn't surprise her that it was Ryder who put up some opposition to this idea. He was a by-the-book kind of guy. And truly, Pansy had to be grateful for that. Because it was her brother's stalwart sense of right and wrong that had made him give up so many years to raising his siblings. But that meant sometimes he was rigid, hardheaded and completely unsympathetic when people didn't behave in the way that he did.

He was grounded, levelheaded. He'd never done a spontaneous thing in his entire life.

Sometimes she thought that was why he was such good friends with Sammy. That Sammy was, in some ways, his expression of a part of himself that he could never let out.

He didn't mean to be unkind, and he didn't mean to be harsh, but he often was.

"Yes," she said. "I think it's a good idea. I think it's the only thing that will work. And I'm already putting up with opposition from City Council. So, I don't need opposition from my own brother."

"I'm just saying," Ryder said. "I don't like the idea of some kid getting away with criminal activity. I don't feel like that teaches him anything."

"I know you're a big fan of harsh punishments," she said,

somewhat dryly, since Ryder had essentially never laid out a punishment in his entire raising of them.

"I just think that sometimes going too soft on somebody causes more harm than good."

"Well, when you make a study of the community, and of effective outcomes for crime and punishment, we can have a chat. Otherwise you have to respect that this is my area of expertise."

Now she felt like she was back in control. Felt like she was back in the saddle, being herself.

Sammy tapped Ryder on the hand. She could always reach him with a small touch, and he always let her get away with it. Their relationship was something else altogether. "We're not all as lucky as you are. I mean…not that you didn't have losses. But I mean, we don't all have family that's waiting to pick us up when we fall down. And if we don't have that, what do we have?" She looked around the table. "Community, I hope. A group of people willing to care just because. To create a support, a family just out of…goodness. You did that for me." That last, soft part was directed at Ryder.

A muscle in her brother's jaw tensed, and relaxed when Sammy removed her hand.

Pansy had to wonder if Iris had her assumptions about who had crushes, and where they were directed, all mixed up.

"Okay, Pansy, whatever you think," Ryder conceded. "I mean, it's your job, after all."

Only when that was over did she dare sneak a glance at Sammy, who was gazing at her slyly.

Pansy narrowed one eye as subtly as she could.

Thankfully after that the conversation turned to other people and their pursuits, and she allowed herself to get lost in the shuffle, which was one of the fantastic things about having a big family. A big, loud one, that didn't like you to get much beyond what they thought you were.

It was so interesting to spend all this time talking to West, who saw her in ways that she didn't even see herself, and in ways her family *certainly* didn't.

It made her feel prickly and strange. And she wanted badly to hide away. That was exactly why she couldn't. Why she couldn't allow herself to give in to this.

Because she'd hidden once before. Hidden after she'd disappointed her father. She had been weak.

She wouldn't be again. She was stronger now, stronger than she had ever been before.

She just had to buck up and deal with herself. Yes, she was in a different situation than she had ever been in her life. She had a lover. She was trying out for a new job. But she had built herself on a more solid foundation that she was currently allowing herself to feel.

She was Officer Pansy Daniels.

She was the daughter of Gregory Daniels.

And she would do his legacy proud. She had to.

There was no other choice.

She had disappointed him in life. Even as a little girl, she had. And the sad thing was she was sure that if nothing had changed, that if he had lived, she would have disappointed him later too. Because what would have changed her? If not his loss, then what?

Her father's death had been a defining moment in her life. It had changed everything she was.

So she had to stand firm in that.

She wasn't going to crumble now.

No way.

CHAPTER NINETEEN

"It seems as good a day as any for you to learn to ride," West said, dropping a pair of boots next to the edge of the couch, where his half brother was lying and playing a video game.

West had spent a stupid amount of money buying electronics for the dumb kid.

He didn't deserve it.

But West found that he was busy compensating for something. His own childhood, most likely.

He hadn't had a damn thing that he'd wanted or needed. And sure, he would have taken a mother's love over video games, but neither had been on the table. And he couldn't be the kid's mother. But, he *could* buy him video games.

His ex hadn't left him *that* strapped. Not in comparison to how he'd started life anyway. All things considered he supposed he should be thankful. Not to her, she didn't deserve his thanks. But the life he had here—the life he was building here—was a hell of a lot better than what he'd left behind.

"Ride what?" Emmett asked.

"A horse," West said. "You said you didn't know how to ride. Well, I want to teach you."

"Gabe said we would learn at school," Emmett said, and West was struck by the fact that Emmett seemed to believe he was staying here. That he had a sense of security. It was…it was good. It was damned good.

"That's fine. And it's great if Gabe wants to teach you. Or, wants to let you ride. But, I want to teach you. Because I'm your brother. Then maybe if…maybe if we weren't such a dysfunctional mess then I would have taught you a long time ago. So, can I teach you?"

"Sure," Emmett said, sliding off the couch and looking at him skeptically. He slipped his foot into one boot, then the other. "These are big."

"Sorry. You ought to grow into them."

"I'm not ten," Emmett said.

"Still. Come on, let's go."

West clapped his younger brother on the back and led him outside. He had tacked the horses up earlier, and left them so that they would be ready to go when Emmett was.

"All right. Get on."

"How?" Emmett asked.

"Left foot in the stirrup," he said. "Grab the horn. Pull yourself up."

"Like this?" He planted his foot in the stirrup and swung himself up, throwing his leg over the top of the big animal.

"Yep. You're on the horse, you're facing the right way and you're not on the ground. All good indicators that you did everything just right."

West mounted his own horse, and looked back at Emmett. "All right, now urge him forward. Just a slight nudge with your heels against his flanks. Just like that."

They continued on with the instruction, moving through the basics as they made their way through the countryside.

They'd been in each other's company a while now, and this ride felt like a step forward. He'd been treading carefully with Emmett, on account of the kid seemed more than half-feral and West didn't want to put a foot wrong. Or at least, not too wrong.

But he'd agreed to let West teach him to ride. And West thought maybe that meant…maybe they could talk.

Like he'd done with his other half siblings.

"So, how was camping out?" West asked, as they continued on slowly and steadily.

"Fine," Emmett said. "I mean, not ideal."

"No. I wouldn't think so."

"I just… I guess maybe I should have tried to call you, West, but I figured that since you were coming out here to meet your other family you wouldn't want anything to do with…us anymore."

"Who told you I was doing that?"

"It's what Mom said."

West sighed. He'd told his mother he was coming back, and he'd told her up front he was going to get to know the Daltons, but he hadn't said *that*.

"That's not true. I came for you too. But when I got to Oregon you weren't around and Mom put me off for a couple of months, and then admitted she didn't know where you were. You weren't in Gold Valley the whole time, were you?"

Emmett shook his head. "I crashed with friends in Sweet Home for a while. Then when you didn't come there I… I came here."

"I'm sorry you thought I didn't care about you."

His brother's shoulders went stiff. "It's not like it hurt my feelings or anything."

"It did though," West said. "And it would have hurt mine too. You're not weak because it bothered you."

Emmett scowled. "I just figured you might remember me. All things considered."

"I did."

They rode on in silence for a while. It was a minute or

two before Emmett spoke again, and when he did his voice was calmer.

"I mean, I get that we don't know each other very well, but you're basically all I've got. It's nice for you, that you had this whole other family just waiting to discover that you existed. A dad that's happy to meet you. But I don't have that. I don't have any of that. And if I didn't have you…well, then all I've got is Mom and she doesn't care. You know that."

"I know," West said. "But that was never what I meant to do. I went away for a while, and being in prison gave me a lot of time to think. Which sounds like a cliché, but it's true."

He lifted his head up and looked at the wide expanse of blue sky. At the mountains covered with pine trees and the endless green hills spread before him.

"I'll never take this for granted again," he continued. "Being able to go for a ride when I choose to. Being able to look at the outdoors and all its glory. But I was… I've been lost for a long time. Most of my life. I thought that if I could make money I could find a way to buy myself some kind of normal. And I thought that was what I wanted. What I needed. I've been a lot happier here. Not with status. Not with money. Just with what I've got. With myself. With what little freedom that means. I don't need to be normal, I don't need to fit in. Neither do you. That's not what you're supposed to do in the world. Fit in. You're supposed to walk your own path."

"I thought I was supposed to walk on yours, because you knocked down all the bushes for me or something." A scowl wound through Emmett's voice.

"You get the idea," West said. "I'm trying to make a metaphor."

"Well, stick to riding lessons. You're actually okay at that."

West chuckled. "Thanks for the compliment. Pretty sure that was a compliment."

"Yeah, I guess so," Emmett said.

"I know it hasn't been a good road for either of us," West said. "I know it hasn't been easy. But you can count on me." He looked back at the kid. "We're brothers. And that matters."

Emmett didn't say anything. He just nodded. But West had a feeling there was a wealth of meaning in the nod.

He could only hope that it meant he was reaching the kid.

Because he was reaching West somehow, this whole place was reaching him. He felt like he belonged, sure and simple. And it wasn't the land or the trees or the sky, as much as he liked them. No, it was the people.

His family.

In his mind, pretty brown eyes glittered.

Yeah, this place was really getting to him. Including one particularly pretty police officer.

IT WASN'T HER birthday that made her feel different. Not this year. She hadn't even really been thinking about it. But then, she had told her family a long time ago that she didn't want a big deal made out of her birthday, and they respected that. She wished it weren't her day off.

She didn't like sitting around doing *nothing* on her birthday. Not that she wanted to do a birthday thing. She just wanted to distract herself.

Because sometimes she felt dissatisfied with her years-old sweeping statement that she didn't want a party or presents or cake. A card with a cute animal on it.

But the other night was a great example of why she

didn't feel like she could. It was just…it was just that she felt like they all had their roles. And it was important that they stuck with them.

Iris had taken her to coffee that morning. Then Pansy had gone back home and done chores. Caught up on cleaning, which she did not do a very good job at.

Come to think of it, she did most of her cleaning on her birthday every year, to distract herself from the fact that she both wanted and would be appalled by a big party.

She was on her hands and knees reaching underneath her couch to see if there was anything down there—there was no reason for there to be, she was just on the quest for busywork—when there was a knock at her door.

She got up, her heart hammering.

It could be her family with a surprise birthday cake. But it wouldn't be.

Given she had left them under the impression that she didn't want that.

She made her way to the door and jerked it open. And there *he* was.

Holding a cake.

"What are you doing here?"

"It's your birthday," West said. "And I was going to come by anyway, birthday or not."

"How did you know it was my… *How?*"

"That is a matter of public record, Officer. These kinds of things are posted on the internet for all to see."

"You looked me up?"

"I did."

She wasn't sure how she felt about that. "Why?"

"Well, in fairness I looked you up after I ran into your police chief, who mentioned to me that it was your birthday. And I then confirmed it."

"Why did he...why did he tell you it was my birthday?"

"I imagine he's aware that we have a connection."

"How?"

West stepped inside of her house without waiting to be invited in and he touched her cheek with his fingertips. The look in his eyes burned all the way down.

"It's easy to see, Pansy. To anyone who wants to take a look."

Heat sizzled through her. "Really?"

She wasn't exactly horrified by that.

The idea that someone could see that this man wanted her felt special somehow. Wonderful.

"The cake is strawberries and vanilla, I hope you like it. For some reason you seemed like the kind of woman who liked those sorts of flavors. A little bit sweet. A little bit tart."

He was right. She didn't know how the hell he was right.

"I do," she said, her insides tensing up, on the verge of *something*. On the verge of giving in to this entirely, or pulling back completely, she didn't know. She really couldn't pinpoint it.

"Well, that was really nice of you," she said.

"I have ulterior motives," he said, winking and heading into her kitchen. He moved around in there like he had every right to. Like it was normal. Like she had asked him to, or like he had done it a hundred times.

When she followed after him, she saw that he had put two cake slices onto two small plates, then closed the cake itself back in the box. "I don't sing," he said, handing her the first piece. "But happy birthday."

"If you don't sing I... I don't know," she said.

She was holding onto the plate too tight. But she couldn't

quite make herself ease up. She didn't know what was wrong with her.

Her fingers were bent back slightly at the first knuckle, straining against the bottom lip of the porcelain. "You really don't want me to sing," he said, "trust me." He took a bite of his cake, then set it back down on the counter.

He started to walk toward her, and she backed up slightly, the counter hitting her right in her lower back.

He took her fork from her hand and moved it smoothly through the cake, holding it up for her.

It was silly. She wasn't going to let him feed her. He had brought her cake, which already felt sort of ridiculously over-the-top in terms of taking care of her. She didn't need to be taken care of. She took care of herself. She made sure she was okay.

But he brought the fork to the edge of her mouth and she opened for him. He slid the fork in and slowly, she felt an erotic echo move through her entire body. "Good?" he asked.

"Yes," she whispered, looking down. Because if she looked at him she was going to spontaneously combust. Over cake. And that would just be embarrassing.

"It's fine," he said. "But I bet you taste sweeter."

He took the plate from her hands and set the cake on the counter behind her. And then he leaned in, pressing his mouth to hers, slowly, gently. He slid his tongue between the seam of her lips and the sound he made reverberated inside of her.

"Just like I thought," he said against her lips. "Delicious."

"West…"

"It's been too long, Pansy. I'm starving for you, don't you know that?"

"You brought me cake," she said, the words shaky. "And then you took it away."

"You can have it later," he said, his voice husky. "I need you."

The pleasure of those words shot through her, sharp and swift. He needed her.

It made her feel like maybe she hadn't needed to hold on to that cake plate so tight. Like maybe she wasn't losing her mind. Like maybe everything would be okay. If he needed her.

Maybe the weakness she felt inside of her wasn't so weak after all. But then he put his hands on her hips, and he kissed her again, taking it deeper and harder, and she started to shake.

Need.

That word kept rolling around inside of her head.

She didn't like it.

It terrified her.

He could need this. In the moment.

That made sense.

And maybe if he could then so could she.

Maybe that's all it was.

Maybe it had nothing to do with *need* in the big, wide sense, that might fill her whole world and her whole life.

Maybe it was just this moment in her kitchen with those big hands bracing her in place, and his mouth all hot and hard and searching over hers.

With his tongue slick and perfect as he tasted her deep and long. He angled his head and consumed her. And she let him. Just stood there and let desire riot through her. Let him take what he needed. Because somehow that felt easy. Easier than grabbing hold of his shoulders and clinging to him. Admitting that she needed him too.

He was going too slow, though. And eventually she got restless, rocking her hips against his and trying to urge him to go faster. To make his hands rough like he had done the last two times they were together. To take her up against the counter, with the lip biting into her body so that she had a counterbalance to the sweetness that he was pouring over her like honey. Like frosting. Like the best cake she could ever imagine.

But he didn't go faster. And he didn't get rougher. He kept it slow, and he kept it sweet, and she began to whimper in frustration.

He moved his hands to her hair as he continued to kiss her, and she moved her hands to his stomach, pushing them up his shirt so that she could feel his bare skin. So that she could try to urge things along.

And then he pulled her ponytail. "Hey," he said, his eyes burning into hers. "Don't get ahead of it. Relax."

She was ready to argue. To tell him she didn't respond to commands.

But then his mouth was back on hers, and she couldn't think of a single compelling argument for why they should do anything differently. Because his touch was magic, and his lips were magic, and he made her feel magic.

She had never felt magic in her whole life.

She had felt restless. And she had felt wrong. She had felt triumphant. And she had felt self-righteous.

But not like she might contain something bright and brilliant that existed inside no one else.

But West Caldwell needed her.

This big, handsome cowboy *needed her*.

And if he did, then maybe there was something special in her. Not just something wrong. Not just something wild that needed to be tamed. Something bad that needed to be corrected. But something that shimmered like gold, just like the sparks of pleasure inside of her.

This was the best birthday gift she'd ever gotten, and for some reason the realization made her throat feel tight. Made her feel like her emotions were trapped there, growing and building, expanding down her chest, into her stomach. Building pressure behind her eyes.

So she tightened her hold on him, because it made her feel like she might be closer to holding herself together, if she could brace herself on all his strength.

At the dinner table she'd had to be strong. Rigid. Self-contained.

But she could be contained in West's arms. Stand solid against that broad, muscular chest.

She could rest.

His hands moved achingly slow over her curves, and when he picked her up off the floor, she didn't even think to protest.

"Which way to the bedroom?" he asked.

This was pivotal, and she knew it. Letting him into her house like this, into her bed.

If he laid her down on that mattress and had his way with her, as he had done against the wall, as he had done on that couch in the barn, well, it would be different. This was her space. Her bed, where she slept every night.

His skin would be against her sheets. And when it was over her bed would smell like him. Like the scent of his skin and hers together.

She was already changed. But this was different. This was him in her home, changing the shape of her mattress with the weight of his body. Changing the shape of her life.

"Second door down the hall," she said, her voice rough.

Because she couldn't tell him no. No matter how much she might fear this. No matter how intense it might seem.

She couldn't turn back, because she wasn't made of that sort of thing.

Because once she had been wild. And once she had run across the property with her hair flying in the wind, not trapped in a ponytail.

Because once she had gone barefoot in the fields.

And that girl would have grown into a woman who hadn't feared this at all.

But that girl felt locked behind a wall inside of Pansy. And for the first time she wanted to let her out.

He walked into her bedroom and set her down at the foot of the bed. Then he closed the door behind them.

He took his shirt off slowly, giving her a good view of his body. Then he worked his belt buckle free, pulling his belt through the loops on his jeans as he toed his boots off. Then he slowly undid the button and the snap on those jeans, and she felt her internal muscles clench in anticipation.

He pushed the denim down his thighs along with his underwear, leaving him gloriously naked in front of her.

She took a step toward him, then another. They had gone so fast all the other times. So desperate. And he had set the pace this time, keeping it slow.

It made her ache, but the idea of taking the time to explore him a bit… That made it seem worth it.

She reached out and touched his chest, licking her lips as she dragged her fingertips down over those hot, hard muscles. When she wrapped her hand around his hard length, his breath hissed between his teeth.

"You know, I've seen a lot of half-dressed men running around in my life. Hazards of growing up in the kind of house I did. But I've never seen a naked man like this."

His response was nothing more than a guttural sound.

"I didn't know that I'd think...you're kind of beautiful." She squeezed him, and he jerked in her palm.

"You're the first woman who's ever called me that," he said, his voice gritty.

"I find that hard to believe."

Suddenly, she hated the woman that had married him. Hated her with everything inside of her. And Pansy hadn't known that she possessed the ability to hate that way.

She had always taken the stance that life was too short for negative feelings. But forever would be just long enough to hold a grudge against the woman that had taken this man, this beautiful man who saw her for who she was, whose body was a damned work of art, and seen him locked away in a prison cell.

How had she not appreciated him? How had she not appreciated this?

She pressed herself against him and kissed him hard, not letting go of his hardened length as she did. She wanted... There was no way she could ever be close enough to him. She wanted to make up for those lost years, somehow. She wanted to fix the fact that he'd given his heart to someone who'd done that to him.

She wanted to protect him.

Ex-convict West Caldwell, and she wanted to protect him.

With all of her five feet four inches.

A tear slid down her cheek, and it was embarrassing and ridiculous, but she didn't even care. She just kept on kissing him. His hands were big and firm on her butt as he held her against him, as she kissed him and kissed him and tried to pour all of the confused feelings that swirled around inside of her into that kiss.

She kissed his neck, his chest. She remembered the way that he had explored her body, and she moved her way down his body. Her lips blazing a trail over all that hard packed muscle. He took a sharp breath and they shifted beneath her mouth, and her stomach tightened in response.

She dropped to her knees, examining the deep line that ran just below his hip bone toward that hard, male part of him that jutted out away from his body. She wrapped her hand around him again, and leaned in, tasting him shyly.

The deep groan that vibrated through his body told her that she was doing it right. Then she followed that. Exploring him in a way that she hadn't realized she needed to. Taking him in deep.

Taking every harsh, fractured sound he made as her due for the pleasure that she gave him.

"Enough," he said, panting hard.

He hauled her up off the ground, and then kept on lifting until her legs were wrapped around his waist and he was walking her back toward the bed. He stripped her top off. Her bra.

Then threw her down on the bed and took her jeans off, leaving her panties on.

He followed her onto the mattress, his breath hot against her stomach, just beneath her belly button. And he kissed her there. Just above the waistband of her panties. He pushed his finger beneath the gap in the fabric where the seam met her thigh and he teased her. Finding where she was slick and hot for him and dragging his fingers through her folds. He teased her until she was arching up off the bed, but still he didn't take the underwear off. Then he pushed them aside and spread her thighs ruthlessly, dropping his head and dragging his tongue directly down the center of her body, the center of her need.

She gasped.

He wasn't tentative. He wasn't shy.

He consumed her like a starving man. Pushed her to the brink, then pulled back. Using his lips, his tongue and his fingers to create a symphony of madness that stretched tight through her body. Then he let her fall. Let her go over the edge. But he didn't stop.

He kept going. Until tears of pleasure were streaming down her face. Until she couldn't breathe.

Until every carefully placed stitch that she had used to sew herself up tight over the years was undone. Unraveled.

And so was she.

Completely and utterly unmade on her very neat bedspread.

And then he was tearing a condom open—she hadn't even seen him retrieve it from his wallet, but then she had lost her sense of time and space—and rolling it over himself.

Then he gripped her hips and pulled her toward him as he entered her slowly. His big body over hers like this with the bed soft beneath her was a new experience. She touched his face, watched as pleasure overtook him. As he buried himself in her completely.

Then he reached up and gently, very gently, slid the rubber band out of her hair.

Ran his fingers through it.

And she felt wild.

She gasped when he pulled out and thrust back in. And he tortured them both. With long, slow strokes that took their time to build, until they got hard and fast. Until he was holding her thighs tight against him as he slammed home.

And she held on to his shoulders, because she could do

nothing else. Could do nothing but surrender to him and to this.

And then he gritted his teeth and froze above her on a shout, and she could feel him hard and thick pulsing inside of her, and she was pushed over the edge once again.

Shattered.

Into a million, brilliant shining pieces of herself.

And at the center of the rubble was Pansy, wild and free, with her hair blowing in the breeze and her feet bare on the rocky ground.

West hadn't created this wild woman. He had simply set her free.

And it terrified her. But she couldn't go back either.

He left her there for a moment as he went to the bathroom to take care of practicalities. And when he returned, he got into bed with her, pulling back the covers and dragging her beneath them, fitting them against his naked body.

"What about the cake?" she mumbled sleepily.

It wasn't that late, but she was exhausted.

"It'll keep," he said, kissing the back of her neck.

She believed him. And it didn't take long before she closed her eyes. And right as she drifted off to sleep the last thought in her mind was that someone had finally tucked her in.

CHAPTER TWENTY

WHEN WEST WOKE up the next morning, Pansy was curled up against him, her dark hair loose over her face. She looked young just then. And like she might not have a worry in the whole world, which he knew wasn't true at all, because poor Pansy seemed to have worries worked all the way through her.

He got out of bed and put on his jeans, not bothering with anything else, and then he went into the kitchen, where he found the cake.

The piece that they had left out on the counter last night was a little bit dry, but the cake itself had been shut back in the box, and was just fine.

He started a pot of coffee and cut her a fresh piece of the cake.

He didn't know how a rule follower like Pansy would feel about birthday cake for breakfast, but given that he had pushed a lot of her other boundaries, he figured it wasn't so bad to push this one too.

When he went back into the bedroom, she had stirred. She was lying on her back, her arm thrown over her face, the sheets low, revealing her breasts.

"Good morning," he said, injecting every bit of his appreciation of the view into his tone.

"Hi," she croaked, moving her hand and peering at him like she was a mole emerging from the ground, wounded by the sun.

"How are you doing, sweetheart?" he asked, bringing the mug of coffee and the cake over to the nightstand.

She blinked. "What's this?"

"Breakfast in bed." Then he kissed her. "Happy birthday."

"I…" She stared at him, like she was dazed. Wonder overtaking her features. "It's not my birthday anymore."

"Birthday week," he said, smiling.

She blinked three times in rapid succession. "Thank you."

He cupped her cheek, dragging his thumb over her skin. He didn't think anyone had ever looked at him like this. Like she was. Like there was something special in him.

He had sent money home to his mother every time he'd won an event in the rodeo. He had sent money home after he'd started to do well in his career.

He had bought his wife the biggest house their money could buy, on a man-made lake in some housing development all full of McMansions plopped down in the middle of two acre lots.

His wife had never looked at him like this. Neither had his mother.

No one had.

No one had ever looked at him like he had given them much of anything, much less looked at him like he'd given them the world because he'd brought them a piece of cake in bed.

"How come you weren't with your family on your birthday?" he asked.

She shrugged one bare shoulder, taking the cake off the nightstand. "We don't make a big deal out of birthdays."

"Why not?"

"Well, we do something for Sammy's birthday, because she likes it. It's fun. But…the rest of us aren't really big on them."

"Because you don't care or because you don't feel like you should ask for one?"

"It just didn't seem like it mattered. After our parents. And you know, for a while it was mostly because we were sad. We didn't want to get out all the birthday things Mom used to do. We didn't want to get the banner back down, or the pineapple platter that she got from her grandmother that was used in her family since the nineteen twenties. We didn't want any of that. Because it just felt sad. And eventually… We just got used to it. When Sammy came… Well, she'd never had a birthday party. And so Ryder decided that she should. And Sammy likes to have a big deal made out of her birthday."

"But Sammy does make a big deal out of you?"

"I've asked her not to," Pansy said.

"I'm sorry, that seems stupid," he said. "You make a big deal out of somebody's birthday whether or not they want you to."

"*That* seems stupid," Pansy said. "What if someone doesn't like their birthday?"

"What if they just haven't had the right kind? You seem pretty happy to have your cake."

She dug another bite out of the piece and chewed thoughtfully. "Well, this feels different. It's just you and me." A blush stained her pretty cheeks. "It doesn't remind me at all of the kind of birthdays I used to have."

"No?" he asked, amusement tugging at the corners of his mouth.

"No," she said. "I can honestly say this is the first birthday I've ever had with a naked man."

"I'm still a little bit smug about that."

"Me too," Pansy said. "If only because it feels good to have finally handled that."

"Is that what this is? You *handling* something?"

She shrugged. "What else could it be?"

But she was sitting there with a birthday cake that he had bought for her. He cared about her birthday.

And so the question felt like it might have an answer out there that he wasn't quite ready to find.

"No clue," he said.

She smiled and grabbed hold of her coffee mug. "How did you know how I like my coffee?"

"I pay attention to what you're drinking when I see you in town."

It wasn't actually that hard. Piecing together the details of who Pansy was. He was interested in them.

He found everything about her pretty fascinating.

"I didn't know men like you existed," she said.

"I didn't know I could be so observant," he said.

Because he didn't know what else to say. Which was unusual too. And really, he didn't know that he possessed the capacity to care quite so damn much about what kind of coffee a woman drank, or what kind of birthday cake she might want.

Or whether or not her parents had tucked her in at night, or if anyone in her family had done it since they'd died.

He didn't know what the hell was wrong with him.

Or what was *right* with him.

"I guess I better go check in on Emmett," he said.

"Oh," she said.

"Do you work today?"

She nodded slowly. "Yes."

"Can I come over later?"

She looked like she was pondering that. "Yes. I would like that."

"Good," he said.

Because he might not know a whole lot of things right now, but he knew that he wanted to spend the night with her again.

He knew that he wanted answers and satisfaction for the desperate need that was coursing beneath his skin.

That he wanted to find a name for this thing that was shifting things around inside of him.

Right now, the only name he had was Pansy.

But that felt good enough for him.

"Do you know which day you're going to visit the school?"

She nodded. "It'll be tomorrow."

"Well then," he said. "I reckon I'll come too."

He expected her to tell him he didn't have to.

But she didn't.

"Okay," she said. "That sounds good."

As West collected the rest of his clothes and headed out of the house, he reflected on everything he had now.

He had expected to come here and forge some relationships with the family he hadn't known he had.

He hadn't expected to end up with Emmett living with him. Hadn't expected he would have more than just a tenuous bond with his siblings.

He hadn't expected to start feeling the roots of his soul growing down deep into the soil of this place.

Hadn't expected those same roots to start tangling around a woman.

But they were.

And he was actually pretty damn glad about it.

THE DAY THAT Pansy was supposed to talk to the kids at the school she felt strangely nervous. But less so because West was at her house that morning and had gotten dressed with her. She was slightly worried that Emmett would pick up on the fact that West was spending the night with her, but West had pointed out that Emmett never woke up before noon if West didn't make him. He also asked why she thought it would be a problem.

"Because," she'd said. "He should have a decent example."

"Is there something indecent about this? Because we are both adults, we're not dating anyone else. We both want to do this."

"My brother never brought women home."

"How nice for you," he said. "Our mom brought men home all the time. I assume she hasn't changed any over the years. So it's not like it's behavior that would shock him. And anyway, considering you're not hanging around in the house with your shirt off drinking beer out of the fridge, it's a huge step up from what the guys my mom brings home do."

"I just… I don't want him getting the wrong idea."

West had dropped it after that. But he'd still made it clear he was planning on continuing to stay the night.

She had insisted they drive separately to the school, because she would need her car later. He had pointed out that he could take her to the police station, where she would collect her police car, but, the first class of the day was a huddle in front of the barn, she had learned from West earlier in the week.

And there they all were, standing there when she arrived. Even Emmett.

The camaraderie among the boys was surprising and touching.

They seemed to have already accepted him. And she

couldn't help but feel that she was watching Emmett with the first thing he might have ever been able to call family. His uncle. Those kids.

The Dalton family.

She parked her car and got out, wearing her uniform.

When West looked at her, she tried not to blush. But it was hard.

Because all she could think about was what had gone on between them the night before.

It had left her scorched.

But every night with him did.

She had come to a place of acceptance there.

Her needs with him. And she felt no guilt about finding pleasure in his arms.

It was the *after* part that made her uncomfortable.

That when he held her close against his body in the warmth of her bed she wanted to weep.

That she felt small and cherished and protected, not weak and helpless.

That she felt like she could rest, and it was the wrong time to rest.

She felt wrong about a whole lot of things.

It was just that the sex wasn't one of them.

"We have something a little different happening today," Ellie said.

Pansy vaguely knew the other woman from around town, but she didn't know if they had ever interacted directly. She was the head teacher at the school, and she was engaged to Caleb.

"Officer Pansy Daniels from the Gold Valley Police Department is here to talk to you."

"Shit! Run!" one of the boys shouted, and the rest of them snickered.

"That's exactly why I'm here to talk to you," Pansy said, bracing her hand on her belt buckle. "Because I know that a lot of you are going to have a negative impression of people like me. And that's probably fair enough. But I want to talk a little bit about what the day-to-day job of a police officer actually entails, at least in a town like this one. And a little about myself. And what it means to me to be part of this community. None of you have to grow up to be police officers."

"I think my criminal record would make that impossible," a dark-haired boy in the back said.

"There are always second chances," she said. "But either way. The point isn't to talk about that, but how a community functions. And how you can find a place in it. I bet some of you were made to feel like you didn't have a place. Whether that was in your homes, or in your neighborhoods. In your towns. But you can always make a home."

She started to tell her story. Of how her parents died and of how she and her siblings had made a family. About the responsibility she felt to Gold Valley.

What surprised her was that they paid attention.

Tragedy respected tragedy, and she could see that. That once they realized she wasn't just another person lecturing them from her easy, perfect life, they thought she might have something worth listening to.

And then West stepped forward. "I was in prison for four years," he said. He didn't elaborate. "I'm here now. I'm Emmett's guardian. I'm starting my own ranch. I like to think that I'm going to be part of the community." He said that last part with a bit of a smirk. "But the point is that it's never too late. Especially for you. Because you're young. And starting over is a lot easier now. Don't wait until you're my age. It's a hell of a lot harder."

THE REST OF the morning was spent on ranch chores and general conversation. West watched as Pansy maneuvered her way around the crowd of boys and talked to each and every one of them.

She was something, this woman. So strong after everything she'd been through.

He had thought that his attraction to her had to do with the fact that he wanted a little bit of carnal revenge on the system, but that just wasn't true.

He was drawn to her inner strength.

That certainty in who she was.

Because he had spent…he had spent a life holding back parts of himself. He wasn't enough for his mother, so there was no point giving her everything he had.

He had brought that into his marriage. He had twisted himself, altered himself to fit the life that he thought he should want. Prison had stripped him of all of that. There had been no pretense, and there had been no status that could make him matter in that environment.

All he had was himself. Brought right back to basics he had spent a whole life denying.

And that had led him here. To her.

Her and Emmett.

He turned to his half brother, who was busy tacking his horse for the midmorning ride they were going to take.

"Pretty decent school, right?" he asked.

Emmett shrugged. "Pretty decent."

"I'm glad that you're here," he said.

He looked at him suspiciously. "Really?"

"Yeah. I'm going to go talk to our mom on Saturday.

Get some guardianship paperwork signed off on just so it's all kind of official and whatever. We'll have to do some court proceedings later I suppose. I had my lawyer draw some stuff up."

"You actually want me to stay?"

"Yes," West said again.

And he looked at his brother, that boy he'd been. He had given him lectures. About how he should do better. Because he had been trying to be an older brother.

But the poor kid needed a parent. He never had one. Not really.

And West didn't know why it had taken until this moment to realize it.

Not only did he need a parent, he needed someone who wasn't going to hold back parts of himself.

West couldn't afford to protect himself. Not now. Not when Emmett needed guidance. Not when Emmett needed somebody who was all in.

He reached out and pulled his younger brother in for a hug, clapping him on the back. "I want you to stay with me. And that's going to mean going to school, going to bed on time, getting up when I tell you, watching football with me and doing ranch chores."

"That...sounds like it sucks," Emmett said, but he could see pleasure behind his eyes.

"Yeah, well tough. Because you're a kid. I'm going to treat you like one. That means I'm going to tell you what to do. I'm going to pay your bills. I'm going to make sure you're not hungry. So, if you think you can handle all those trade-offs..."

"Yeah," Emmett said, his voice hoarse.

"Good," he said. Emmett finished tacking up the horse and mounted him.

West cleared his throat as Emmett headed off in the same direction as the other boys. This whole having family thing weighed on a man in strange ways.

And he didn't hate them.

Not at all.

West looked back and saw Pansy, who was getting in her car. Heading down to work, he knew. But also maybe avoiding him a little bit.

Things had been intense between them. They'd spent the last two nights together, and he'd stayed all night. He could tell that she was uncomfortable with that aspect of it. With him taking care of her. But she also wanted it. And he...

Well, he wanted everything. He was starting to be able to identify that feeling inside of him. But he knew that in order to make it mean anything, he was going to have to give everything to her too.

And he didn't know if she was ready to hear that.

He didn't know if he was ready to say it. If he was really ready to try and identify all those feelings in his chest.

But he supposed he was going to have to get to a place where he was.

First things first, though. He needed to go talk to his and Emmett's mother.

He was going to focus on that for now.

WEST HADN'T BEEN back to his childhood home in a long damned time. When he did go, paperwork in hand, he thought that he was prepared. But he wasn't. The whole house seemed smaller, which was silly, since it wasn't like the last time he'd been he was a kid or anything.

It *shouldn't* seem smaller. He'd been the same height the last time he walked up this cracked old sidewalk.

He knew his mother would be home, because she worked

night shifts, and it was a pretty decent time of the day for her to be up and around. He charged right to the front door and knocked.

She opened it a crack at first. Then the rest of the way. He couldn't read the look on her face. Her brows were drawn together, her eyes shining a bit bright.

Her lips were pressed together firmly, as if she was holding something back. But for the life of him he didn't know what it might be.

"Hi, Mom," he said.

"Come in," she said, backing away from the door.

To be honest, he had expected her to leave him there standing on the porch.

She invited him in, and he accepted, following her into the tiny kitchen.

One side of the table was clear, with a coffee cup still sitting in one of the seats. The other side was stacked high with magazines and scratch-off lottery tickets. It looked basically the same as it had when he left.

"I just came to talk to you real quick."

"What?" She was guarded.

"Emmett is with me," West said. "And I have him going to school. I need to be his legal guardian. I have some paperwork for you to sign. We may need to go to court and make it all official."

"We don't need to do that," his mom said. "I can sign whatever."

"All right," West said, pushing the file of papers forward.

"How have you been?" she asked, flipping the folder open and staring down inside at it.

"All right."

"You staying in Oregon?"

"Yes," he said. "I bought a ranch."

"That's good," she said, finding the places that he had highlighted and adding her first signature.

West hadn't meant to come here to question his mother. There was spare little point. What was done was done. To both him and Emmett. But when she signed in the second spot he couldn't stop himself. "Do you love him?"

His mother looked up at him in confusion. "Who?"

"Emmett," he said.

She huffed a laugh and picked up a pack of cigarettes from the table. "He is my son," she said, lighting it and taking a slow drag off of it. "I love him more than anything in the world."

A laugh caught in West's throat. "Is that so?"

"I did my best by you boys. I did the best that I could. But the money that Tammy Dalton gave us was only enough for this place. Sorry if it was too modest for you."

"We could've lived in a trailer park, Mom," he said, his voice rough. "We could've lived in a cardboard box. It didn't matter. What mattered was knowing that you cared about us. And I can't really speak for Emmett. But I can speak for me. You never did seem like you cared that much."

"What more did you want? I care for you as much as I care for my own self."

"We didn't always eat. The men in your life… They treated us awful. The house was never clean and…" And suddenly as he said all those words he realized that what his mother had said was absolutely true.

She had cared for them the best she had known how.

She had loved them as much as she loved herself.

The problem was she didn't love herself. Or she didn't know how to. She didn't feed herself. The men in her life treated her badly. She let herself live in a house that was falling down around her.

She didn't know how to give more than that. And it started with the way she saw herself.

West was lucky enough to have some youthful idea that he deserved more. But he had thought that he had to change himself first.

And he was suddenly staring at the evidence that until a person accepted themselves. Until a person found some way to love themselves, they really couldn't figure out how to give it to other people. Because they didn't know what the hell it looked like.

"I'm sorry," West said. It didn't make what his mother had done to them right. And it didn't mean that if she started loving herself tomorrow everything would magically change.

Love meant wanting better. Love meant trying.

Love wasn't a passive acceptance of the way things were, or the way a person was.

Love was active. The evidence of it would show up everywhere. If she loved herself, her life would look different. She would look different.

So would his. So would Emmett's.

And he'd done a whole lot of thinking since last night about what it would look like if he could accept himself. If he could find a way to stop holding bits of himself back. But maybe that was it.

Maybe it was just finding out a way to be all right with all that he was. From those white trash roots to the mistakes he'd made escaping them. His failings and his relationship with his mother. With his wife.

Even with Emmett. Accepting it and finding a way to be open in spite of it.

He was the man from here. The man who had married his wife. The man who had gone to prison.

That was all him. All decisions he'd made that had led him to those places. He was ready now to embrace this new life. This new path. To be the man that Emmett needed. The man that Pansy needed.

And in order to do that, he knew what he had to do.

"You did the best you could," West said. "I'm just fine. And Emmett…he's going to be just fine too."

He could see relief winding down his mother's spine. Relaxing her posture. "I always was proud of you," she said.

He put his hand over hers for a moment. Then took it away.

She finished signing the paperwork, and he took it and headed back out the door, headed back to Gold Valley.

Back to create the life that he'd never known he wanted.

CHAPTER TWENTY-ONE

WHEN PANSY ARRIVED home from work there was a picnic basket at her door.

There was a note attached to the top of it, but even without the note she would have known who it was from.

She smiled and bent down, looking at West's bold handwriting.

Dinner for two.

She looked around, wondering where he was. And suddenly, she saw him. Riding up to her on an actual white horse.

"What are you doing?"

"I think it's called a romantic gesture," he said, maneuvering the horse right up to her front door.

She straightened, taking hold of the basket.

He looked…well, he looked like some damned fantasy come to life. He was wearing a white Stetson, a white T-shirt and battered jeans, along with some well-worn and expensive looking cowboy boots. He had one of those big rodeo belt buckles that she had never thought she would find compelling, but did now. And she was just wearing a plain T-shirt and jeans.

Which…was what he was wearing, but somehow with all the cowboy trappings it seemed a bit more spectacular.

Her bad boy was on a white horse, at Redemption Ranch.

And it all seemed so surreal, so perfect, she could hardly wrap her mind around it.

"Let me give you a hand up," he said, reaching out his hand.

"You're kidding," she responded.

"Nope."

She hesitated, then took his hand with the free one that wasn't hanging on to the basket, and he hefted her up off the ground right in front of him on the horse.

"Shouldn't I ride on the back?"

"This is fine," he said, his breath hot on her ear.

He put one hand on her stomach, and used the other to guide the horse out of her yard and onto one of the trails that lead away from the house.

"What if I had plans?" she asked.

"I'd ask you to cancel them. For me."

There was something about that request. That he would ask her to make him a priority that…unsettled her. Because they had been doing this thing as if it were convenient. And getting to a place where they worked to spend time together was something else entirely. Something she wasn't sure she was ready for.

But then she forgot to be concerned, as they rode up a steep trail that eventually let out at a clearing. It was beautiful. All yellow and lavender flowers and sunshine.

In late May the evening air was warm and wonderful, and the sun was beginning to cast a rose gold glow all around.

"This is beautiful," she said.

"It is." He helped her dismount, and then tether the horse to a tree nearby. Then he took her hand, and the picnic basket, and they picked through the tall grass, just up and over a rise that offered them a stunning view of the valley below.

"That's why they call it Gold Valley," he whispered.

The sun was spilling over the town below, like liquid gold illuminating the vineyards, the barns, the houses. She could just make out Main Street, the red brick set ablaze in the light.

The whole thing had been turned to miniature up here. This place that held her heart so deeply. That mattered so much. She could see it all at once.

It was incredible.

"I don't think that's really why they call it Gold Valley," she said softly. "I think that has to do with the gold rush."

"Well, now there's no gold in the hills. But there's definitely gold on them."

"I guess so."

He reached into the picnic basket and took out a blanket, spread it out on the grass, and then settled onto it.

"You know," he said as he got food out of the basket—sandwiches, potato salad and some kind of pasta salad, "when I moved here I had the thought that I didn't know the place yet. I found something in Texas. Something that made me a better man. I found out that I could work and I could make change in my life. And that was an important lesson. Trust me. It was when I needed to learn. More than that, because I figured out what kind of man I was going to be there, I felt like the land was in me in some way. In a way that I didn't feel here. Texas felt like home. Until I got out of prison, and I realized I didn't know it anymore.

"Then I came here, and I didn't feel any more connected. But I've been coming up here a lot. I feel like I found my roots. This land, this dirt... It gets in your blood. I'm happy that I'm staying here. I'm happy that I'm going to ranch here. That this is the ground I'm going to work. I had to go somewhere else to find it, I think. Redemption. It's what I've been searching for all this time. I found it here. I found home."

"For me too," she said softly.

"I love the big skies in Texas. But here they're tall. Taller than the trees. And the mountains stretch on forever. Makes you feel small. Like you could walk into one of those thickets and never come back out. You feel your insignificance here. I needed to find my insignificance. Because I spent a whole lot of time being concerned with what I looked like to other people. Inflating their thoughts about me into something that mattered the most. And I built a scaffolding of a person around what I was." He cleared his throat. "I went and saw my mother today."

"Oh," she said, her heart twisting.

"I've been angry at her for a long time. But I realized something today. She just hates herself, Pansy. She doesn't think she deserves for things to work out. She doesn't really think she deserves anything nice or good or lovely. And that's why she couldn't give anything to us. I can't hate her. But I can damn well make sure that I take that lesson and learn it. For myself. Because I don't want to be sitting by myself in the same old house in twenty years bent by bitterness and the weight of the world. And I could be. I could let my time in prison define me. I could let what happened with my ex-wife define me. But I have to be willing to let it go. I have to be willing to care about the future more than I care about the past. To want something good in the present more than I want to hang on to my anger."

He stared out at the scene below, the light reflecting in his blue eyes, setting sparks of fire off the color there. "I have to stop hiding myself away. Because the truth is I was in prison a long time before I went there physically."

His words scraped uncomfortably close to her bones.

And she didn't quite know what to say in return. So they just sat. She ate her sandwich in silence, and looked out at the view.

"How are you feeling about your interview?" he asked, shifting his body, shifting the conversation.

"Oh," she said. "Good."

Except she didn't know what she felt about anything. She didn't feel particularly confident. In herself, yes, but in what was going to happen? No.

"You're the best person for the job," he said.

"You don't know that. You don't know everybody else they're considering."

"Do *you* think that you're the best person for the job?"

"Well, yes. If I didn't I wouldn't be going out for it."

"I think plenty of people would, whether they thought they were best or not."

"Well. I wouldn't."

"Which is exactly why you are best for the job. I've never known anyone quite like you," he said. "So sure in yourself. I mean, I've met a lot of people who had confidence in themselves. Who had an inflated idea of who they were. But you... You're strong. You're steady. I know that you want the best for the community. I admire how much you care. In spite of everything that life has taken from you."

Pansy didn't know quite how to respond to that. She felt like she had always been fighting to be good. And he just seemed to think that it was something she was already. That she was worthy of praise for some reason.

"I..."

She started to argue with him. But then, she didn't want to. Because the man had literally ridden to her door on a white horse.

Because he was the epitome of a hero.

And she would have never thought that she would look at an ex-convict, a man like him, and see that. She had spent her entire life with a very rigid idea of what it meant to be a hero.

Of what it meant to be good.

But West made her see layers. Depth and richness that she hadn't before.

She looked at him and saw a hero. And for just a while she wanted him to be hers.

Because she had lost the only other hero she ever had far too soon.

And now she had this man only a foot away from her. Strong and solid and real.

Arms that could hold her.

She leaned in, and she pressed her palm against his chest. Felt his heart beating.

Strong and certain.

This man was so incredible. So solid and alive.

He kissed her. He kissed her, and she surrendered to it. Surrendered to him. And she shivered when his hand skimmed over her curves. When he pulled her shirt up over her head, and the cooling air drew breath against her skin. She should be embarrassed. She supposed.

But in the arms of her hero, she couldn't be anything but his.

Cherished.

Cared for.

So many things that she had decided she didn't need to be.

He stripped her bare underneath a blue sky that was fading to purple. And then he stripped himself down, and it felt like the most honest thing she had ever experienced in all of her life.

West. Pansy.

Naked and in the open.

She had spent so much time fighting against her nature. Fighting against her name.

As if she had to prove she wasn't her namesake. Wasn't weak or wilting.

But out here on this blanket of flowers she didn't think of those blooms as weak.

Bright and striking and resilient.

Because they came back every spring, didn't they? No matter how cold the winter got.

West had talked about growing roots into this land, but as he laid her down and settled between her legs, she thought it wasn't the land that had become a part of her. It was West.

He didn't feel like a rebellion. He felt like reality. He felt like part of her.

Maybe even the largest part.

Like his heart was making hers beat in return.

Like his touch was fueling her breath. Her vision. Her pleasure.

He drove her to the edge, over and over again. He made her feel unbreakable. He made her feel unashamed.

And when it was over, she drifted to sleep in that tall grass, until he bundled her back up on the horse and rode them both back home.

Until they slipped beneath the covers together and found heaven one last time there in the secluded darkness of her bedroom. She didn't know how many times she woke up in the night and turned to him. She lost track of the heights he took her to. She was reduced. To nothing more than a shattered, glittering thing. And yet, she felt like more as well.

Like she had never been so in touch with all of the places of her body. With every beat of her heart.

When they finally did sleep for real, the sky was turning gray. And she fell asleep dreaming of what it had meant to be with West during each evolution of the sky. From gold to a midnight of stars, and back to that pale morning.

It felt like them.

Like the way they were together. Fiery and passionate. A sweet blanket of comfort. The beginning of something new.

Those thoughts spun around in her head until her eyes drifted shut for real.

SHE SAT UPRIGHT before she realized she was awake. The sky was far too blue. It was not early. It was much too late.

West was lying next to her, and he was never here this late.

She looked at her phone.

"Dammit," she said. She stumbled out of bed in a panic. Her interview was in twenty-five minutes. There was no way she was going to be able to get ready and get there in time. It took her ten minutes just to drive into town.

She started moving around in a tear, trying to find her uniform. Which of course should be exactly where it always was. It wasn't, though. Because she had left it in the car, because she had gotten distracted when she had come home and seen the basket. She ran out of the house wrapped in a towel, and dug through her car, taking the uniform bag and running back in. Then she started dressing as quickly as possible.

"What's going on?" West asked, his voice gravelly.

"We overslept. I have an interview."

"Shit," he said, getting out of bed. "Emmett is probably late to school. Awesome first day of guardianship."

"I'm never late," she said. She couldn't even care about him or Emmett. It was all too... She squeezed her eyes shut and tried to keep from panicking. Then she grabbed her phone and dialed the number for the city manager.

"I'm going to be late," she said. "Can you delay the panel by ten or fifteen minutes?"

"I'm afraid I can't" was the response. "We'll discuss among ourselves until you arrive."

She gritted her teeth, angry that she had taken time away from getting ready to make the call.

"Okay," she said. "I'll see you there."

She let out a frustrated growl and continued getting ready. Her hair was in a ponytail. She didn't often bother with makeup anyway.

"Is there anything I can do?" West asked.

"Don't talk to me," she said, her heart hammering. She couldn't think through all the implications of this. She just couldn't. She was too frantic. And she had to get there. And she needed him to *not* talk to her.

"All right," he said. "If that's what would help you."

"It would," she said.

She tore out of the house and got into her car, driving as quickly as she could down into town without breaking any speed laws, because God only knew how horrific it would be if she got pulled over for speeding on her way to the job interview.

When she walked in, there was clearly a discussion happening. She took a breath and sat down at the table. "I'm sorry I'm late."

"I think we're close to being finished here," Barbara said.

"Don't you have questions for me?"

"Well," Barbara said. "We might have. But we are on

a schedule. And we have another interview directly after. This is your chance to make a final statement."

Everyone was looking at her, and she felt herself falling apart. Felt herself losing her grip. On everything.

"I'm qualified for the job," she said, her voice breaking. "I'm the most qualified person. It's not…it's not actually a debate. Just because Barbara doesn't like me. I'm sorry I was late today. It's the first time in eight years with the department I've been late to anything. My superior officer can attest to that," she said, carefully not looking at Chief Doering. "I care about this town. Nobody else cares about it more. I hope you'll do the right thing."

"Thank you, Pansy," the city manager said. "We will keep all this in mind as we make the decision."

She stood and walked out of the room on numb legs. Then she stopped just outside the station, clutching her chest. She couldn't breathe. She really thought that if she were going to have a heart attack it would be now.

A couple minutes later the panel began to file out the front door and Pansy wished that she could melt into the sidewalk.

No one said anything to her, but when she chanced a look, it was Barbara who met her eyes. The older woman practically smirked.

And Pansy had only herself to blame.

She had brought all of this on herself. She had gotten involved with West. She had gotten involved with Emmett. She had thought…

She had thought for a moment that she could have more than the thing she had been focused on for so many years, and she had done it at the worst possible time. She had compromised everything for herself. Everything. Over what?

Over that man. The man who was supposed to be nothing more than a diversion.

She had lied to herself. She had tricked herself into believing that she was being more than just a naughty kid with him.

That she somehow wasn't the same girl that she'd been.

She wanted to hide. She wanted to hide like she had that day her father had left for Alaska.

That day that he died.

She gritted her teeth, and made her way to her car.

She drove home slowly. And when she walked inside her house, West was there.

"What are you doing here?"

"I just came back to clean up."

"Get out of my house," she said.

"Is everything okay?"

"No," she said. "How can you ask me that? Everything is not okay. Not at all. The interview went horribly. I got there and it was just about finished. I'm not going to get the job now. I'm not going to get the job. Because of this. Because of *you*. I worked my whole life for this, and you took it from me."

"Did I?"

"Yes." Except she knew that she had taken it from herself. "You did."

"Pansy," he said, keeping his voice low. "If they don't give you the job over this, that's some bullshit. You've gone in what? Two other times? And you did an excellent job. You have history working for the city. You've never made any mistakes. Your boss thinks that you should have this job. He thinks that you should be his successor. If they don't give it to you, then they were looking for an excuse."

"And I gave it to them," she said. "I gave it to them, and I swore I would never do anything like that. I would never do anything that opened myself up to censure. I'm young, and I'm a woman, and I knew that all that was working against me. And still, I let myself get distracted. I… When I was a kid this was what I did. I messed things up all the time. I misbehaved. My dad was so… He was so disappointed in me all the time. And right before he died I made him so mad…" She squeezed her eyes shut, tears falling down her face. "I never got to fix it. He never got to see."

"Sweetheart," West said, closing the distance between them, his voice filled with tenderness that made her hurt.

"Sweetheart, you weren't bad. You were just a kid."

"No. He was right. I swore that I'd make him proud, West. I swore it. But we can't change. It's all still there. And I… I can't do this."

"Pansy," he said, keeping his voice measured. "Not getting a job isn't a failure."

"It's not that. It's *everything*."

"Honey," he said, his tone stern. "I love you."

She hadn't expected that. Of all the things that she had expected to come out of his mouth, it hadn't been that.

"You don't," she said, her voice choked. "You don't love me. This is a fling. And I was a virgin, and you're…you're older than me, and you're more experienced than me, and you don't ever want to fall in love because of your ex-wife."

"All true," he said. "But I did just the same. You showed me something," he said, his voice husky. "About being brave. And I can be at least half that brave."

"I'm not brave," she said. "I'm just a mess. I'm a mess who doesn't need you up in the middle of it. I have to… I can't do this. I can't be this person."

"I didn't think I could be either. I had a whole plan for myself, Pansy. I was supposed to be mega rich by now. With a big corner office. Because I thought that's what I had to be to be important. But I've never felt more important than when you're holding me, darlin'. That's just true. It doesn't matter to me what anyone else in the world thinks. What matters is what you think. I've never given myself to someone wholeheartedly before. I've always kept parts of myself back. My wife couldn't love me, because she didn't know me. And I couldn't love her because I didn't give her all the pieces of myself. Because I didn't really trust her. Not ever. Good thing, as it turns out. But still."

"I need… I need to…"

"You don't need to do anything," he said. "You don't need to change a damn thing. The woman you are reached in and saved me somehow. And I want to spend my life drinking Coke with you in the middle of the day in a bar. Having sex in a basement at a museum. I want to watch you put your uniform on in the morning, and then I want to take it off you at night. I want to meet this big family of yours that raised you and made you who you are. Because that woman, I love her."

"It's not enough," she said, everything in her pushing against these declarations.

"Why not?"

"I'm not… I'm not enough. I'm just not. I need to get this job."

"Why? To build a monument to a dead man? I'll tell you what, it's a lot easier to do that than it is to look around you and fully embrace the living people that care about you as you are. You're having conversations with someone who can't talk back. You don't know what your dad would say with all these years and all this hindsight. You don't know if he'd be proud or not."

"He would be proud if I…if I did what he did."

"Maybe, maybe not. Maybe he didn't like the man he was, Pansy. You don't know. You were a child. Let me tell you what I think. I think he would've been proud of you if you would have become police chief, an artist, a dancer. Whatever. I think at the end of the day he would've wanted you to be happy. You know why I think that? Because you love him so damned much. Which means that in spite of whatever issues you had with him sometimes, you loved him a whole lot. Because his opinion mattered to you. And you wouldn't want to make him proud if he weren't a really great dad. And if he was a great dad, that means he would've loved you always."

She pushed back. She rejected it. She couldn't believe him. She couldn't. And she didn't quite understand why she couldn't with such desperation. She only knew that it was so.

"No. Get out of my house, West. I have to deal with the fact that I'm going to have to call a man that I want to punch in the face my boss in the next couple of weeks, because lord knows Johnson is closer to getting the job than I am. I just lost the one thing I cared about."

"Pansy…"

"I don't love you," she said. "I just wanted to lose my virginity. That's it. I was so focused on *this* that I forgot to do *that*. And then big surprise it turns out I don't do balance very well. Well, my lesson is learned. And I'm done. Please get out of my house." He looked at her for a long moment, his blue eyes filled with pain.

Pain she had put there.

Only a week or so ago she had thought that if anyone ever hurt West, if she could find the people who had been responsible for putting him in prison, she would have to fight against her desire to put them in the hospital.

And now she was the one hurting him. But she had to. She had to. To save herself.

He said nothing. He only nodded once, and tipped his hat.

And then West Caldwell turned and walked out the door.

Pansy couldn't catch her breath. She had been struggling with it since she'd left the interview, and now it was even worse. She collapsed onto the ground, breathing hard and heavy.

And suddenly she remembered the day that her parents had died.

Remembered the pieces of it that she had forgotten. This. On the floor. Breathing hard. Thinking she was going to die too.

Grief.

Whole body grief. Stole her breath. Stole her ability to think. But she didn't know in this moment if she was grieving for the loss of her job, or for the loss of West.

West.

She had lost West.

She didn't think she'd ever be okay again.

CHAPTER TWENTY-TWO

WEST DIDN'T FIND himself on the Dalton ranch at night all that often anymore.

And of course, he wouldn't be able to just run into his half brother Caleb by happenstance, seeing as his brother was now happily engaged, and didn't have any reason to be out doing late-night wandering.

So he called him.

And few things had pained him more.

But his brother had come. Even in the darkness.

The two of them mounted up on their horses, with headlamps as guides.

"So what's going on?" Caleb asked.

"I thought… I thought we might re-create our late-night ride. Because I'm in desperate need of a similar miracle. Crappy thing is, it's not anywhere near Christmas, and it's entirely possible that a little bit of holiday magic played into your success story."

"Well, I don't know about that," Caleb said.

"No," West said. "But then, I don't know much of anything."

"You might need to start from the beginning."

So West did. Starting with the ticket Pansy had written him when he had rolled into town, ending with her rejecting an offer of love he hadn't even been planning on making.

But he realized that he couldn't hold a damn thing back

from her if he wanted to keep her. Because she deserved more and better. Because she deserved a man who was certain of his feelings.

When his wife's betrayal had sent him to prison, it was the consequences of that which had hurt him.

Being in prison sucked.

But this actually felt worse. And it was simply because a life without Pansy wasn't one he wanted to live in.

"I'm a goner," he said. "I would have told you that I couldn't have ever loved a woman like this. Not ever loved anyone like this. It's all your fault," he said.

"How is it my fault?" Caleb asked.

"All y'all," he said. "Gabe, Jacob, you. McKenna. Emmett. This whole family thing. You said that all of your significant others helped you deal with the situation with your family. Well my damn family made me think that maybe I could fall in love. Because look at all of you. None of you are less of a mess than I am. And *look* at you. Married. Engaged. Happy."

"Not for lack of fighting it," Caleb said.

Silence settled over them as they continued to ride the horses under the cover of the darkness. West knew that to be true. He knew that Caleb fought for what he had.

He knew that he had encouraged him to do it.

"She said no," Caleb said. "She said no to me too."

"Yeah. And I had no idea how fucking miserable that was."

"You gave some pretty good advice all the same. The thing is, I had accepted that I loved Ellie a long time ago. I had also accepted that I couldn't have her. I spent a lot longer sitting with my feelings than she did with hers. So when I was ready to make it all or nothing…she wasn't."

"She thinks she messed up getting the job she wanted because she was late. Because of me."

"Why exactly was she late because of you?"

"I'm giving you a look right now," West said. "I know you can't see it. But if you could, you'd get it."

"The usual reason then," Caleb said.

"Yep. That part we've got no problem with. It works a little *too* good. Kept us from talking when we probably should have. But then, I think we were using it as an excuse to be together." He snorted. "Yeah, burn out the sexual attraction. Keep it physical. I mean, it's a damn fine excuse. But mostly, I think we like to be together. I think neither of us wanted to admit it."

"I relate to that too," Caleb said. "Here's what I know. Love is complicated. And it's a damn scary business. Pansy's lost people. And…that's tough. It's tough to move on from."

"She's got this idea that she has to be something particular to honor her father's memory."

"Deals you make with the dead are pretty damned hard to get out of later," Caleb said. "As a man engaged to my best friend's widow, I can speak to that pretty solidly. I promised him I'd take care of her. But the trouble was, I was also in love with her. And what I had to realize was that when you lose a person…they're gone from here. What they don't need are promises from the living. Because their concerns aren't here. I'm not saying I know what Clint would've wanted or not wanted from me or Ellie. I just know that we're the ones that are here having to live. That she's the love of my life. And I'm the love of hers, as hard as it was for her to admit that. I get it. She and I railed against more than one ghost. But we found love with each other. And that's a beautiful thing. And it's worth the fight. It's about the only thing I can think of that is."

"So what should I do? Go to her door and beat it down?"

"No. But you seem to think that she's the strongest, smartest, best woman around. And if that's true…she's going to come to these conclusions on her own. Even though they're hard.

"What can I do for her?" West asked.

"Well. I suppose you could always submit a personal statement to the city manager. To the mayor. About all she's done to help Emmett."

"Yes," West said. "I can do that."

"And then I suppose Gabe and I could do the same. Talk about what she did for the kids here."

"All right," he said.

"And you still might not get her back, you know. Even if she does get the job."

"I know that," West said, his chest feeling tight. "But she deserves the job whether she chooses me in the end or not.

"You really *do* love her."

"I know," West said. "What a way to find out that I can love like this. It's kind of a bitch."

"Yeah, this part of it kind of is. But when you get it back, it's the most beautiful thing in the world."

"But I might not get it back."

"That's the risk. It's always the risk. That's why you don't do it till you find the person worth all that risk."

And West knew that no matter what happened, that person for him was Pansy.

Whether in the end she broke his heart or not, he wanted her to have her dreams.

For the first time ever, the dreams of another person felt more important than his own.

CHAPTER TWENTY-THREE

PANSY PRACTICALLY SNUCK into Iris's room, creeping up the stairs and dashing into her older sister's room.

Eventually, she supposed she would have to talk to everybody. About the job.

She would have to admit that she had messed up. And somehow not talk about West.

Sammy and Rose would want to know.

But Iris... Iris was the one that Pansy felt most closely understood her.

"What's going on?" Iris asked when they were safely ensconced in the private space.

"I ruined everything."

The whole story came pouring out of her. Down to West saying that he loved her.

He loved her.

The very idea made her heart pinch.

"You sent him away?" Iris asked.

"I can't accept it. I can't. Look at how I messed up the interview because of all this distraction."

"If you're not going to get the job why not at least take the man?" Iris was looking at her genuinely incredulously.

"Because I can't. Because I don't... I don't deserve him," she said, the words slipping out, surprising her.

"You don't deserve him? How can you think that?"

"You remember what I was like when I was a kid," Pansy

said. "How I misbehaved all the time. How I… You prob-ably don't remember this, but Dad got so angry at me be-fore they left. And I hid from him. And it's the last memory that I have. It was the last he ever knew of me. And I just wanted it to be different. *I* wanted to be different."

"Pansy," Iris said. "You were a little girl."

"I built my whole life around this. Around needing to be good."

"Why?" Iris asked. "Do you really think that he would've been mad at you for the rest of your life for doing some-thing naughty when you were a child? Do you really think he died thinking what a bad girl you were?"

"I don't know," Pansy said.

"I think you do," Iris said. "I think you do. Is that all you remember about Dad? Him being disappointed in you? Because I remember him being really proud of you, Pansy. I remember him laughing at your jokes. And thinking you were so silly and so clever. I remember one time you drew a picture of him in his uniform and he had it on the fridge for months. Ryder didn't take it down until…way after they died. I remember one time we went on a walk around the property, and him and Mom held your hand and swung you between them."

Pansy's throat started to get tight, a lump building there.

"Don't you remember how they would read to us?" Iris asked. "How they would tuck us in?"

Tears started to fall down her face, and she hadn't even been aware of them building.

"No," she said, her voice a broken whisper. "I don't re-member."

"Why not?"

"It hurts too bad," Pansy said. "And there's nothing I can do about it. It's just sadness. It's just loss. At least when…

when I was going to be police chief for him there was a reason. It meant that he…that he mattered. That him dying mattered. That it changed me. How can you lose your parents and not have it change you?"

"Of course it changed us," Iris said. "But Dad would have wanted you to be happy. More than anything else. You know that."

Something broke inside of her. And pain washed right on through.

He would want her to be happy. Because suddenly she didn't just remember his stern face, but his smiling one. Him lifting her up in the air, putting her on his shoulders.

You wouldn't want to make him proud if he weren't a really great dad.

And West's words echoed in her head.

He *had* been a great dad.

He had tickled her and teased her and he had tucked her in at night.

And he had disciplined her when she needed it, because that made him good too.

He'd worried for her. He'd tried to teach her his values. But he'd loved her. Above all, he'd loved her.

She hadn't been able to let herself remember just how much.

"It hurts to remember," she whispered.

Iris put her hand over hers. "I know. I know."

"I'm afraid to love West," Pansy said. "I'm afraid it will make me weak." She swallowed hard. "When he left I cried. And I thought I might die. It felt like when we lost Mom and Dad. And I never wanted to feel that way again ever in my whole life. And he makes me feel that way. I'm so scared of losing him."

"Honey," Iris said. "You lost him already."

"No," she said, stubbornly. "I sent him away. It's different."

"Is it?"

"It feels like it," she said.

"It's all the same in the end."

Seconds ticked by, marked by the clock that hung on the wall. Old-fashioned and steady like Iris herself.

"I'm afraid of being happy," Pansy said quietly.

"I know," Iris said. "I know. But you have a real chance at something here. And I think you need to take it."

"Is that what you would do?"

Iris shook her head slowly. "No. I have a feeling I would run away scared. I'd hate myself for it later. But I'm not brave like you, Pansy. I bake pies and knit sweaters. You arrest bad guys."

"You are brave, Iris," Pansy said. "You took care of us. If it weren't for Ryder and you and Logan…"

"I know," Iris said. "But I like to be here. I like to be safe and it's why…it doesn't matter. Be brave enough to remember the good parts about love, Pansy. Be brave enough to let him love you. And to love him back. Because our childhood wasn't all grief. And your life shouldn't be all about it either. We'll always carry the loss with us. It's part of who we are. But there's plenty enough that we get to choose."

"I don't know if I can."

"It's up to you," Iris said. "You know I've always admired you," she continued. "I admired the way that you left the ranch, and went out and did all this stuff. I never knew you were afraid of anything."

"I'm pretty much afraid of everything," Pansy said. "And up until recently I could pretend it wasn't true."

"It's hard when you know that the world isn't safe," she said. Pansy nodded.

"But rejecting him won't make it safer," her sister said, gently. "It'll just make you sad."

Pansy sniffed loudly. "I came to you because I figured you would be practical about it."

"If a gorgeous man who is also good in bed tells you that he's in love with you, rejecting him is not the practical choice."

And then her sister got up and left her sitting in her bedroom. And Pansy was left to wonder if she was right.

WHEN SHE WAS called into Chief Doering's office the next morning she was sure that it was going to be to have him delicately tell her that she did not get the job. So when he told her that she in fact had gotten it, it took her thirty whole seconds to actually process the words.

"What?"

"The job is yours, Pansy."

"How?" she asked.

"Oh there was vigorous debate," he said. "Especially after you showed up late to the last interview. But believe me when I tell you that Johnson put in a pretty piss-poor performance over his interviews, and the prospect of hiring an outsider didn't thrill anyone. Not even Barbara. Combined with your track record, and the results of your evaluations…it was a unanimous decision in the end."

"I have the job," she echoed flatly.

"Yes, you do," he said.

"I can't believe it."

"Believe it," he said.

"I…"

He stood up from behind his desk and walked around it, pulling her in for a brusque hug. "I had to give your brother the worst news anyone could have given. It means a lot to me to give you some good news, Pansy. Your dad would do that if he were here. And he would be damned proud of you. The youngest police chief in the history of the town. The first woman with the job. You've done him proud, Pansy. You've done us all proud."

She had done it. She had done exactly what she wanted to do. Exactly what she had felt like she needed to do all her life.

Her photo would go on that wall, the same as her father's. The Police Chief of Gold Valley, Oregon. She was finally good enough.

She had finally done it.

Those words kept playing in her head over and over again as she went about her day, went about her job.

And she waited to feel done. Waited to feel changed. Waited to feel as if she had walked through some magical, mystical veil and crossed over to the other side.

But she hadn't.

She hadn't even come close.

She didn't feel changed at all. She felt hollow. And worst of all, the person that she wanted to tell most in the whole world was West.

And she… She didn't have West.

And it all felt pointless.

Because her dad—as much as she loved him—wasn't here to celebrate this. And West would have been. But she'd rejected him.

She had been so sure that this moment would change her. That it would make her feel like she could sit down and rest after running a long race. But she just felt numb.

And her dad was still gone.

Nothing had changed. Nothing at all.

She thought back to what Iris had said about their parents. About the way they had loved them. Hugged them.

And it all blurred together like a montage in her mind. These beautiful moments with her parents that didn't come with a directive, or a sense of shame. These memories that she could do nothing with except feel.

She had wanted so much to avoid feeling.

Because action was so much easier than pain.

Like West said, it was so much easier to build a monument to the dead than it was to try and live. Really live. With her whole heart. With everything.

West.

He loved her.

He loved her just like she was. He loved her when she was cranky and mean and handing out tickets, and pushing him away.

He loved her in spite of everything he'd been through. And he called her brave.

But she wasn't the one who was brave. It was him.

He was all the things that she'd been afraid to touch. Beautiful and wild, and he made her feel like she could be too. And suddenly she knew what she had to do. She knew where she needed to be.

She went into Chief Doering's office. "Can I just take a couple of hours?" she asked.

"Why don't you take the day off?" he asked. "We'll start going over everything you need to know tomorrow morning."

"Thank you," she said.

She changed quickly out of her uniform, got in her car and drove back toward home.

Toward Redemption Ranch.

Not her little house, but the place where West was.

When she got there, she tumbled out of her car, and ran up to the front door of his house. She knocked, but he didn't answer.

So she started walking out toward the barn, and there she saw him, off in a distant field. She stood there and looked at him, at his broad back as he stood facing away from her, looking at the scenery. At this place where he had grown roots.

This place of redemption.

And her heart filled to overflowing. With love and pain and all the things that she had been afraid of for so long. But most of all, that sense of bursting, boundless excitement that had filled her when she had been a girl. For life. For everything. Until the death of her father had killed it.

Not her father. Not his words. Not a fear of disappointing him.

But that sudden, awful blow delivered by death. Something that she had learned could happen far too soon.

Fear.

All of this was because of fear.

It was nothing to her to be a police officer, to put on a badge and promise to protect other people.

But it was everything to her to risk loving someone that she might lose again. Trusting that things could be okay, when she never knew for sure if that was the case.

But the love that West made her feel was stronger than that.

And it returned something to her that she thought she'd lost forever.

And they were two people who lived on land named Redemption and Hope.

Fear had no place in either.

She grabbed hold of the rubber band that held her hair

up in its ponytail, and she released it, shaking her hair out. She put the rubber band in her pocket, then reached down and untied her shoes, toeing them off along with her socks. Until she was barefoot. Until her hair was free.

And then Pansy Daniels ran, like she hadn't done since she was a child.

Not jogging in formation around the town, but like a wild spirit that couldn't be contained.

Right toward the man who held her heart.

"West! West," she repeated.

When he looked at her, he smiled.

CHAPTER TWENTY-FOUR

WEST THOUGHT HE had never seen a more beautiful thing. Pansy, her hair tangled, her cheeks red, her breath coming in short, hard bursts.

Her feet were bare in the squishy grass, and her eyes were bright.

He loved her. More than anything.

And she had come back to him.

"I'm ready," she said.

He let out a whoop and grabbed hold of her, lifting her up off the ground and spinning in a circle.

She threw her head back, and she laughed.

And it was the best thing he'd ever heard.

"I love you," he said.

"I love you too," she answered, brushing her fingertips along his jaw. "I'm sorry that I was afraid."

"There's a whole lot of things to be afraid of in this world. And they're not foolish. Because God knows life can hurt. There is no shame in being scared of something like this."

"But it could've ruined everything," she said. "I had an excuse in my head for why...for why being police chief was the most important thing. Why honoring my father's memory was the most important thing. I held on to the idea that I needed to make him proud because I didn't just want to feel... Losing him hurt so much. It hurt so damn much."

"I know, sweetheart," he said, his voice rough. "I know."

She was so beautiful now. Wild and vulnerable. It killed him to let her keep talking because he could see that it cost her.

But he needed to let her.

She needed to say it. And he needed to hear.

"Losing my mother hurt." Her shoulder shook. "And I realize I didn't even ever let myself think of her because that just hurt. She always accepted me the way that I was. And you know, my dad did too. But I wanted something to do with the feelings inside of me and just missing them didn't feel like anything. Anything but pain. And I held on to all that like a kid hiding from the truth for the last seventeen years."

She wiped her tears on her arm, and kept on going. "West, you make me feel like that person that I used to be. Who never lost anyone. Who could still be filled with joy and excitement about the world. And who sees mischief and fun in it all. You make me want more. You make me want everything. And there's just no room inside of me to be afraid anymore. I haven't felt this free in so long."

Her voice broke, something inside him breaking along with it. But it felt fixed too, and he didn't know how that was possible.

Being broken but whole.

But with her he was.

"My love for you has filled me up all the way," she said. "And I just don't have the space for anything else. I tried to fight it. Losing you was like grief, West. Telling you to leave made me hurt like I did the day my parents died. So it isn't that I don't know what it would cost me if something ever happened. But I just… I want you anyway. Because all the colors in my world are brighter with you in it."

"I feel the same," he said. "I spent four years in prison thinking about where my life had gone wrong. Thinking about the man that I had decided to be. The person that I thought it was so important I become. It was all for other people. It wasn't until I came back here. Until I met you. Until I found Emmett. Until I met the Daltons, that I realized the man I want to be for *me*. For you. I thought that being the right kind of person meant changing everything that I was. Because I looked at the life that I had, the life that we had with our mother, and I thought I had to be something different. But this feels right. This is more than fitting in. It's finding home."

He stroked her cheek, her skin so soft beneath his touch. She was precious and perfect. The kind of beauty he'd never imagined he might touch in his lifetime. But she was here, with him.

With all the pieces of himself.

"And it all came together when I met you, sweetheart," he continued. "That's when I started to grow roots here. Because this place is your heart. And I want to be where your heart is. I always believed in love. I've seen it in a lot of places, I've seen it go a lot of different ways. But my feeling on it was that you couldn't see how it would turn out in the end, so I wasn't willing to risk it. But this isn't a risk, Pansy. It's a baptism. I feel like I've come out clean, saved. For you. With you. I was never in love. Not before. I thought I knew. I saw my siblings with the people they fell for, and I thought I understood. But I didn't really. I had a lot of bitterness in my heart. A lot of resentment. But anything that would get in the way of me loving you has to go. Because I've got to be able to open my arms as wide as they can go, and that's what you do for me. I wasn't really free when I walked out of that jail cell. I was still in bondage. Until you."

She smiled up at him, and he kissed her, hefting her up into his arms and looking down at her beautiful face.

"I made police chief," she whispered.

"Well hell," he said, his heart expanding even more. Damn he was proud of her.

"I know. And I… I waited for that to feel like it made me perfect. Like it fixed all of this. But it didn't. And that was how I knew. That's how I knew it was never going to. Because it's not about pictures on walls or job titles or building a monument to a memory. It's all just about love. That's what sustained us when we grew up. All our noisy family dinners and holidays and showing up to school with mismatched clothes that had holes in them, love was what made it work. But somehow I missed that I needed it in the rest of my life too. It's not a job that'll make me happy. It's loving you."

"Well, I'm damn glad you got your job anyway," he said, sharp, hard emotion slicing through his chest.

Loving her this much hurt. But it was the best hurt he could have ever imagined.

"Me too," she said. "I never thought it was possible to have everything."

"Well look at you. You seem to have it all now."

"Of course, I know what I could live without. And it's not you." She touched his face. "As long as I have you, I have it all."

West Caldwell hadn't been happy to get pulled over by the cops. At the time, it had seemed like an annoyance. But now, it seemed like a damned blessing.

If he could frame every ticket his wife had written him, he would.

"You know," he said. "If you want to keep your last name when we get married, I understand. Because you thought about being Police Chief Daniels for a long time. And I know you want to continue your father's legacy."

"Did I say that I was going to marry you?"

He smiled. "You will."

"You know, I don't think I need to keep his name. Because he's with me, and in my heart. Because he's part of who I am. And because I'm going to be the police chief that *I* am. Because I know what things I want to do to change the community, and whatever name I use, it's going to be more than a monument."

"Well I'm damn glad to hear it."

"West," Pansy said. "You still need to meet my family."

"Well," he said. "Then let's go to Hope Springs."

She paused for a moment, and the corner of her mouth tipped up. "You know, for the first time since my parents died, I actually think it's a fitting name."

And West had to agree that it damn well was.

More fitting than whoever named it could have imagined, that was for sure.

These two ranches that between them they called home, had been the answer to what ailed them all along.

When he'd felt damaged beyond fixing, when Pansy had believed she was bad, redemption had called to them.

And when everything seemed dark and grim, hope had remained. It had sheltered his Pansy for all those years when she was a child.

Redemption led to hope, and it was hope that had brought them to love in the end.

And love had led him home.

* * * * *

HARLEQUIN
DESIRE

One man's betrayal can destroy generations...

Fifteen years ago, a hedge fund hotshot vanished with billions,
leaving the high-powered families of Falling Brook changed forever.
Now seven heirs, shaped by his betrayal, must reckon with the sins
of the past. Passion may be their only path to redemption.

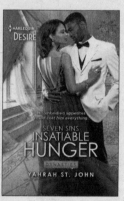

Book 1   Book 2   Book 3

Experience Dynasties: Seven Sins!

Jessie felt the anger emanating from Ryan and knew it was directed at her for
not confronting the kiss earlier. She'd run because she'd been too afraid to
face what had happened. She'd tried to put the mask on, layer by layer, but had
failed miserably. Was it any surprise that when she'd tried to go to bed, she
couldn't sleep? She'd tossed and turned until she'd finally given up the ghost
and realized that until she settled things with Ryan, sleep would elude her.

She'd wondered if she'd pushed Ryan away enough to make him leave, but
instead she'd found him on the deck looking out over the ocean, his button-
down shirt nearly undone and still wearing his jeans.

"You're angry with me."

"Does that surprise you?"

She shook her head. "No. I suppose not. I deserve it for being a coward."
The kiss had left her feeling vulnerable and exposed.

"Go on." He sipped the drink in his hand.

"The kiss caught me off guard. We've always been friends, but everything
has changed and…"

"That scares you," Ryan finished. "Do I scare you? Or is this because you're
still with Hugh?"

"I—I'm not with Hugh anymore. We're on a break."

"A break?" Ryan asked, straightening. "Since when?"

Jessie walked over to him at the balustrade and glanced at the dark ocean.

"Jessie?"

She turned to him and his gaze focused on her. "Since the night of the
reunion."

Ryan's eyes darkened and Jessie forced herself to swallow. "Why didn't you tell me?"

Jessie cocked her head to one side. "Do you really have to ask me? Because everyone, especially my parents, think Hugh and I are supposed to be together. But they couldn't be more wrong."

"How long have you been feeling this way?"

Jessie shrugged. "A while. I've been restless and unsure of our relationship for some time… But I've felt so ruled by Black Crescent's fall and my parents' expectations to marry a guy like Hugh, from an established wealthy family, that I've pushed aside my own feelings. And when we nearly kissed at the reunion, it threw me for a loop. Just like tonight did. I couldn't continue seeing him if I had feelings for another man."

Ryan's gaze locked with hers and then he drew her to him. He pinned her against him and his mouth sought hers. Sky and earth tilted on its axis for Jessie as Ryan's lips parted hers in a kiss that was everything she'd ached for but hadn't realized she needed. And in that devastating moment, Jessie knew that she would die if she couldn't be with him.

When Ryan pulled away, he held both sides of her face and peered into her eyes. "Tell me to stop, Jessie, because I don't know if I can."

"I don't want you to stop, Ryan. I need you."

He leaned his forehead against hers, his lips a fraction away. "You're temptation for even the strongest man. You have no idea how much I want to make love to you."

She gasped and, that very instant, his mouth was back on hers. Jessie didn't have any doubts. She wanted Ryan. She didn't know if she always had. She did know that in this moment she had to have him…

Don't miss what happens next in…
Insatiable Hunger by Yahrah St. John,
the third book in the Dynasties: Seven Sins series.

Is passion the only path to redemption?
Experience Seven Sins.

Available July 2020 wherever
Harlequin Desire books and ebooks are sold.

Harlequin.com

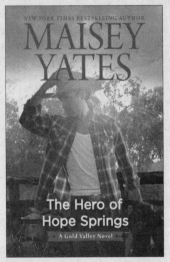

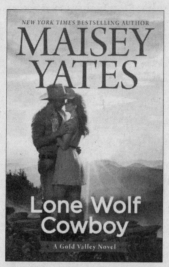

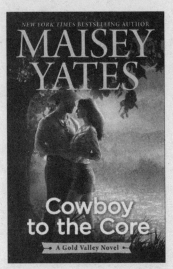

Get 4 FREE REWARDS!

We'll send you 2 FREE Books plus 2 FREE Mystery Gifts.

FREE
Value Over
$20

Both the **Romance** and **Suspense** collections feature compelling novels written by many of today's bestselling authors.